THE RED DISEASE

Dana Berlin

Copyright © 2017 by Dana Berlin

All rights reserved. No part of this publication may be reproduced, distributed or transmitted in any form or by any means, without prior written permission.

Dana Berlin
1616 Main St
Susanville, CA, 96130
instagram.com/dana.berlin.writes

Publisher's Note: This is a work of fiction. Names, characters, places, and incidents are a product of the author's imagination. Locales and public names are sometimes used for atmospheric purposes. Any resemblance to actual people, living or dead, or to businesses, companies, events, institutions, or locales is completely coincidental.

Book Layout © 2017 BookDesignTemplates.com
Edited by Blake Gowing
Map by BMR Williams
Book Cover Design by Faith Hostettler using Canva.com
Cerulean Blue: The Red Disease/Dana Berlin. -- 1st ed.
ISBN 9781705406250

Dedicated to my siblings: Eve, Eli and Jonah.

You're the most creative, caring, beautiful, and intelligent people I know. Also, we are collectively the funniest people in existence. I love your hearts.

I live for you three.

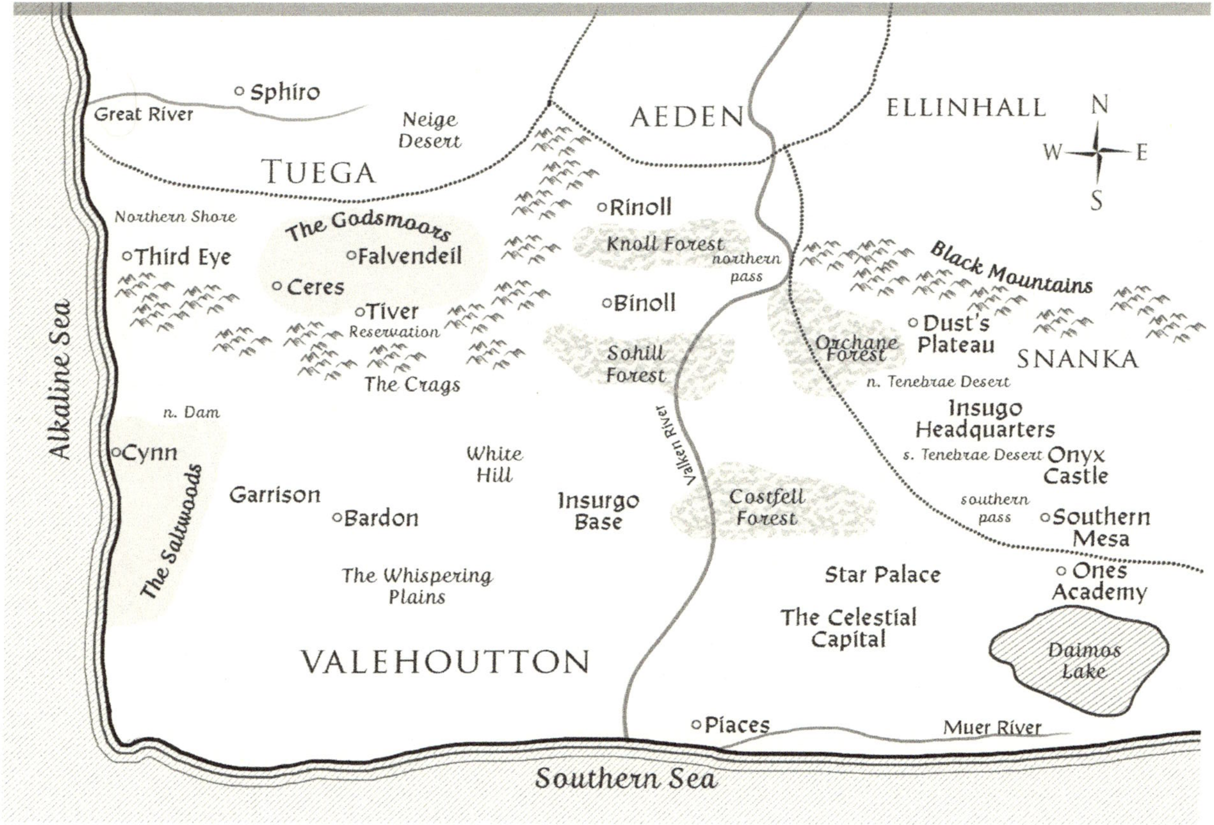
Sphiro
Great River
Neige Desert
TUEGA
AEDEN
ELLINHALL
N
W
E
S
Northern Shore
The Godsmoors
Third Eye
Falvendeil
Ceres
Tiver
Reservation
The Crags
Rinoll
Knoll Forest
northern pass
Binoll
Sohill Forest
Black Mountains
Dust's Plateau
Orchane Forest
SNANKA
n. Tenebrae Desert
Insugo Headquarters
s. Tenebrae Desert
Onyx Castle
southern pass
Southern Mesa
Alkaline Sea
n. Dam
Cynn
The Saltwoods
Garrison
Bardon
White Hill
Insurgo Base
Valken River
Costfell Forest
The Whispering Plains
Star Palace
Ones Academy
The Celestial Capital
Daimos Lake
VALEHOUTTON
Places
Muer River
Southern Sea

1: BLOOD & WATER

SEPTEMBER 1837: CYNN, VALEHOUTTON

It had been two months since the royal occupation, or at least that's what Ash kept saying. Every day he would tell her how long it had been; how long they had been prisoners in their own city. Venell could feel herself growing listless as the early autumn sun blazed down into the city's open square. The sun's rays reflected off the white pavement and walls, making the square blindingly bright. There was plenty of shade opposite the makeshift fence that separated those who were infected, and those who had not yet contracted the disease.

    Venell waited in line behind Ash, but ahead of her father. Men in red and white uniforms bearing the royal seal of King Sireh Redal on their breast pockets stood in front of the fence, checking everyone for signs of illness before letting them pass into what they called the safe side of the city. Even at her age, she knew better. Nowhere was safe anymore.

It started shortly after she and her family returned from the Snankian border. Their journey had taken them across the kingdom of Valehoutton, then back to their home in Cynn, one of the new western colonies near the Alkaline Sea. They had barely found themselves settled when the panic started. There were rumors that in other coastal cities near Cynn, a disease that caused murderous madness was rapidly spreading. First the heart would beat too fast, and the victim was stricken with fever. Then all symptoms would seemingly disappear, but the infected couldn't be roused from sleep until they finally awoke with blazing eyes. They would no longer be the person they once were. It was said the infected had red eyes and sometimes their teeth would grow long. They would kill and eat anyone they could catch, no longer aware of friends or family. That's what the soldiers said. Her father reasoned that it was more likely the soldiers' horror stories were just based on tall tales. He said that fear was more dangerous than any disease.

After the rumors, soldiers arrived from the Capital. They isolated the city. All the gates were closed, and no one was allowed in or out except the soldiers. The people of Cynn trusted King Sireh's decision to quarantine the city, thinking they would be kept safe from the reach of the disease. No one thought it would last long, all orders were obeyed without question. As the weeks dragged on, Cynn began to run low on food and water without outside trade. Waste began to accumulate without access to the sea. The constant, sulfurous odor from the alkaline water was overpowered by the growing stink within the walls. Still there were no answers from the soldiers about what was going to happen or what was going on outside the city walls.

Like caging a wild animal, the people began to grow angry and violent trapped within the great fortress their forefathers had built. After standing completed for nearly four decades, the great wall was entirely unmarred. Neither invaders nor the crashing waves at high tide had left the slightest wear. It reached to the sky endlessly; a smooth, seamless barrier of luminous, pure white rock with an ever so slight curve as it carved its path surrounding the city. Small crystals in the rock would reflect the setting sun every evening, creating a dazzling show of sparkling lights cast all over the city. Venell thought it looked like a second starry sky. This triumph of men's hands was meant to keep them safe, but now it was killing them.

Throngs of city folk began to gather in front of the main gate where most soldiers were positioned. For hours they would shout to the heavens. They demanded answers; they demanded to talk to someone. For days their calls remained unanswered. Her mother was still alive then.

Venell leaned back against her mother's chest as they both stood just outside the town square. She admired the floral embroidery on her mother's shawl, the same one that Venell would wrap about herself when she would dance around the apartment, pretending to be a grown lady. Her mother used one hand to shield her daughter from the midday sun, while the other calmingly stroked Venell's hair. Both she and Ash strongly resembled their father with their straight black hair and almond-shaped blue eyes, while Celidian had soft auburn curls and earthen brown eyes.

Ash and Father had left early to scavenge for food now that rations had run out. The soldiers weren't even allowing the fishermen to their vessels to harvest Cynn's famous brine shrimp. Venell and her mother had spent most of the morning in their apartments, but the noise growing outside had drawn them out, as it had for many.

The citizens of Cynn were either starving in the streets or pounding on the main gate with the ever-growing mob. There was still no sign of any disease besides panic. Finally, a rope ladder was thrown down the side of the great wall surrounding the city. Men in the mob shoved each other aside as they each fought to be the first to reach the ladder. Women screamed to take the children first. Soldiers poked their heads over the side of the wall.

"Step away from the ladder! We will come down and deliver the royal orders from King Kras to you if you step away from the ladder!" The soldiers ordered.

"Kras!? King Kras!? What happened to Sireh!?" voices roared from the mob. The men climbing the ladder refused to back down. More and more began to climb up the wall. The mob began hurling bottles and rocks against the wall, though no throw could reach where the soldiers stood at the top.

Venell felt her mother sit upright very quickly, her eyes focused on the wall. Venell looked to the top, trying to see what her mother was so intently staring at. A metal rod placed over the wall caught the sun's light and glinted sharply. It was followed by many other rods appearing over the wall. Then there was a deafening crack, and the head of the first man on the ladder suddenly disappeared into a rain of crimson that showered onto the mob below him. The same thunderous noises continued to explode from more of the iron rods being held over the wall. Screams rose through the air, taking over all other sound.

 Venell's mother grabbed her hand and began to run. Venell's ten-year-old legs could not keep up with her mother's strides, but she was much too heavy to be carried. She soon began to tire, slowing her mother even more. The mob was heading their direction. More sharp cracks rang out, and with each the mob gained more terrified momentum. Venell saw a young boy behind her suddenly grasp his red, slick shoulder before falling to the pavement. They were soon overtaken by the sea of panic.

 Venell looked up so see an old woman running near them with blood pouring down the side of her head and across her face. The woman tripped and was swallowed by the storm of feet. Venell's eyes widened with fear as she witnessed the woman's body being crushed flat under the feet of the mob. She knew her mother was trying to lead them back to the apartments, but the flow of the crowd cut them off from the route home. People shoved their two weary frames to the side, nearly knocking them to the ground. They crouched behind a long-forgotten delivery cart. Venell climbed inside, taking shelter beneath some of the empty burlap sacks.

    Her mother placed her hands on either side of Venell's face. They were taunt and bony and felt like a stranger's hands now. Her dark brown eyes wavered, and her thin brows knotted. "You have to stay here. If you move, I may not find you again. I must go back to the apartments for Ash and your father. They're looking for us and they'll never find us in this crowd. Please, Venell, promise me you'll stay here no matter what." Venell nodded. Her tears wouldn't stop and her hands shook with fear. Mother was crying also. It made her nose and cheeks flushed so that her light freckles stood out more strongly than usual. Her mother kissed her on the forehead, told her she loved her, then covered her with some of the sacks before disappearing into the chaos.

Night came soon, as did the cold. The streets were empty except for those kneeling over the bodies of their loved ones. The city was quiet for the first time in days. Only the hushed sobs of those still alive and the constant lullaby of the sea echoed through the dark. Venell had already tossed aside the sacks she had been hiding beneath. She waited on the edge of the cart with her feet dangling off the edge. It seemed like no one was coming for her. She had been battling with the promise she made to her mother all night. Finally, she let her feet touch down to the pavement and let her legs lead her through the deathly silent streets. She followed Cynn's white pebble streets until she came upon the building where they had made their home four stories up; where her mother said she was going when she left. She stared up to the empty, dark windows.

    No one was there. Venell stood before that spot, feeling all the hope she had left draining from her body. She couldn't even cry any more, she was too dehydrated. Suddenly, she felt herself being lifted off the ground by a pair of strong hands. She was turned around and held tightly. She buried her face in the warm, familiar scent.

Her father cried softly into her ear. "I can't believe we found you. I thought for sure you both..." he let his voice trail off as he embraced her. Venell could see over his shoulder that Ash was standing behind him. Her brother's icy, blue eyes narrowed as he held a bundle of ripped and bloody clothes closer to his chest. She could see an outline of embroidered blue and white flowers on the beige linen, even through the stains and grime. Venell looked worriedly between her father and her brother, searching for the truth in their faces. Father softly told her that her mother had been trampled to death in the riot. Her body was too mangled for them to recover, so they had decided to remove her coveted shawl to keep as a grim memento.

The memory played over and over in her mind every day. She felt her throat clenching with grief. It felt as though it had been ages since that day, as her world had changed so much since, when in reality it had only been a little over two weeks. "Sixteen days." Ash had told her that morning. Their remaining little family unit felt empty without their peacekeeper.

Her consciousness suddenly shifted back to the present as it was Ash's turn to be checked for the disease. The soldier nearest to the gate roughly grabbed her brother's wrist and waited to feel his pulse. As the seconds ticked by, Ash's glare upon the man grew more and more intense. Venell felt herself shiver at the thought of that gaze being upon her. She stared up into the cloudless sky that was so unusual for coastal weather. The sun burned her eyes and she quickly lowered her head, only to cause the beads of sweat to trail down her forehead, collecting dirt and grime as they rolled into her eyes, continuing the sun's stinging assault.

"He's good." The soldier said as he released his grip on Ash and beckoned for him to move forward through the fence.

Venell blindly stumbled up to the soldier, barely able to see with the agony going on behind her eyelids. The soldier ignored her evident pain and mercilessly pulled her arm forward to check her pulse. She began to cry softly and felt the relief of her tears washing away the dirt and sweat. He carelessly tossed her forward toward the fence, and she clumsily plodded to the other side of the barrier. Both she and Ash waited on the other side for their father to come through so that they might rejoin what was left of their family.

Jet Keoneo stepped forward and offered his arm to the solider. The soldier placed his fingers on his wrist, though he kept studying Jet's face curiously. "Did you ever serve in the royal army?" the soldier asked. His voice was oddly soft for such a large man, but it matched is soft, callow body. His uniform jacket looked thick and heavy. Sweat beaded across his forehead and his breath sounded ragged.

"I fought in both battles against Tuaega." Jet replied while keeping his gaze lowered. He scratched the scar on the side of his neck with his free hand like he always did when he was nervous. Father usually had his long, black hair tied back in a ponytail at the base of his neck, but he let it down before having to cross the checkpoint. His scruffy beard was more grey than black now, and deep lines rippled across his forehead, but the blue of his eyes had not faded.

"Thirty years ago? You must've been young."

"I was, but I'm much older than I look. I've been retired for many years."

"Just a foot soldier? Not an officer? Because I swear you look familiar..."

"Cavalry, actually. Never gained any ranks."

The soft soldier just kept staring at him. Venell looked over to her brother and asked what was taking so long. Ash didn't reply, but he kept staring the scene intently.

"No, bullshit! It's General Keoneo! I knew I recognized you! Seize him! You Red disease-ridden scum! Seize him!"

Jet shouted for his children to run before he was overtaken by other soldiers. The line to get to the safe side of the fence was broken as everyone fled to get as far away from one of the infected as possible. Venell confusedly called for her father before Ash grabbed her hand, and the two took off into the maze of the inner city. Venell dared to look over her shoulder to see four or five soldiers running after them.

She knew where her brother was headed: to the canal at the northernmost point of the city that led through the wall and to freedom. It was a small opening and not many people knew where it led, but the siblings often used it as a shortcut to get to the meadow outside of Saltwoods before the quarantine started. Now it was guarded at all times, but it was their only chance to escape alive. All other canals emptied over sheer cliffs and into the Alkaline Sea. She kept glancing over her shoulder to see if the soldiers were closing in on them. Ash roughly pulled her along and shouted for her to keep up.

They darted through narrow alleys and through crowds of the lethargic, starving citizens. Each turn put their pursuers further and further behind.

The canal was in her sight. Only a single guard stood outside it, most likely since little protection was required now that the people of Cynn barely had enough life left in them to move, much less fight. Ash swiftly pulled a dagger from the side of his boot. He let go of Venell's hand and kept up his pace as he approached the guard.

"Hey, what do you—" His sentence was ended as his vocal cords were severed by Ash's blade.

"What are you waiting for?" Ash shouted at his sister.

Venell stood frozen with shock for a few moments before rejoining her brother at his side. She just stared at the gash in the dying man's flesh. Ash hadn't even hesitated before taking the man's life. As she looked over her brother, he suddenly seemed much older than fourteen. Turning away, she began to climb into the canal when a thought struck her. "Wait! If they see that dead guard, they'll know we escaped this way!"

Ash cursed under his breath, and she knew that she was right. She grabbed the dead man's arms while Ash grabbed his feet. She walked backwards into the canal while dragging the dead weight behind her, while Ash continued to shove the body further into the canal. As they crawled deeper the light began to disappear, and they had to rely on touch. The siblings were separated by a corpse, and only their grunts and groans echoed through the bricked tube. One of Venell's feet scraped over an iron grate, moving it slightly. As she gave another heave on the dead guard, holding him under the armpits, the grate was pulled off further and the guard's legs began to slip down the uncovered hole. Ash lost his grip before Venell did, and the weight of the body's bottom half was too much for Venell to hold on her own. The body slipped into the darkness below, and a thud echoed as the body hit the ground below.

"I guess that was for the best." Ash muttered as he wiped his bloody hands on his trousers. She could see his ever-present scowl, even in the dark. "We should wait until night to make our run. They'd spot us too easily during the day and we'd be dead before we ever reached the cover of the Saltwoods." He paused, and suddenly refused to look his sister in the eye. His tone turned even colder than before, and she knew he was about to say something she would like even less. "I'm going back to see if Father is alive. You just have to promise that you'll wait here until I come back."

Weeks of grief finally released like a flood at these words. "Ash, please! When Mother said that to me, she died! Please don't leave, Ash!" She grabbed onto his sleeve as she sobbed to him helplessly. "It's only us left! Don't leave me alone!"

"I'll come back just fine before night, quit crying!" he snapped at her. He turned around and crawled back through the canal and into the city.

Venell hugged her knees and buried her face in her lap. She didn't want to wait for someone to never come back, again. The stench of the guard's body was beginning to fill the tunnel. It was rapidly rotting in the damp environment. Both ends of the tunnel were still light after what seemed like hours. No sound reached deep enough into the canal to let her know what was going on outside. The end of the tunnel that led outside to the Saltwoods was showing hues of pink and orange, meaning that the sun must be setting. Nights on the coast were always freezing this time of year, and Venell could already feel the temperature start to drop without the sun.

She felt her alertness fading as she began to drift off. It had been days since she slept. She was abruptly startled by something scurrying across her feet. She couldn't see what it was in the dark. She ignored it and closed her eyes once more. Something moved across her feet again in the same direction: from the city to the forest. She pulled her feet in, only to hear the growing hum of insects and the scampering of tiny claws across the walls. She squinted, trying to see in the dark. It looked like the floor was moving. She realized in disgust that the entire bottom of the canal was covered with bugs and rats fleeing from the city, she tried to stand as best she could with such a low ceiling. She kept backing up, closer and closer to the far end of the tunnel as she tried to stay out of the path of the herd of vermin.

Soon she was at the end of the canal. The rats poured out, rounding her legs and crawling all over her feet before dispersing into the wide field that separated the wall from the forest. It was nearly night and Ash still hadn't returned. She looked back into the tunnel, hoping to see his figure approaching. There was nothing. As she scanned the field, she could see the tracks of carts, men, and horse hooves. There were holes left in the ground where tents had been pitched and piles of debris where fires once burned. It looked as though all the soldiers were gone; their entire campsite abandoned.

As suddenly as they had appeared, the hordes of pests were gone. She glanced back into the tunnel again, only to see a dark pool gathering at the far end. It spread across the floor of the tunnel, some of it disappearing into the hole where she and Ash had dumped the guard's corpse. It began to form faster, and soon the dark mass reached out to touch the tips of her outstretched fingers. It was wet, but as she pulled her hand back, she saw that it was clear. It was just water, but it kept coming. The tunnel soon began to fill, even as it emptied itself at an increasing rate into the field. She couldn't stay in the tunnel any longer. She made the three-foot drop to the ground where the canal protruded from the wall. Her brain felt muddled with astonishment as the water refused to cease, for she could not comprehend where it could all be coming from. The corpse of the guard floated with the current and fell with a heavy thump onto the soaked grass below.

More and more water flowed out from the canal and from smaller tunnels that lined the city, constructed in case of a flood. Soon it was too much for all the canals to handle. Water shot out in streams, then began to leak through unseen cracks in the wall. She turned face the North, then she saw what she feared: smoke in the distance. There was a black, menacing cloud billowing into the sky where the largest dam in all Valehoutton had been built to allow the coast to be colonized.

Venell lifted her skirts and began to run, but the water was gaining strength and rushing past the city walls on the East and west sides. There was a loud groan that boomed from the city. The sound of rushing waves thundered over the crashes of buildings collapsing within the city walls. Venell dared to slow and watch her home breathe its dying breath. With a final exhale, the great wall gave way. Once a few stones were cracked and shook loose, the water gained power and tore down the mighty barricade. The water swallowed the city whole, and now it was coming for her with all its new-found tyranny.

As she ran toward the Saltwoods, she could feel the water begin to lap at her boots. It quickly rose, making it too difficult to run as it crept up her legs. The water maliciously swirled around her as she tried to lift her legs higher with each step to keep her footing. The river was hurling pieces of her broken city at her; it was doing everything it could to capture the last part of Cynn. She desperately grasped onto a splintered plank of wood just as the water reached her waist and swept her off her feet. Now she was the river's puppet.

Venell could barely keep her head above the water. Adrenaline took over her mind. Rushing water filled her senses. She gasped for breath every time the water allowed her to surface before being pulled back under. Somewhere within her head she kept hearing her father's voice calling her name. Even though her eyes were open she could barely turn her head to look for him with the force of the river at her back. Venell closed her eyes. She knew that she heard him calling her. He must be dead, and this must be the end for her as well. He must be waiting for her on the other side. He and her mother were waiting for her with open arms.

The current suddenly rammed her into something with such force that she felt a huge crack on her side as her ribs took the brunt of the impact. It was a tree. Her body and mind reawakened, and she dug her hands into the bark. Some of her fingernails snapped off as she gripped the tree so fiercely, but even the river and all its might could not pull her away from this savior. Inch by inch, she pulled herself up the side of the tree until she was above the water. As she climbed, she began to look around, but all there was for miles was water. Cynn was gone. She continued her ascent up the tree, the water was still rising. It was unbearable just to inhale, for with every breath she could feel her broken ribs digging into her lungs. She kept hearing her father's voice shouting her name. He was nowhere in sight.

Then she saw him: soaked and clinging to another tree only a few feet away. "ASH!" she screamed. She had only just seen him, but he looked at her as though he had been watching her all along. She screamed his name over and over, trying to get him to move or yell back so that she could tell if he was real or not. His eyes locked with hers, and their gazes didn't part the rest of the night.

The bark of the tree dug mercilessly into the flesh of her fingertips. As the sun completely disappeared beyond the horizon, her hands became numb from the cold and the pain. She shivered uncontrollably; her dress was still soaked from the river. Her neck became stiff where her wet hair began to freeze, while her ribs throbbed with hot pain and oozed warm liquid. The branches she stood on were slick, so to stay upright she had to tightly grasp the trunk of the tree with her thighs. The paper white skin on the Keoneos was the only thing illuminated in the sea of darkness. Venell could still hear the water rushing below; a constant reminder that death awaited should she lose her grip. Sometimes she would dare a peek down, but she couldn't see anything but blackness. And Ash's eyes, those icy blue eyes, stared into hers through it all.

The sunrise brought little relief. Venell began to feel some warmth spreading over her frosty skin. When she looked down, she could nearly see the bottom of the trees, though the water remained in shadow. Knowing the worst was over, Ash began to climb down. She tried to do the same, but even though she willed her limbs to move it took several minutes before she was able to do so. As she approached the ground, she could see that the water was no more than a foot high and the current was weak. Her feet hit the earth with a splash, and she quickly had to grasp her injured side in pain. The entire right side of her dress was stained dark red. She gathered her skirts up in her hands and hobbled toward her brother. She threw her arms around him and sobbed deeply into his chest. He held her in mourning silence.

Ash cradled his sister as if she were a babe and began to trudge through the water and floating debris. The two soon came upon a small stone hut with some walls still standing, though the roof was gone, and all the doors and windows had been ripped off or caved in. Ash cleared the rubble off a child's bed that was floating around the little cottage and laid his sister upon it. Her entire body felt stiff with the pain. It was becoming increasingly difficult to breathe with her ribs digging further into her with each inhale. Ash collapsed in a heap in the corner of the room, causing water to splash up all around him, and he rested his head against the wall and closed his eyes.

"They had already killed Father by the time I got there." Ash said breathlessly. He didn't open his eyes to look at her when he spoke.

Venell didn't think her heart could break anymore, but still she felt it sink lower in her chest at the news of her father. Somehow, she had known, but somehow, she still had hope. She really was alone with Ash.

"They slit his throat and dropped him in the dirt. The other people of Cynn started to fight back.

The soldiers were cornered, so they started shooting everyone. I had to hide. I waited until it was quiet. Almost everyone was dead. Those who weren't... their eyes still looked dead."

Ash continued, "The soldiers were gone but the gates were still locked. The sun was setting... and then I saw the water. The city filled up so fast. The North side was completely drowned. I kept running, trying to find another canal or some other way out. I finally found a tunnel that I could fit through, but it was covered by a metal grate. The water was up to my knees as I tried to pry it off with a knife. It gave way just in time, and I escaped the city, but there was too much water for me to get back to you. I knew you would go to the Saltwoods, so I just kept running until the current swept me up and carried me the rest of the way to you."

He gasped for air. He was speaking with such vigor that he had forgotten to take a breath. Venell couldn't move her head to look at him, she could only move her eyes as the rest of her body grew heavy.

"But while I was hiding, I listened to the soldiers. Sireh's son: Kras, is king now, and he is terrified of the Red disease reaching the capital. He ordered for Cynn to be put back underwater! They dug trenches on the Eastern side to direct the river here and destroyed the dam! He killed everyone."

He crawled through the water to Venell's bedside. He grasped her slick, bloody hand and held it to his lips. "You have to promise me this now. You must promise me that we'll kill that man responsible for this: that false, evil king. It's his fault Mother and Father are dead; his fault Cynn is dead! Promise me!"

He held her hand tighter even though her consciousness was beginning to fade. "I promise." She forced out before her eyes closed. And all she could think about was Ash.

2: THE BEAST

JUNE 1849: BARDON, VALEHOUTTON

The sweet smell of a woman's skin was so intoxicating to Ronnock. Sometimes he would forget himself on nights like this. Although the room of the inn was darkened, he could still clearly see the raven-haired girl's face twist up with pleasure as he thrust himself deeper inside of her. She let out a soft moan; the sound was as sweet as her smell. Her skin was dark, the color of cinnamon, which contrasted with the milky white hands of the fiery-haired, freckled girl that grasped her breasts. Both their bodies were covered in a sheen of sweat. It had only been minutes past dusk when they began, but now even after midnight the women still begged for more. Ronnock knew it might've been different if they had seen his face in the light.

Ronnock grasped the red head by her waist and turned her over so that she lay on her stomach. She felt so good, warm and slick. With his other hand he pulled the dark-skinned girl's mouth to his own. She tasted strongly of wine, but his thoughts remained on the pulse he could feel through her tongue. He felt a familiar tingle in his gums, and this time he knew he could not suppress the feeling. He nuzzled his face in the crook of the dark-skinned girl's neck. She closed her eyes and tilted her head back. He began to feel the Red taking over him. To lose control was an incomparable release.

Relief and pleasure washed over him as his elongated eyeteeth slid down from their sockets to reveal how fearsome a creature he really was. He graciously kissed her neck as he continued to bounce the red head against himself. Slowly, slyly, yet hungrily he pressed those teeth onto her delicious flesh and penetrated her skin. She moaned;,her mind too clouded with pleasure to realize that everything was almost over for her.

The red head suddenly sat up, nearly foiling his plans. She began to wiggle her hips against him as she cried out in ecstasy, pushing the other girl closer to him as his lips closed over the punctures on her throat. Blood was always hotter than could be imagined by one who had never felt it filling their mouth and taking over all their senses. As he drank from her, the Red completely consumed him. After holding it back for so long, it was both thrilling and cathartic to let the beast run free for a night. As one of the girls died, the other reached a peak and shuddered. The dark-skinned girl fell away, dead.

Thinking it was over, or that it was the other girl's turn, the red head began to turn around. Ronnock knew his changed appearance would be seen, even in the dark. He held her head down in the pillows and knew that it was time. She let out a moan with every thrust, grinding her ass against him again. He bent over her, grabbing her throat and pulling her to his mouth. There was no going slowly this time, the beast had already been awakened and there was nothing to stop it until it was satiated. The excited look on her face told him how blissfully unaware she was to her rapidly approaching doom. They never knew what was coming.

He bit down onto the side of her neck, tearing into her and spilling the sweet nectar of her life all over his tongue. The blood ran down both sides of her body, even coating his hand where he grasped her breast. She made no sound as she died, she just slowly began to lay her head down on the crimson-soaked pillow.

 He pulled away from her and the beast began to recede. Then Ronnock was alone. He wiped the blood from his chin and began to dress himself. The black linen sleeveless shirt and loose fitting shorts were truly all he wished to wear in the humid heat that plagued Bardon in the summer, but that would neither hide nor protect him. He fastened his breastplate of boiled leather over a long-sleeved, dirty grey shirt and put on his black leather greaves and arm braces. All his leather work was studded with steel as to better protect him from a blade as well as keep his mobility. His long, black cloak was the last accent to help him disappear into the night.

 He climbed out of the inn window and rounded the corner to the hitching posts where he had left his horse. The black stallion stood proudly, looking like no more than a shadow in the night. After he had succumbed to the Red, it proved incredibly difficult to find a horse that wasn't afraid of him. Even with the beast buried and hidden, the animals could still sense it boiling inside of him. He patted the stallion's neck. The horse nickered quietly under his touch. Ronnock felt himself smile;

it felt good to be understood. "I suppose I can't just call you 'horse' forever. I'll think of something." He said as he began to saddle his mount.

He couldn't remain in Bardon for much longer. His haste was not brought about by the gory mess he had left in the inn; that was mild compared to what that inn had previously seen. Bardon was filled with the vilest scum of the earth, so Ronnock felt he was just one of many. It used to be a bustling merchant town full of travelers and exotic finds, but through the years the inhabitants and the visitors became rougher and crueler. Every man would rob and kill an innocent passer-by if he got the chance, and every whore would do worse.

He was headed east out of the city. Just beyond the reach of the cloud of stink that spewed out of the city was a block-shaped stone fortress that served as a base to the Insurgo. It was small, no grandeur or intimidation, but it was incredibly effective when it came to repelling enemies. The Insurgo held the most firearms in the country after the royal army, much to the king's anger. They had become the rebellious force that King Sireh and his successor, his son Kras, had been working so hard to prevent. As a boy, it had never been Ronnock's desire to become a soldier, especially not one that belonged to a resistance. Many things changed after the Red.

Ronnock and the black stallion rode off into the night with a fearsome fury. He and the stallion were one in the same; invisible in the darkness, preceded only by the thunder of hooves. There was no moon tonight, and the light from the city could no longer reach them as they tore across the Whispering Plains that surrounded Bardon on every side. He could not hear the whispers over the sound of hooves. Dark clouds covered the sky. There were no stars tonight. Even though he was part of the darkness, Ronnock always missed the stars.

In his dreams every night he would see the moon shining on a single, white flower that was pushing its way through the muck and mud of a forest floor, freshly after a rain shower. The flower needed the sun. He would stoop down towards it, feeling the humid air fill his lungs, and slowly brush his fingers over the delicate, velvety folds. A petal fell from the flower and became immersed in muddy earth around it. A whispery voice would shudder in his ear, and in his mind, he would see a pair of blue eyes widen. The eyes always woke him. Sometimes he would wake up alone, sometimes with a woman beside him, or enemies surrounding him. He would try to remember where it was that he was seeing in his dream, for it felt as though he had seen it before. The trees were old, yet very much alive, with huge gnarled roots that rose out of the earth, covered in dark green moss. He could smell the moisture in the air and feel it cling to his skin. The sky was visible, the moon was bright, but still there were no stars. There was a single path, strewn with muddy puddles and fallen leaves. There were two fresh pairs of footprints, but he was alone.

    The stallion's snorts brought Ronnock back to reality. The horse must've sensed they were close to home. The horse's home, that is. The base was growing larger upon the horizon, and before long two riders arrived at his side to escort him. He vaguely recognized the man riding a chocolate brown steed: a long-time soldier of the Insurgo whose name always seemed to escape him. The other must have been a new recruit; the boy didn't have a single hair on his chin.

    With an enormous groan, the black metal gates of the base open inward to give them passage. Carvings of valiant, ancient horselords known as the Rhanians that once ruled the plains around Bardon decorated each gate. In those times they were called the Thundering Plains. Now the plains were silent besides the occasional rush of wind through the tall, dry grasses. As the gates closed behind him, Ronnock turned to stare at the carving of Khazar the Storm. Khazar's fist was raised to the sun, the god of the horselords, and held a feathered sabre. His helmet was also feathered, but his eyes still burned with vengeance and fury even though they were only made of black ore.

    The ancestors of the Aejons, the race that inhabited most of Valehoutton, found a great foe in Khazar and his riders. The plains may have never been conquered and colonized if the Aejons had not stolen away Khazar's wife in the middle of the night, forcing him to surrender if he wished to have his love returned to him with all her limbs and digits attached. The gates finally shut and Khazar's black eyes were gone.

    Ronnock dismounted and left the stallion with a stable boy. He probably should have gone into the commander's quarters to report on the status of his mission, but he decided it could wait until the morning. Instead he passed by all his comrades without a word and went straight to his chambers. He shut the heavy wooden door behind him, leaving the room pitch black without a candle lit. With a crack of sparks from the flint, Ronnock lit the end of a blood cigarette rather than his lamp.

His chambers were nicer than most, thanks to some strings his sister pulled with the commander, and it was significantly better than being housed in the barracks with all the young male recruits. When he first arrived, he bunked with four other soldiers, and there was no privacy. His room now had red brick walls, a small crank-open window, and even his own washbasin and mirror. His furniture was sparse and used, just a bed and a worn sitting chair, and he had no décor to make the room home. Because it wasn't.

He stood near the open window, staring down into the courtyard as the men of the Insurgo prepared for their day to end. Red puffs of smoke left Ronnock's mouth and bonded with the humid summer air. He loved to watch the small clouds dissipate and become one with the night. He took another heavy drag and let his fangs slide down from his gums. The blood soothed the Red while the smoke soothed his nerves.

"I am nothing." The whispery voice of his dreams echoed through his room. "I am nothing." She always said the same thing.

"You don't have to be." He would always tell her. Over the years he had become more comfortable talking to an empty room than when he caught himself doing it the first time. He tilted his head back and exhaled red smoke through his nostrils. Sometimes when he heard her voice he felt like crying, and he didn't even know who she was. He could feel her soul touching his own, but he couldn't even remember what she looked like. All he could see were tears clinging to her eyelashes as his hand reached out to her.

The dawn was cruel. Ronnock had forgotten to close the window before he went to bed, and the light poured into his room and attacked his eyes. He rose slowly. Every morning was such a struggle. He washed his face in the silver basin near his bed. The face he saw was no longer his own. When he was younger, he had many girls fawning over him. He would dress handsomely, keep his face shaven clean, and kept his hair short. Now he had seen thirty and two winters, but the jagged scars of countless battles across his face suggested he had seen more. He knew his face made people uncomfortable. No one ever looked him in the eyes. Unless he was about to kill them, then they most certainly did.

His hair was a black mess, sticking up in some places and matted in others; he looked like a crazed old crone. He sighed and sat down to roll his thick locks between his palms, but then he could not concentrate on the task with his hunger gnawing at him and he had to smoke another blood-soaked cigarette before finishing. He liked the glass and wooden beads that remained woven into the strands of his hair; each was a gift from one of his sisters. The red bead was from Krisae, the youngest, the gold and purple one was from his twin, Hellan, and the green one from his half-sister, Rheena.

Ronnock left his room and made his way down to the mess hall, this time greeting a few of his fellow soldiers as he passed them. He grabbed a heel of bread and a plate of messy, bloody steak that the cook had left out especially for those with the Red. When Ronnock was first infected, he thought it would be best for him to be around others that were diseased as well. He knew now that it made no difference, for in his head he was always alone with the beast.

He took a seat next to his teenaged nephew, Mayan Ankatez, and one of his old companions, Giness Anshee. Mayan immediately looked up from his food, "Uncle! My father is about to piss on all of us if you don't go see him soon."

Ronnock grumbled and stuffed his mouth full of meat instead of answering.

Giness leaned over, "A group of nearly thirty greth arrived in Bardon this morning. You know what that means." Giness waited for Ronnock to reply, but he said nothing still. "One of the higher-ups is in town, you shit." He finished and elbowed Ronnock roughly. Ronnock coughed as a chunk of poorly chewed meat caught in his throat from the nudge and coughing it back up sprayed blood back onto his plate. Both men laughed and Giness clapped him on the back.

"Do you really have to eat that in front of us?" Mayan said, disgusted.

"You can't expect to be a soldier if you can't handle a little cow blood." Ronnock retorted.

Mayan looked much more like the commander, a descendant of Rhanians, than his mother. He was dark-skinned and black-haired with a firmly set jaw and narrowed, dark eyes. His hair was always wild, nearly sticking straight up no matter how long it seemed to get. Even though he decided to join the Insurgo while he was very young, he still was never set on potentially dangerous missions. Most said it was because his father feared for his safety, but Ronnock knew the young man lacked the skill to keep up with most of his seasoned comrades.

Giness was attempting to turn his life around by means of the Insurgo. He has spent most of his life imprisoned all over Valehoutton for various petty crimes and was downright lucky to not have been executed when he was arrested for thievery in Snanka. He was lanky and pale with a mop of light brown, loosely curled hair. He was almost as scarred as Ronnock, but fortunate enough to have avoided receiving most of those on his face.

Ronnock finished his meal and made his way to the commander's quarters. Iratez Ankatez was not known for his patience. Before he could even knock on the door, it swung open and Iratez grabbed the front of his shirt and yanked him in the room. "Ukon! You bloody bastard, too busy pouting last night to report back from a scouting mission?"

"Yes, sir. Pouting." Ronnock replied. It was best to agree with whatever Iratez said until he calmed down, otherwise he would be stuck listening to him go off for hours.

"That's how all you bloody Red devils are, always brooding off in corner. Jet was the same way; may his soul be at peace." The commander thumped his fist over his heart like he always did when Jet was mentioned.

Jet Keoneo had once been a general in the royal army and was a decorated war-hero through the many years of conflict with Tuaega, the kingdom to the North, over thirty years ago now. Despite all his service, he was banished from the Capital upon it being revealed that he was the Red. It was even rumored that King Sireh was aware that Jet was infected, but let Jet win his wars for him and waited to exile him until his throne was no longer under threat. Through it all, Iratez had been by Jet's side. They left the Capital together, eventually forming the Insurgo to forever torment Sireh and his family, the Redals. Jet had left Iratez to manage their project and retired to the coastal colonies shortly after he and his wife, Celidian Sloe, welcomed their second child. After the destruction of Cynn and no word from his dear friend, Iratez had come to terms that Jet and his family were among the thousands drowned in the flood.

"I'm sure you've already heard there's a startling amount of greth in Bardon now. I want you and your sister to go clear out anyone in a uniform in the whole stinking town. And get rid of and those beasts you run in to, I can't stand the sight of the things." Iratez said, his volume slightly receding as he settled back down into his armchair.

"Krisae doesn't have to—"

"YOU and YOUR SISTER!" Iratez boomed and slammed his fist onto his desk. It still surprised Ronnock how red the commander's face could get despite his dark skin.

"Alright, yes, sir." Ronnock muttered and bent slightly before taking his leave. He knew the commander was upset with him, that's why he was sending Krisae as well. She would be there to mind him as if he were a child that needed minding.

Ronnock found his stallion hitched near the front of the stables, next to Krisae's spotted horse, Kunzite. "Of course," he thought to himself. He patted the stallion on its neck before reaching for its reins and saddle. The animal's black eyes watched his every move. "Ready to run, Khazar?"

3: GHOSTS OF CYNN

JUNE 1849: CYNN

It seemed impossible for those days to move to Venell's memories instead of remaining forever intact at the forefront of her mind. They could not be pushed away, much less forgotten. The colors, the sounds, all the vivid details refused to fade. Since then, everything appeared grey to her. Nothing was alive, nothing could feel, and nothing moved except some rubble that would catch in the wind. Cynn was always deathly silent except for the ghostly echoes that haunted it when night fell. To Venell, her life was simply grey.

It had been twelve years since the royal army had quarantined then extinguished Cynn, yet nothing had changed since its destruction. There was no rebirth in this cycle. Nothing grew from the ruins, nor did any animals seek shelter within its broken walls. Nothing returned to the city except for the Keoneos.

The flood had carried the thousands of corpses left in the city to the vast ocean. The great, crystalline wall of the city had been destroyed, while many of the shorter buildings within the city had remained intact if something taller hadn't collapsed upon it. The Keoneos returned to the pick the bones of Cynn after the water receded a few weeks following the flood. They found most of what they needed to survive from what had been left behind by their deceased friends and neighbors. They had managed to tend a small garden for years to help feed themselves, but lately harvests had been meager, and Ash was forced to hunt deeper and deeper within the Saltwoods.

Ash was consumed by his dreams of revenge. Venell could only watch as the hatred continued to eat away at his heart over the years. She knew that he was still intent on killing the king, as if it would set everything back to the way it was. They would never discuss his plot, nor would either sibling mention anything about what they saw or felt during the quarantine, but both knew that the other was constantly thinking about it. Venell could always see it in her brother's eyes. She saw the same scene replaying over and over across those eyes, and then everything would become cold. The emotion would radiate from him: raw hatred. Hate is not a fire, it is very, very cold. Sometimes Ash would force her to spar with him so that she might fight alongside him to avenge their parents, but each time he would give up on her when her physical limits fell much shorter than he expected of her. She just couldn't do it. She just wasn't strong.

They had moved homes often at first, using everything left behind in one abode, then moving to the next. They had been in their current shelter for over two years now. It had two bedrooms, an outhouse, and most importantly a roof. The glass from the windows was long gone, which made it hot in the summer and cold in the winter, but they had little other choice. Moss grew between cracks in the stone walls, and grains of salt left behind from the humid night air clung to nearly every surface. They had used up the last of the oil in the city years ago, so nights were always dark unless they lit a fire.

It had been twelve years since the quarantine. Twelve years they had been isolated here, but Venell knew their time in the ruins was coming to an end. Ash had come back from the Saltwoods empty-handed for almost a week now, and the last of their garden squash was boiling over the fire. His haul today would determine their fate.

The thought kept repeating itself in her mind, growing louder and more forceful as she heard Ash's footsteps approaching the front door. She tried to swallow her anxiety. She tried to look like she was thinking about something else as the door slowly opened and shut behind her brother. Ash didn't even look at her as he entered. He went straight to the fire and began poking the coals around. He finally took a seat next to her before removing his boots. He kept his eyes fixed on the fire.

He sighed, "What?"

Venell quickly shook her head and tried to concentrate on the tunic she was mending. She cursed quietly under her breath after accidentally jabbing her fingertip with the needle. She placed her finger to her lips. The metallic taste of her own blood filled her senses and she instantly recoiled.

"It's long overdue." Ash said in his usual brooding tone. "We have to move on. Don't worry about packing until morning. And try not to bring too much." Ash stood and made his way to his bedroom, he had nothing left to say to her.

The fire hissed as the pot of water she had been boiling began to spill over. She moved the pot off the fire and sat alone in the growing darkness. This lonely, grey fog may yet begin to lift. For so long she had been afraid of leaving and terrified of what could be out there beyond the small world that she and Ash had built. She never realized that instead there may be color out there; bright, beautiful colors that she had yet to experience. Anything had to be better than being trapped in this shell of an existence; this icy fortress. Anything, bad or good, was better than years of nothing. She remained in the ruins because she was too afraid to be without Ash. His insistence on staying in Cynn had made him feel like her captor at times, but now he was her escape.

The next dawn brought warm, spreading hope. She had ignored Ash's advice and packed the night before. She was ready to step out into the real world after being trapped in the shadows for far too long. She yearned to know how much the country had changed, or if anyone would even know of the disaster in Cynn. It wasn't until the previous night she had even felt hopeful about leaving since she had been too preoccupied fretting over her old promise to her brother. Now it seemed that new doors were opening all around her. The early sun cast a golden glow upon the forest, making it seem much more inviting that usual.

Ash stood waiting for her just beyond the ruins of the city wall. He set out on a path straight into the Saltwoods as he saw her approaching. She quickly followed at his heels. They first had to cross the meadow where they and the other children of Cynn used to play. Echoes of their voices still rung in Venell's ears. Even when she would explore the rest of the ruins, she would never come to the meadow or to the small apartment that had once been their home. Ash marched on the most direct route to the forest, even if it meant mercilessly trampling all the flowers in the meadow. Venell did her best to avoid crushing the delicate things.

Venell had only ever ventured into the Saltwoods after the flood a handful of times, when Ash brought her with him to hunt. Even then, she had never traveled very deep into the labyrinth of trees. All the stories she was told as a child of its danger must've really stuck with her. She hated going into the forest. She always felt like an unwelcome intruder, but the Saltwoods were full of life this early in the day. Birds sang to each other high up in the trees, and the buzz of insects passed by her ears from time to time.

Although the light was blinding atop the trees, little sunlight filtered through to the forest floor. The shade was broken up by patches of light that made it through the leaves, casting speckled shadows over her and Ash. It was an odd forest; the salty sea air made the trees dry. Unlike the rainy forests to the East, the vegetation appeared washed-out in color. The trees were tall and skinny with brittle bark and brown leaves. Many of the leaves had already fallen for the year, even though summer was not even halfway over.

It didn't feel like she was finally leaving Cynn forever, although she knew she was. She didn't even look back as she walked away. No matter the outcome of their search, she knew that she would never return to this place.

They were only a few miles deep into the woods when Venell saw a tree with knotted branches and thick, white bark. Its pattern was identical to all the other trees of the Saltwoods, but Venell still recognized it immediately. Something deep within its bark seemed to recognize her as well. Its roots rose from the ground, gnarled and ancient. She ran her fingers over a dark stain on the bark; a stain she left. She grasped her scarred side, still able to feel the burning pain of her broken bones.

By evening the forest grew silent. The quiet was eerie, like something was stealthily planning an attack. It made sleep difficult. Venell listened intently for the rustle of branches or the vibrations of approaching footsteps, but there was nothing. It was completely dark in the woods except for the campfire Ash had built. She kept fretting that the light would bring unwanted attention from whatever lurked in the depths of the Saltwoods. "How long until we reach the nearest city?" She asked Ash in a hushed voice. She knew that his answer would be made with the assumption that all the cities and towns they had known twelve years ago were still in existence. She also knew that the flood had destroyed the road that led from Cynn to Bardon. All they could do was keep walking east.

He only shrugged in response. It seemed so stupid to her that they could've left Cynn years ago. They could've gone to Bardon right after the flood and gotten help and tried to live normal lives. Maybe it could've never been so, for her brother's deepest desire was to exact revenge on the ruler of the country. Perhaps they would've been immediately killed if it was revealed that they were survivors from Cynn, for the king obviously wanted everyone there dead. But she knew in her bones that the real reason she and Ash never left Cynn was that they could have never gone back to the blissful mundane of everyday life. Something in the hearts of the Keoneos had changed forever.

"I think we're being followed." Ash finally whispered to her from where he lay in his pile of blankets on the other side of the campfire. "I've felt eyes on me all day, and every time I look behind us, it's as if something had just moved."

Venell hadn't felt anything of the sort. She agreed with her brother anyway, for there was no sense in arguing with him when he was sure he was right. He would just make her feel stupid until she gave in. There wasn't anything they could do if someone chose to follow them. If they were prey in the black of the night, then they were certainly defenseless. No amount of Ash's rigorous training could make him see in the dark.

Vivid dreams always gave her the most restless sleep. She dreamed of the woods that separated Snanka from Valehoutton: the muddy paths of the Orchane Forest, surrounded by vivid, green life. It was there she would meet with the prince.

He said he was the crown prince of Snanka; his name was Aconite and he had been tall and handsome. His voice soothed her, and his kindness warmed her frozen heart. She dreamed of soft, white moonlight upon his smiling face. His concern for her touched her, but still she shied away.

Then his face faded away and she was in Cynn before the quarantine. She could taste the salty air as she looked out over the sea from their home. Four small residences were below them, and at least three on either side. At the top of the building she could see over the great wall and gaze out upon the horizon. It was bright, brighter still with the reflection of the sun off the white wall and the water. She blinked and looked for her parents, but only skeletons walked through her house. There were only two at first, smiling through fleshless mouths, but then they doubled. Soon there were so many skeletons they were spilling out of the windows and falling five stories down.

Venell felt completely unrested when she awoke the next morning. Her dream of the Orchane Forest was one she has seen many nights before, but the turn to the dead in Cynn was a new nightmare. Ash looked like he had sat up wide-eyed the entire night, yet he was on his feet and ready for travel before she was. She felt so discouraged, knowing entirely too well that she was slowing her brother's progress. She was constantly lagging behind him and had to stop to eat and rest twice as much as he did. Throughout the day Ash kept muttering to himself about them being followed.

It must have been midday when she found herself deeper into the forest than she had ever been. It was surprisingly bright. Much of the sunlight was able to reach the forest floor and cast a radiant glow upon everything it touched. Birds were soaring over their heads, chirping louder and louder as they pressed on. A small stream ran through the clearing that they had come upon. Thinking nothing of the new surroundings, the Keoneos crossed the threshold. It seemed as though all the life in the forest fell silent the moment Ash's boot touched that stream. Ash looked around suspiciously. His hand was steadily placed at the hilt of his sword as his icy blue eyes carefully scanned the forest all around him. The wind mysteriously picked up, carrying leaves in its invisible current.

At the far edge of the clearing, directly in the siblings' path, stood a young woman. She was the first human either had seen besides each other for more than a decade. Ash stopped dead in his tracks, while Venell carelessly kept walking forward. She had forgotten about danger and evil; her heart was too excited by the notion of interacting with another person. As she drew closer, the other woman suddenly unsheathed two knives and readied herself to attack. Venell quickly stopped and put her hands up. She looked to her brother for direction, but he remained focus on the woman before them.

 She wore rough spun clothes of a loose weave; the top was sleeveless and ended above her bellybutton, while the bottom only covered her to mid-thigh, less than even Venell's undergarments. The exposed skin across her body was patterned with tanned and pale patches, even on her face. A brown pelt was wrapped around her shoulders, while a thick, leather belt hung diagonally from her left hip to right thigh. Knotted, flaxen hair was tightly pulled back on either side of her head.

 "Stop where you stand, miserable curs. Are you some of Kras'?" She barked out in a husky voice that seemed so strange to be coming from her petite frame. She accusingly pointed one of her daggers at the Keoneos.

Ash nearly spat with anger. "No, we would never follow that tyrant."

"Oh, then what are you doing so near to the garrison? Just taking a casual stroll?" She asked facetiously while nonchalantly spinning one dagger around her hand, then catching it again on the hilt.

She let out an animalistic growl from deep in her throat and then lunged at Venell. She covered so much ground in a blink of an eye. Venell quickly, though not gracefully, ducked out of her way. The woman turned her attack onto Ash. He drew his short sword and skillfully blocked many of her attacks; though he never had the opportunity to strike as he was far too busy trying to defend himself. She was lightning fast; Venell could barely see her moving. The woman's eyes were flooded with bloodlust, making them narrow and cat-like.

"We're survivors of Cynn!" Venell suddenly shouted out loud. The woman immediately stopped her attack to look Venell's way.

Ash took the opportunity to trip her and pin her to the ground with his blade pointed to her throat. The sharp edge ever so slightly grazed the flesh on her neck, causing a small trickle of blood to ooze from the wound and trickle down to her chest.

The woman lifted a single hand to the cut and wiped away the blood, revealing that the wound had sealed itself in a matter of seconds. Venell thought her eyes were playing tricks on her at first, but she could plainly see that there was no longer any mark on the woman's skin. Ash stared at the woman, completely bewildered. She angrily grabbed onto his sword and pushed it away from her. She looked angrier that he had bested her than worried about her life being in danger. Venell could see the truth in her eyes; the two siblings were no threat to her.

She bared her teeth and hissed at Ash. "I am no fool! There was only one who survived Kras' massacre-" The air around them was suddenly pierced by an incredibly high-pitched whistling. Ash and Venell both dropped to the ground helplessly with their hands covering their ears. The woman got to her feet and dusted the dirt off her clothing. In the same place they had seen her so suddenly appear, another figure emerged. It must've been a man, but the enrobed entity was over seven feet tall. He kept his head lowered so that the hood of his dark blue cloak concealed his face.

He approached the Keoneos slowly. It felt as though it took him forever to reach the spot before them, and the air became thick and stagnant. He raised his head slightly, and they saw that a white, porcelain mask with a painted face upon it covered his real one. Venell felt his gaze wash all over her entire being, looking into her soul and most distant memories. She felt as though she was re-experiencing all the visions that played across her eyes.

Relief warmed her as his gaze turned to her brother. The look on Ash's face told her that he experienced the same phenomena she had. He finally came to rest near the young woman, whose chest was heaving with the adrenaline of earlier battle. She remained focused on him, waiting for him to give her an answer or an instruction.

"Ash and Venell Keoneo, I would like to introduce myself. I am Aldrion."

Venell felt her spine prickle. The omnipotent presence he spread was all-consuming. It was experiencing both fear and awe simultaneously. Her legs trembled, but tears of joy sprung into her eyes.

His voice boomed so deeply it seemed to echo across all the Saltwoods in all directions.

"This is Nalahi Daaine. She is more like you than you know. She also lived in Cynn twelve years ago."

4: THE MATRICIDER

JUNE 1849: TIVER RESERVATION, VALEHOUT-TON

The fog was beginning to roll in. Minortai inhaled deeply and fixed his gaze, then exhaled slowly. The black wood was smooth under his fingertips as he methodically drew them down the length of the arrow until his hand was fixed at ear level. The lion was completely unsuspecting. Minortai could tell by its sluggish movements and taunt skin over bones that it was nearly starved to death. The poor creature was probably one of the last of its kind: the white lions of the Godsmoors. The maneless, white coated cats had once shared their homeland with his people. At one time they were mutually respected kin. Now as food grew sparse for both with the loss of their homes, each became prey for the other.

This should be an easy kill. The valley grew dark as the clouds blocked out the remaining sunlight. He let the arrow fly, his aim straight to the animal's heart.

The arrow noisily clattered against the rocks behind the lion. He misjudged the distance to his target, again. The animal quickly darted away into the thick vapor and vanished from Minortai's sight. He rubbed his eyes and angrily cursed at himself under his breath. Two days of traveling this far into the land of mists had proven futile and he would have to return to camp empty handed.

He only had three arrows left in his quiver, and they would not be enough to defend himself if he had the misfortune of running into any mercenaries. The only other weapon he carried was a small flaying knife that had yet to be used, seeing that he had never made a kill. It was difficult to see the stars through the heavy fog, yet Minortai could sense the pull of his namesake constellation from the East. He slung his bow over his shoulder and began to traverse the slick rocks that lined the path of his way back to camp.

All the people of the Godsmoors had patterns of white or silver speckles across their faces that matched a constellation, and it was from those patterns that they received their names. The large, triangular pattern across his own was that of Minortai: The Matricider. It was an ancient yet easily distinguishable pattern that no one had been born with for generations. While it was impossible to know exactly how long it had been since a Minortai had been born, as their records and histories were all destroyed when greth mercenaries sacked Falvendell, he knew that he was the only one since his people had lost the Godsmoors.

Minortai had traveled far beyond Tiver in his younger days. He had been to the capital as a child with his father, and he had been the borders of Snanka more recently with his brother, Nehlas. The people of Valehoutton outside of Tiver were always in such a rush. Their decisions and emotions were so rash, and they lacked the vision for long term consequence. Now he feared that he and his people would have to live like them or die.

Even after only three decades away from their sacred land, his peoples' lives grew shorter, the stars across their faces became sparser and less clear in meaning with each generation. There were children born that had never known the Godsmoors. They were forgetting the old ways. The ancient Deep flow of life and power that constantly courses within the earth, that all but his people had forgotten, was as strong as ever, but he could only just feel its constant beckon. He had been too far from the Godsmoors for too long.

    The people of Valehoutton that studied the old ways and tried to use the earth's power for themselves never succeeded. His people were the only ones that understood. The people of Valehoutton could not be taught, for they only tainted the purity of the cycle. He feared that the only way for his people to regain balance would be to regain their land, but it was becoming increasingly apparent that if too much time passed their connection would be severed forever. His race would be lost to the world.

    He could still remember how Tiver had been thirty years ago, before the Redals allowed the greth to overrun their home. The southern lands of the Godsmoors were blanketed with meadows, rolling low hills, and small creeks that trickled across the land from waterfalls spilling over the surrounding mountains. Mists from the Northern Shore settled into the valley every evening and lingered throughout the morning. Fields of purple, yellow, and orange wildflowers turned into woodlands of pine and sequoia as the land elevated into the Crags, which surrounded the sacred Godsmoors to the west, east, and south. He could still smell the life in the air when he recalled those days. He clung to his memory of that Tiver, though he knew well enough that the lands of his ancestors were no longer an idyllic sanctuary for his people.

Black smoke rose from the West; from the heart of the Godsmoors. The land was overrun with the scarlet-skinned, reptilian, Tuaegian-native greth and their primitive forges; fueled by fire and blood. They had arrived during the reign of Sireh Redal, and had continued to multiply during his son's reign, though less regulated by the crown. They were a violent race, always focused on blood and conquest. They had no regard for life or sustainability. It was no wonder the elders sadly proclaimed they could no longer hear the world's voice, for it was drowned out by screaming and weeping. The greth were killing the land.

He recalled the fear and confusion they faced when Redals soldiers and greth arrived to remove them from their homes. Rumors had reached Tiver that Godsmoorians were being uprooted by the Tuaegian mercenaries in the North and East, closer to the border, but to see them at the center of their hallowed grounds was demoralizing. Resistance was met with violence, and his people were not a violent race. Even the strongest amongst them were nothing compared to the blood-thirsty mercenaries. Their long era of peace had made them complacent.

They had only two days to pack their belongings before they were led in caravans to the sanctioned reservation in the South, which was a high desert of desolate land. The terrain was rocky, and the flora was nothing but sagebrush and juniper. So far their attempts to renew their agriculture had been fruitless, and as the years went on they became more and more isolated on the reservation itself. It was dangerous to venture off alone with greth crawling around every crevice. Even now, Minortai felt fear and adrenaline pumping through his body when he thought of those hellish, yellow, bulging eyes and mouthfuls of long, pointed teeth.

He had been born in Ceres, over a hundred years ago now, though his memory of the city was not as clear as that of Tiver. It was an ancient, wealthy city carved into the side of the Crags. The buildings and roads were part of the mountain itself. He remembered his father, an aging war hero with sad eyes, and how even as a child Nehlas followed exactly in his footsteps. His paternal aunt and uncle lived with his family in their river-side home. He remembered seeing them much more than he saw either his father or brother. Minortai was still a child when his father died; the old soldier had let go of life long before his body followed. Nehlas was never the same after their father was gone. The boy was forced to become a man with far too much resentment locked in his heart.

Nehlas: The Noble Warrior. His brother's path was one of both honor and glory; named for one of the greatest ancient heroes of the Godsmoors. He always walked with his head raised high and his chest held out broadly. Nehlas was born with such skill that it crackled like lightning through his soul. Everyone was drawn to his radiance. His bright, blue-green eyes were the only thing that outshone his perfect, glittering smile. Women swooned over his muscled arms and long, wavy white-blonde hair, but he had yet to take a wife even though his centennial year had already come and gone.

He was fortunate to reach the border of the reservation without being usurped by any mercenaries. He had not seen any sign of the beasts. It was only a few more miles to his village from the boundary line. There were still remnants of those that lived so close to the edge of the reservation, old fire pits and tent stakes, but they had been the first to be killed when the raids began. Now their makeshift tent-village was set a mile in and surrounded by warriors and sentries on every side.

Ten years ago, when he had just become a young man, he had his one success as a warrior when he saved a woman from three greth mercenaries. He had no weapon with him, for during an earlier fight a huge greth had wrestled his sword from his hand and he was forced to flee. In midflight the woman's screams reached his ears as a greth tossed her over its shoulder. Two others nearby argued about killing her on the spot since she wasn't young enough to be sold into slavery.

Minortai picked up a rock that was a little larger than his closed fist and sprang into action. He slammed the rock onto the greth's kneecap. The greth shrieked and dropped the woman as all three of the mercenaries turned to him. He smashed in the greth's other kneecap, and then quickly rolled out of the way of the second one's massive club. He wasn't even thinking anymore, he was just reacting. He tackled the greth with the club, tore off the creature's helmet and smashed the rock into its face. The third one was the biggest of them all, and it picked Minortai up by the neck while baring its yellowed, needle-like fangs. Its breath smelled like rotting flesh, and Minortai felt himself growing dizzy from either the smell or the lack of air. The creature continued to curse him in Tuaegian.

With his last ounce of strength, Minortai lifted his hand that held the rock and forced it into the greth's mouth, breaking off most of its needle-like teeth and causing it to release his throat. Minortai gasped for air as he fumbled around on the ground, trying to find the rock before the greth regained itself and finished him off. His hands instead found a rope. The greth was still writhing in pain next to its unconscious comrade with the broken knees. Minortai looped the rope around its neck and strangled the beast to death.

He sat back to catch his breath for a moment. He had almost completely forgotten about the woman until he heard the crack of the kneecapped greth's head splitting open when she struck it with a heavy wooden shield. She pulled Minortai into an embrace but didn't say anything. He remembered that she smelled like the purple flowers that used to bloom on the Godsmoors during late summer. Her hair was soft and brown, and the shape of Siyah the Lover sparkled across her cheeks beneath her gentle, lilac eyes.

He felt his mouth curve into a smile as he walked. Just the thought of her made him smile. Nehlas has taunted him for marrying her since she was not only widowed, but also nearly a half a century his senior. Siyah was wise and reserved, but she could still always manage to surprise him. He had never known someone to be both so tender and so fierce. Delicate lines from years of laughter around her mouth and eyes only made her more beautiful.

Siyah's entire body radiated her beautiful soul. He could listen forever to her voice tell him about her childhood, her home, and about all her hopes and dreams for the two of them. The thought of her honey-colored skin sliding under his palms and that husky tone her voice always got in bed was enough to make his face flush even though he was alone. She was at home now, waiting for him, ready to greet him with a kiss.

Minortai passed the line of sentries, he heard one of them chuckle to the others about how he was returning empty handed again. A funeral was being held as evening turned to night. Someone named Owreh had died, for the pyre burned to the North under the constellation of The Great Bird of Morning. A fever had broken out among the children on the reservation, many of them were laid out under the stars in hope the earth might spare their lives. Their families sat around them crying and praying. The candle inside Nehlas' tent was still burning. Minortai guessed his new favorite girl was paying him a visit.

Siyah was waiting outside their tent for him, watching the sun set. She turned as she heard him approach. She smiled, but he could see the tears in her eyes. She held a small woven doll meant for a child. "My niece..." she began, but her voice trailed into quiet sobs. Minortai dropped his bow and quiver and took his wife into his arms. He inhaled her scent deeply and felt her warmth against him. He wanted to comfort her, but just to hold her made his heart swell with such happiness that nothing seemed sad anymore.

Siyah's brother and niece were her only living relatives, and the child had fallen ill not three days before. Her brother had been badly wounded during a recent raid and had still not begun to recover. Minortai knew the blows of losing your loved ones did not lessen with each added on, but it was sadly almost expected to lose someone you knew every day. Their race was dwindling. Minortai's aunt and uncle had both died on the journey to the reservation. Nehlas had been forced to care for him until he came of age. But all those tears and all the bitterness were lost as he lay down next to Siyah and caressed her lips with his own.

She shuddered under his touch and brushed her fingers through his hair. There was something to live for even if they lost everything: love. From that first day he found some untapped power in his soul to save her, and for every day after, he knew that she was the greatest meaning to life that he had ever found. Years of being shunned for the marks across his face, years of feeling the underlying hatred of his father and brother for when his mother was forced to trade her life so that he might live, years of constant struggles and failures to overcome the slightest of life's obstacles, nothing mattered. She knew him, understood him, and still loved him. Siyah had shown him love and his heart had changed forever.

Morning always brought reality back to his mind. Siyah lay with him under his arm, naked except for the sheet she had wrapped herself in. He lay there for a while, letting her sleep and remain in a better place. The sounds of the village grew louder as the sun rose higher. There used to be many voices: some just talking, some laughing and there had been the sounds of children playing. Now there were only stern conversations met by weeping and pleas to the Deep earth. He kissed Siyah and her eyes fluttered open, though they were still heavy with sleep. He told her to stay in bed, then got up and dressed himself. He stepped outside to find Nehlas and the other warriors sitting with the remaining elders.

"We won't make it through another season with what's left of the reserves compared to our daily intake. A party will have to venture further south than we've ever gone in hopes of bringing back enough food and supplies. Whether it be by trade or by sword, it has to be done." Nehlas argued with the other captains.

"We can't leave our people so vulnerable." The last female elder replied.

"There hasn't been a raid in months. We haven't even seen mercenaries anywhere near the border. We'll leave enough men to defend the village, but it will still take many of us to be successful on this trek," said Nehlas.

The other two elders exchanged glances before lifting their heads and nodding in approval.

The female elder looked down dismally and muttered something to herself.

"Good, we leave today!" Nehlas shouted to the warriors before taking off to supply himself with weapons. The warriors dispersed, leaving the elders sitting by the fire alone. All three sat with their arms folded and were looking older every day.

The woman saw Minortai passing, "Your brother grows more reckless."

Minortai stopped and let his shoulders drop. He ran his hand through his hair before taking a seat across from the elders. "Who is he leaving behind? Will it really be enough to protect us if the mercenaries do come?"

"He's taking twenty of the best warriors." The bearded elder replied. He coughed harshly. "The other soldiers and the sentries will remain, and arms will be given to every able-bodied man and woman left." He began to cough again, though this time there was no reprieve until a healer hurried over to give him a cup of soothing nectar.

"Maybe if you and the other useless young men brought a kill back when you ventured out, we wouldn't be in such a sorry state, Matricider." The other male elder cursed at him.

Minortai didn't respond, he stood and left the fire. He found where the warriors were gathering to prepare for their journey. They were taking all the remaining horses in the village. Wives and mothers embraced their husbands and sons before they readied their steeds. Nehlas stood at the head of the crowd like a proverbial hero. One hand was on his long sword and the other held his silver helmet. A green and blue cloak was draped over his engraved silver armor that had once belonged to their father.

"Nehlas!" Minortai called out to his brother.

Nehlas clapped his hand on Minortai's shoulder and led him aside, "You don't think you're coming with us?" he said in a lowered voice.

Minortai felt the sting of his words deeply, "No, I didn't, but do you really think this is best? There won't be enough of us left if the mercenaries come. Look at us, we're dying by the moment!"

"You think I don't see that?!" Nehlas snapped at him. "Why do you think I'm doing this? We're all going to starve to death in a matter of months if nothing is done. I'm taking action! What the hell have you done to help? Just go back to your crone of a woman and leave the bigger matters to us!" Nehlas put on his helmet and turned his back on his brother, his cloak fluttering behind him magnificently.

In a daze, Minortai wandered back to his tent. He took off his boots in silence as to not wake his wife, and he sat down on the bed. It wasn't even anything his brother said to him, not even the elder's words hurt him anymore. He just had a deep, awful feeling that Nehlas was making a terrible mistake. He worriedly began to wonder if he and Siyah would be better off abandoning their dying people and trying to make a living elsewhere. All he wanted was her anyway. Siyah was awakened by the thundering noise of twenty-one horses leaving the village.

"What's happening?" She asked, startled.

"Nehlas is taking the twenty best men out scouting." Minortai ran his hand through his hair. "We're not going to make it here. I don't know where we would go, but I think we should leave the reservation."

Siyah frowned, "My brother is here. If he starts to get better, he'll need me."

"He's not going to get better." Minortai slipped without thinking.

Siyah's eyes flashed with anger and her hands balled into fists. "How dare you say something like that!? Don't you have any hope at all, Minortai? We can't just abandon everyone and think our problems will go away. No matter where we go, we'll be persecuted for our stars. Our place is here, with our people."

"It's over, Siyah. Our ways, our race, it's all over. We have to save ourselves somehow."

Siyah shoved him back. "Our place is here until the end!" She shook her head and stormed out of the tent.

Minortai began to cry and put his face in his hands. He couldn't leave her. If she wouldn't come with him, he would stay here with her until they and everyone they knew were dead. If she wanted to stay and watch their race's demise, he would stay with her and hold her. She was all he wanted after all.

Siyah still hadn't come back by nightfall. He had never made her this angry before. He knew she was sitting with her brother in the sick tent, but he still knew better than to go after her until she was ready.

Minortai put the last of his sweet leaf into his wooden pipe, the only thing he inherited from his uncle. He lay back under the night sky and inhaled the smoke. His uncle had taught him to blow rings of smoke when he exhaled. The rings expanded until they disappeared against the canvas of the stars. He lay facing southeast, underneath Siyah's constellation. It was his favorite time of year in late summer when he could see her rise over him. Soon he would go to bed and find her there. They would make up and make love.

But then the sentries began to shout

: DESTINY

JUNE 1849: THE SALTWOODS

Nalahi chewed on her bottom lip angrily as she continued to eye Ash and his sister. He felt the fire of impatience burning inside him. "How could you have survived the quarantine, the riots, the massacre, and then the flood? You would've only been children then." She demanded.

"How did you survive?" Ash immediately snapped back. "We only did so with broken bodies." Out of the corner of his eye Ash saw his sister absently, yet self-consciously, lift her hand to where her scarred ribs were hidden under her tunic. "We spent the entire night after the flood clinging to treetops and praying that we didn't lose our grip. Venell nearly died from her injuries, and it took her months to recover from the infection she got from her broken ribs. Don't doubt for a second what we've been through."

Nalahi looked ready to fire back, but the mysterious Aldrion spoke first. "People that have experienced the same tragedy should unite against a common enemy rather than attack the degree of one's grievances. Nalahi comes from a prominent political family in Cynn, so they were taken south and imprisoned where the flood did not reach them. However, when her family refused to give information, they were slaughtered. A kind soul helped Nalahi, her little sister, and two young friends escape to where they took refuge in the Saltwoods. However, I could not reach them in time to save anyone except Nalahi. I raised her, and when she was old enough, she began to take justice into her own hands."

Ash couldn't help but suspect that Nalahi was the presence he had felt trailing him since he and Venell set foot in the Saltwoods. She never ambushed them while they slept, and easily could have. It could be true that she was specifically hunting Kras' men. Ash couldn't shake the feelings of mistrust that still lingered at the heart of his judgment. "You said Kras had a garrison near here, where is it?" Ash asked as he turned toward Nalahi.

She nodded "It is just northwest of Bardon on the Whispering Plains. Kras has been keeping his most profitable city under his thumb for the last decade. If you had ever seen Bardon before, it is certainly no longer how you remember." She wrinkled her nose at that thought. "It is a stinking city of travelers, soldiers, and criminals. All are the lowliest filth of Valehoutton that do not deserve the slightest mercy."

Nalahi seemed incredibly rough and quick to anger alongside her well-composed guardian. Ash still wasn't sure which of them to watch more closely. The woman's eyes even flashed an angry yellow when she spoke of the city, of the king, and of his kin. "I have been trying to force the soldiers to abandon the garrison, but the best I can do alone is make myself a nuisance to them."

Aldrion's booming voice suddenly rang through the air: "Join Nalahi and go to the garrison, Keoneos. Prove yourself worthy allies to Valehoutton and mortal enemies of our kingdom's cruel, unfit ruler. Kras must see the extent of his destruction. The balance of the world will not allow him to tip the scales any longer."

It wasn't a command, nor was it a suggestion. It seemed to Ash as though his fate was speaking directly to him. It was so clear that only a fool would ignore it. The opportunity was perfect, and it was almost too easy. Ash knew he could not refuse the chance to finally close his fingers over the king's throat, even with the looming threat of betrayal.

Ash exchanged glances with his sister. It was the first time he has seen a glimmer of hope within her in years. Venell's eyes were pleading with him. Ash frowned, but he still extended his hand out to Aldrion. "We will join you." Ash said with finality.

Nalahi stepped in front of Aldrion's towering figure and clasped Ash's hand in his stead. Ash was surprised how much heat Nalahi's skin gave off as it touched his. "I will be the one leading you on this task. Our future together will be determined by this outcome. Now follow me."

As soon as she finished speaking, Nalahi turned away and began to jog toward the end of the Saltwoods. She quickly picked up speed and loitered near the threshold of his vision. Aldrion had vanished as well but with no trace. Ash stared at the clearing where the enigmatic man had been standing just seconds before. His natural inclination to be suspicious wasn't nagging at him, to his own surprise. He knew somewhere in his body that that booming voice spoke true. The Keoneos were left with no choice but to hastily follow the wild woman further into the Saltwoods, or be left behind to wonder what could have been.

    Nalahi moved incredibly fast. She knew every inch of the woods. She skillfully ducked under branches and hopped over stones, leaving Ash and Venell so far behind that they kept losing sight of her. She finally stopped for a moment to let the siblings catch up as she glared at them over her shoulder irritably. Before the two could meet up with her, she was gone again. The forest was getting brighter as the setting sun shone horizontally over the golden Whispering Plains and reflected onto the city of Bardon in the distance.

    Nalahi stood at the crest of the wide, rolling plains that lay before them. The city sat flush with the horizon, illuminated by millions of lights within. Venell's eyes were wide and overwhelmed by the glow of civilization. After all this time, Bardon had been so near, yet they remained in ruins of the past.

    Nalahi pointed to a stone tower just north of Bardon and closer to the edge of the Saltwoods. Ash counted three columns of windows stacked vertically up the rounded walls. It wasn't heavily fortified; no bars on the windows, and the wooden door with simple hinges would not withstand a ram. "That is the garrison. Kras' generals and commanders just use it to store supplies. It's not heavily guarded, but whenever I rid it of one minion, another takes his place the next dawn. Most of the soldiers live within the city, spending their earnings on drinks and whores." She spat on the ground in disgust. "If we attack now, the rest will not know until late morning when they finally drag themselves out of bed."

A softer look that Ash had not yet seen on the woman's face took him by surprise. "Tell me truthfully, have you ever taken the life of your own kind? It is a vital threshold if you have not crossed it yet. You must be able to separate their lives from the lives you will save. You cannot think of them as one of your own."

Venell didn't have to answer; Nalahi could see the truth in the fearful look on his sister's face. The girl had never hurt someone in her life. "I have." Ash finally spoke up. His tone was deep and serious.

Nalahi gave him a disapproving look. "But can you do the rest of the things I asked of you? You do not kill them because of the wrongs put upon you. You kill them because you must; for all of Valehoutton."

Ash nodded. He could make all the promises he wanted, but when he finally held a blade to Kras' throat and slowly revealed the crimson within, that cut would be his greatest release. Venell also nodded when Nalahi's gaze turned on her.

Nalahi took off running again, keeping to the edge of the forest for cover. She was much easier to follow on flat land than through the woods. They stood at the base of the garrison in no time. There was only one entrance on the ground floor, but there were several windows that lined each floor around the entire building. Ash followed Nalahi's lead and crouched behind some trees behind the garrison. They were close enough to hear soldiers talking within. Two exchanged vulgar stories just inside the entrance, complete with hand motions. A yellow light surrounded the pair as it poured from the wide-open door.

It felt like their journey was truly beginning. He had just taken his first leap toward the throne room. Nalahi leaned over to whisper to him, "Listen, I will climb through one of the upper windows. As I make my way down, eventually those two morons by the door will come looking to see what is going on. Once they come inside, you two will be completely clear. There are no more than five guards on duty. We corner them, kill them, and then destroy everything in here. Keep the outside of the building clean or we risk being caught."

Without another instruction, she suddenly leapt toward the side of the garrison, skillfully clinging to grooves in the wall and climbing up the tower. She grabbed onto the top of the window and swung herself inside, disappearing from Ash's view. The siblings exchanged glances.

Venell drew her dagger and looked as ready as someone so fearful could. Instead of his short sword, Ash opted for his dart blower instead; for stealth and distance. Each dart had been carefully dipped in a poison he had learned to cook from a combination of plants and snake venom. He claimed one puncture would paralyze in seconds and kill in minutes, but he had yet to use it anything besides squirrels and rabbits. He had doubled the potency of this batch before they left Cynn. Ash crept closer to the entrance and ducked under some bushes. He aimed his dart blower at the pair of soldiers and waited.

"That's some big news, ain't it? Think he'll stop by to make sure we're following protocol?"

"Nah, he never does. He don't give a fuck what we do if the revenue stays the same and no Red scum start spreading 'round."

"I've only met him in person once. Don't think I ever want to again though. He's a hard guy to please, but real easy to piss off."

"Yeah, that's the truth." One guard chuckled. "Good ol' King Kras in our humble Bardon but doesn't invite us to the party."

Ash felt his heart freeze in mid-beat. His fists clenched around the blowpipe. He could almost laugh in the sheer disbelief that engulfed him. Of all the times they chose to finally leave Cynn and to come to Bardon, it was the exact time Kras was there was well. His destiny was so clear. The path was at his feet and all he had to do was follow and all would be set right. And how righteous it would be that he, the son of the exiled General Keoneo and a survivor of Cynn, would be the one to lay the bastard to rest.

There was a loud crash and the sound of grown men screaming. Instead of running into the building as to investigate as Nalahi had anticipated, the two guards in the front fled for their lives.

Ash cursed under his breath as he saw they were coming straight toward Venell's hiding place. He blew a round of darts that hit one guard in the neck and chest. He collapsed instantly, and his body began to seize. His partner cried out and knelt over his friend's body. Ash blew another round and killed the second guard. Venell safely emerged from her hiding spot and approached the front door of the base. Ash quickly followed her. He could still hear fighting within the building. Ash used the flat side of his sword as a mirror to look around the corner before he rushed inside. He nodded to Venell, indicating it was clear.

They charged into the building with swords raised high. There was one bloodied body on the ground, and a second rolling down the stairs with a feathered dagger sticking out of his skull. Nalahi suddenly darted down the stairs, kicking the corpse out of her way. "Did you kill them? Those two fucking cowards that ran?"

"Yes, both of them are dead." Ash replied.

"Good." Nalahi sighed heavily attempting to catch her breath. She placed her foot on the skull of the man's body before her, bent over, and tore the dagger from within his brains. She wiped the blood and bone fragments off on his clothes before returning it to its sheath around her waist. "Was it messy?"

"I don't think so." Ash said grimly. "But there is something more important. We overheard them saying that Kras himself is currently in Bardon."

Nalahi smiled wickedly. "Well, aren't you two the luckiest find I've ever had." She stepped outside, and the siblings followed. She placed her index finger and thumb in her cheeks and whistled loudly. Aldrion's dark silhouette emerged from the shadows of the trees and took his place by his Nalahi's side. Ash felt goosebumps pop across his arms as the air changed with the man's presence. "We overheard guards discussing that Kras himself is in Bardon." She told him.

"You will get what you desire if you venture to Bardon tonight." The otherworldly man boomed.

Nalahi seemed overwhelmed. "I've never been so close..." she mumbled. "I'll return when it's done." She said as she turned to face him. Aldrion whispered something to her before once again disappearing into the night.

"Why isn't he coming?" Ash questioned the wild woman. He couldn't imagine an ally so massive hindering their cause.

"Aldrion is still bound to the Saltwoods, as he has been since he found me twelve years ago." She replied. Her voice was even more curt that usual, as if she didn't want to answer Ash fully, but she knew that she had to give him something to keep their delicate trust intact. "He may know much, but he cannot alter what is to come. That is up to us."

Venell shot him a look he knew all too well. His sister was incredibly uncomfortable, but she wouldn't say anything about it. He didn't acknowledge her pleading gaze.

Nalahi once again turned to Ash and Venell. "This is crucial. The coward would never leave at night for fear of being robbed, so he must be staying at an inn. We probably only have until dawn to find him, but I know we can do it." Her eyes darted back and forth between the Keoneos. "Are you still with me?"

"We would never turn from an opportunity like this." Ash replied.

6: HER EYES

BARDON

The pair moved with silent, deadly perfection. Their prey was entirely unaware as they watched them from their perch in the inn's rafters. Krisae drew the two curved-blade dirks she kept strapped to her thighs. Ronnock watched her eyes fill with Red, and her jaw unhinge as her fangs slid down. It still unsettled him to watch the transformation, knowing that he looked just as fearsome when he let out his own beast. He shifted his weight onto his toes, readying himself to leap down onto their unsuspecting victims.

In a flash of crimson, Krisae descended upon the officers. She had already decapitated three of the uniformed men before the others in the room even realized they were under attack.

Ronnock watched the men fight for their lives as Krisae played her favorite game. Even when a greth's hooked blade caught one of her dirks and tore it from her hand, Krisae threw down the other and ripped out the greth's throat with her bare hands. She threw its long, forked tongue to the floor, where it continued to writhe about.

The greth were scarlet-skinned mercenaries with bulging yellow eyes that were native to Tuaega. They were reptilian in appearance, though they mirrored the stature of a grown human. Kras preferred to use them in his royal army, thinking that gold was the best loyalty. They were terrifying at first, with mouths full of long, needle-like teeth, but after fighting them for many years Ronnock had learned the creatures were utterly predictable in their attacks.

The greth continued to swarm Krisae. She was an unarmed, young woman, and they were trained as soldiers since childhood, how could she stand a chance? But the officers knew better, or some were just cowards, and they rushed to the doors to escape.

Ronnock finally made his descent from the thick, overhead beams. He dropped in front of the only exit and blocked the path of the officers. They shuddered at the sight of his face, taking a step back and shaking in their polished boots. He looked upon the men with his grey eyes, his human eyes, then drew his sword and made an end of them. Only one even managed to draw his sword before Ronnock's blade cut them open. A weak parry was hardly a hinderance to Ronnock's absolute dominance. The long blade of his bastard sword knocking aside the soldier's rapier was the singular clang of metal in the room.

The inn became uncomfortably silent as Ronnock turned to scan the room for any remaining life. An older officer with a ponytail and a crisply pressed uniform cowered behind an overturned table, thinking Ronnock didn't see him. Ronnock grabbed his hair and slashed his blade across the officer's throat. After he released his grip, he began to gather up some of the scattered maps and papers across the wood and straw floor. With only a brief examination of their plans, Ronnock folded the papers into a disheveled lump and shoved them deep into his coat pocket.

Krisae wiped the blood off her mouth with her sleeve, which fortunately was a dark color. The floor was a mottled mess of red and black; human and greth blood. He cleaned the blade of his bastard sword before sheathing it. Out of habit, he ran his thumb over the pommel, smooth and worn from years of his after-battle routine.

The only sound in the building was Krisae's heeled riding boots clicking against the wood floor as she approached him. Her eyes had faded back to grey and her mouth set in a slight, satisfied smile. "I missed you, brother. We never go out anymore."

"That's more you than me." Ronnock replied, really only half-listening to Krisae. It was true, Iratez was no doubt grooming her for leadership since promoting her to lieutenant commander, and it kept her very busy. Krisae had been part of the Insurgo since she was fifteen, shortly after she had become Red. She always pleaded with him to join her at the Valehoutton base from where he had been posted at the headquarters in Snanka, and eventually he caved. He had a difficult time refusing his baby sister anything, and it did not help that she was more than well aware of that.

She punched him in the arm, "Well, we're out now. I could use a drink." She wiped the blood off her blades on the clothes of one of the dead officers before tucking them away into their sheaths. It amazed Ronnock how many weapons she could fit on her slight frame: two dirks, a short sword on her back, some throwing daggers under her belt, a hunting knife under her boot, some flash bombs, some real bombs, and a revolving handgun.

There had been countless ordered purges to remove all firearms from the ordinary citizens of Valehoutton. Ultimately, they were not successful, Krisae was proof, but it certainly made guns a rare find, and well-made ones that wouldn't explode in your hand were even rarer.

They stepped outside into the stinking streets of Bardon. Krisae wasted no time lighting a cigarette and exhaling a red cloud into the evening air. She didn't care who knew she was Red; she never tried to hide it. She embraced it from the moment it was bestowed upon her. If he hadn't known better, he would've thought she was willingly bitten. Most others that were Red were more secretive about their ailment for fear of prejudice. Ronnock refused to exhibit his Red for fear of the violence it would draw. It wasn't for his own safety, but for that of whoever was bold enough to attack him. Almost everyone knew someone that was killed by a Red, and they all seemed to think their vengeance could be satisfied by killing another Red.

He followed her quietly, for he couldn't think of anything to say. Krisae talked though, about everything and anything. She would always just go on about nothing and he would pretend to listen. Krisae looked like their father, more than the other four of his progenies. She had lighter skin than the rest of his siblings and himself, more ivory than beige. Her black hair had a slight waviness to it, and although she kept it cut above her shoulders it always seemed to bounce as she walked. The ends of her hair and bangs were dyed red this month, sometimes they were blue or purple. Her face was young and beautiful; free of any scars with big, pouty lips and straight, white teeth. She was lean and muscular, built like their father, making her a dangerous warrior. Like all the Ukon children she had grey eyes, but hers were much lighter. They verged on silver and shimmered with a lens of child-like wonder that she still saw the world through.

Some people spat at them as they passed. He used to try to confront them, but it was easier to just let it go. He already knew he could kill any of them, what else did he have to prove? Attacking the city folk only produced more fear and hatred toward their kind. "Of course he's a murderer, he's Red" they would say when word reached their ears.

Krisae crushed her cigarette under her boot and turned to face him. Her arched, plucked brows furrowed as she studied his face. "Brother, you act like it's always raining on you."

Even though Krisae was talking to him again, he was watching a line of women, chained together at their wrists, being led by a few greth soldiers. He had never seen the phenomena within the borders of Valehoutton: slaves. It was well known that greth would kidnap women of child-bearing age from settlements they sacked to sell to rich men's bedrooms, but the common practice in Tuaega was slow to take root in Valehoutton. Krisae saw where his eyes were stuck and stopped dead in her tracks. His sister gave him a knowing look.

"Now is not the time." She whispered to him. She grabbed onto his arm to lead him away, but he kept looking back over his shoulder to the line of women. Some were very young, no older than twelve. All of them were crying. "Maybe we should just go back to the base." Krisae said, the wind now out of her sails.

A copper-skinned woman walked with her face buried in her hands. She stumbled slightly, forcing her to look up and around. Her tears were clinging to her long, dark eyelashes. As she looked up her ghostly, pale blue eyes met with his. Those eyes.

Ronnock tore his arm away from Krisae and ran to the woman, ignoring his sister's shouts. The two greth leading the line turned and hissed at him. "You don't look now, you look when they for sale." The greth had long, stringy black hair and its hand was on its sword.

"I can pay you now." Ronnock lied.

"They not ready for sale." The long-haired greth repeated in its thick Tuaegian accent.

The other greth spat at Ronnock's feet, "We no sell to Red filth!" The greth drew its serrated dagger and pushed Ronnock back with its other hand.

Ronnock felt fire burning in his heart. He stepped toward the greth, provoking it to raise its armed hand in attack. Ronnock grabbed onto its fist and crushed its bones in his hand. The greth dropped its dagger and shrieked with agony. All the women gasped and jumped back from the fight.

With its partner rolling on the street and howling in pain, the long-haired greth's buggish eyes widened even more as Ronnock turned his attention on it. "Just take woman you want! Just take her, which?" he pleaded as he fearfully pointed to each one in line.

Ronnock could've ended it and just taken the blue-eyed girl, but he saw each of the six chained women looking at him with a glimmer of hope in their eyes that they had certainly not felt in a long while. "No, all of them."

The greth hissed and threw its arms around wildly. "It take me months to find them all! I work hard to—" His sentence was cut short as Ronnock's long sword entered the bottom of its jaw and exited out the top of its skull. He took an iron key off the dead greth's body and freed the women from their bonds. "Just go wherever it is you want to go. No one will stop you." He told them. Krisae walked up to his side and gently placed her hand on his shoulder.

Three of the women cried more and thanked him repeatedly before leaving together in a huddle. Two scurried off into the city without a word. Then there was only her left: the blue-eyed girl. Small bells woven into her long, black hair jingled as she walked toward him. She smelled of rich spice and perfumed oils. A jewel glistened from her nose and more from her ears. She clasped his hand warmly, making his skin look deathly pale in comparison to her rich complexion. "Thank you." She said in a low, throaty voice, laden with the exotic Tuaegian accent.

That evening Ronnock was still searching for a room to rent for the Tuaegian girl, who said her name was Nai Kint. She strolled alongside him as they went door to door. The bells in her hair chimed in time with her long, graceful steps. Her skin was incredibly flawless except for the raw sores around her wrists and ankles where she had been chained. "I've never been to Tuaega. I heard it's mostly desert." He told her after they were turned down yet again. He wasn't sure if no one would rent to her because she was Tuaegian or because he was Red.

Even though much of the civilian population of Tuaega was also suffering from their near-constant political unrest of late, many people from Valehoutton looked down on all Tuaegians with contempt and blame for the bloody clashes near their borders. Though it had been more than thirty years since Valehoutton had a long, violent war with Tuaega, only ended when Jet Keoneo led Sireh Redal's troops to victory in the Last Battle at Neige Desert, the countries had not fully made peace. Nai bore all common Tuaegian traits and still wore their traditional clothing: spice-scented chiffon and silks wrapped all around her to form a dress, sandaled feet and oiled hair woven with bells, jewels and feathers. Her wraps were almost entirely coral pink and sunset orange.

She laughed in her low, enticing voice. "Mostly. There are very beautiful parts as well. I used to live in a gorgeous city, Sphiro. I could see the Great River Valley from my bedroom. Are you from Bardon, Ronnock?"

"No, I was born in Snanka. I came to Bardon a few years ago to join the Insurgo."

"Snanka! Now that is all desert!" she laughed again.

The name of his home sparked memories of the hazy, red sun that burned over Snanka all day and late into the evening before setting over the western Black Mountains. The obsidian sand that covered the country made the nights dry and warm, but the days were unbearably hot.

"How long were you with the greth?" He asked her.

"A few months, I do not know exactly. They raided the house where I was living and took all the women as slaves. I saw many of my friends sold before we came here to Bardon." She didn't seem very sad about the notion.

It wasn't the most appealing area of Bardon, but Ronnock finally found an older man that would give Nai room and board for a month once he pressed some gold into his hand. "I'm sure you'll be safe here if you don't go looking for trouble." He told her as he walked with her to the door at the back of the building that led to her room.

"You won't come in with me?" she asked him.

He felt his fangs twinge. So that's what she wanted. He reached around her, slyly tricking her into thinking he was going to touch her, and instead opened the door. She smiled wickedly and snaked her arms around his neck before pulling him into a passionate kiss. Her tongue filled his mouth, delicious and warm. She was pulling his clothes off before he even got the chance to close the door.

He lifted her sheer dress over her head and ran his hands over that skin he had been longing to touch. Every inch of her smelled so good he just had to run his tongue over her belly and the swell of her large breasts.

She laid him down and straddled him. He grabbed a handful of that gorgeous, thick hair as she began to ride him. He tried to enjoy the feel of her, but his thoughts kept coming back around to how skillfully she was fucking him. It was almost like she was following a routine instead of actually feeling anything. She opened her eyes and looked down her face at him. They were brown. Her eyes were brown.

He looked up at her doubtfully as her fake cries continued to fill the room. He relaxed his mind and let her have her way with him. After, she cuddled up against him and asked if he would come back soon. For some reason he said yes. Krisae was waiting for him at a tavern across town to return to the base. He had already taken far too long finding Nai a room. Krisae had probably already started a few brawls.

"When they sell my friends, they are given to men and not to houses," she began as she pulled on a silk covering for her bosom, "I think there are not the pleasure houses in Valehoutton?"

He tried hard to hide his disdain. He knew it. He redressed and looked up at her. Now her eyes were green. "No, there are many in Bardon." He muttered more disapproval under his breath as she went on about how she thought she could make good money in this city. "Well, I know where to find you." He said before he left.

    He immediately lit a cigarette. He was frustrated and anxious and needed something to satiate himself. He had forgotten to consider that some Tuaegians had eyes that changed color based on their mood. Those blue eyes were not the ones that kept talking to him in his head. They were a trick, just like everything else about her.

    He angrily stalked through the dark alleys of Bardon until he came upon the Green Roof tavern that he had left Krisae at hours ago. Apparently, no one could be bothered to light the lamps after sunset anymore. Though he supposed the darkness was fitting for what Bardon was becoming.

    Inside, the air was thick with smoke and rowdy noise. He walked in to see Krisae standing on a table with a fat woman, their arms linked and both trying to finish a full tankard of ale faster than the other. Men crowded around the table had fistfuls of money as they made wagers on the winner. Krisae tossed her empty mug into the crowd as a roar broke out. Obviously, no one was betting on her to win. She laughed loudly and belched, as if she were drunken old man with a huge gut, and then comically danced around the fat woman who was unable to even finish her tankard. As she did the last spin of her jig, one of her feet caught on the other and she fell off the table.

Ronnock parted the crowd and scooped his little sister off the tavern floor. There were some calls of disapproval from patrons who though he was taking her for himself. He didn't reply. He knew they were fools for thinking that she would choose any of them over a bed to herself. He had only ever known Krisae sleep with someone when she wanted something from them.

"Aw, Ronnie, c'mon, I can keep going." She mumbled out drunkenly. He wasn't in the mood for her antics. He paid the innkeeper for a room and carried Krisae upstairs. In no time she was snoring and drooling away. They wouldn't be returning to the base until morning it seemed. Krisae was such a powerful fighter and hardworking leader that sometimes Ronnock would forget how young she was.

He took a seat by the large paneled window in the room and lit another cigarette. It was a difficult task for his shaking hands. He hadn't felt real anger for a long while, and as he continued to reflect upon his awkward meeting and even more awkward intimate encounter, he felt like a fool. A group of four greth walking past the inn caught his attention. Krisae was still dead asleep. He left the room and locked the door behind him. He slid the key under the door so Krisae wouldn't break it down when she woke from her stupor. He hurried out onto the street and took to the rooftops.

The greth went into a pub in the prostitute-run section of Bardon. If just one of them stepped outside for a minute, he would hack the creature's disgusting head right off its shoulders. He'd place his aggression in a good outlet. Time ticked by, and he considered just abandoning his quest for violence, until a heavy wood and iron door in the back of the pub that led into the alley suddenly slammed open. A figure draped in sunset hues appeared in the alley. Ronnock rubbed his eyes in utter exasperation. It was Nai that stumbled out into the night, closely followed by a greth. The greth grabbed her by the hair and shouted something at her in Tuaegian as she covered her face and cried.

For just a moment, he considered leaving her to her fate. He felt no need to defend her, but the guilt of leaving her to suffer and possibly die did make him feel obligated to interfere. He was ashamed of the irritation rising inside of him. He had tried to close the door of his life to her, but she was knocking again. He didn't want to answer it. Nai continued to plead with the greth, even kneeling down and kissing his boots that were layered with grime from Bardon's streets. He couldn't just let the creature beat her to death. Despite how much he wanted to be rid of her, she certainly didn't deserve a cruel fate.

He felt the Red fill his senses as he leapt down from the roof. He had to be cautious not to let it take complete control, or he might kill Nai as well. The greth was completely caught off guard. It didn't even have time to reach for its weapon before Ronnock buried his fangs in its throat and tore through the flesh. The creature was still alive, choking on its own blood, until Ronnock gripped its head by the chin and ripped it from the rest of its body. The greth collapsed into its two separate pieces and a pool of black blood around its mangled corpse.

Nai suddenly threw herself at him and wrapped her arms around his shoulders. He felt himself taken aback, and guilt washed over him when he realized that he had to refrain from his immediate instinct to sink his fangs into her delicious skin. She exclaimed her thanks and cried happily. Ronnock began to wonder if she too much enjoyed his new role as a hero to her damsel in distress.

Ronnock heard someone running towards them in old, leather-soled boots. He lightly pushed Nai to the side so that he stood between her and whoever was approaching. A young man turned the corner. He was nearly out of breath, but his eyes burned with blue fire. Ronnock waited for the man to say something while he took note of his odd selection of clothing. He could usually tell where someone was from based on their garments, but this one had him stumped.

The moment passed abruptly; they went from staring at each other awkwardly to the young man's hands clasping for Ronnock's throat. "You Red-diseased monster! You—" He continued to curse at Ronnock while doing his best to throttle him.

Ronnock could have easily crushed the boy's hands and thrown him against the wall with such force he wouldn't awaken until the morning, but there was something about him that made Ronnock feel pity. A young woman suddenly appeared behind his attacker. She had the same blue eyes and black hair. The worried look on her face was outshone by her bold move to grab the crazed young man by his shoulders and pull him away.

Ronnock decided to remove himself from the entire situation. He pulled Nai in by her waist and leapt back up onto the roof. He had killed enough innocent people. When he could escape doing so, he did.

Nai questioned where he was taking her. "You can't stay here." He replied irritably. He brought her to the inn room where Krisae was still snoring loudly on one of the beds.

"Rest now, I'll take you to the Insurgo base tomorrow." He grumbled. She began to object, but he slammed the door behind him and left. He shouldn't care, but he knew if he left her in Bardon she'd be dead in a week, if not less. It only took her a matter of hours to get tangled up with greth. He could smell the moisture from a coming storm in the air. Bardon needed the rain to wash the shit off the streets.

The boy that tried to attack him in the alley was no threat to his life. He should be used to strangers hating him for being Red, but for some reason he couldn't stop thinking about him. Something about the two he had encountered in the alley was weighing heavy on his consciousness. They looked so similar, they must be siblings, or at least cousins. They were dressed strangely; he couldn't tell where they had come to Bardon from. He spoke the common tongue with no accent, so they had to be native to Valehoutton. He searched his memories for the scent of either.

The Red began to awaken as he pictured the blue-eyed boy's face. All the smells of Bardon became much stronger, though he could still find the individual source of each odor. The blue-eyed boy's hand smelled of salty sea air with a touch of blood. He inhaled deeply through his nose. He inhaled again. There. He caught the scent and began to hunt like the predator he truly was.

7: PREY

THE WHISPERING PLAINS, WEST OF BARDON
Venell could barely catch her breath as they came upon the city of Bardon. The last light of the sun sank beyond the horizon. Nalahi beckoned to the Keoneos to follow her before she again took off sprinting across the wide-open plains surrounding Bardon. The grass was tall, well past Venell's knees, but it was wispy and easy to traverse. Instead of heading to the main gate of the city, she led them to the far wall, well-hidden away from the moonlight.

    Thunder would occasionally shake the earth as dense clouds began to gather. Venell feared that the rain would soon come, making this task all the more challenging. Nalahi stopped as she came to the stone wall surrounding the city. It was nothing compared to what the walls of Cynn once were. It was slightly over ten feet in height, and the stacked stone blocks provided plenty of footholds. It was more of an inconvenience for someone trying to surpass using the gate, rather than a barrier. Nalahi waited for the Keoneos to catch up to her before dexterously darting up the wall and hopping down on the other side.

It began to drizzle as Venell tucked the tip of her boot into a crack between the bricks and hoisted herself up to the next niche she could find. Nalahi had made the climb look so easy. Venell could hear her shouting from the other side of the wall that no one would see them if she would only hurry. Inch by inch, Venell moved further away from the ground.

Ash curled his fingers over the top of the wall and pulled himself up onto the ledge. He reached his hand down to her, and with his superior upper body strength, he heaved his sister up over the wall and lowered her down to the ground on the other side. He leapt off and landed easily on his feet. Venell's legs felt oddly weak after running so much, but she hid her discomfort and said nothing.

Nalahi was crouched behind a stack of wooden crates and barrels as she carefully observed the area. "We just have to be certain no one saw us sneak in and then hopefully we will be safe. We should all blend in well enough, Bardon is a crazy place. We'll leave this spot one by one and regroup—"

She was cut off by the heavy sound of a door slamming open in the dark alleyway that lay just before them. The noise from inside the building leaked out as a copper-skinned young woman suddenly stumbled into the night. She looked frightened, and she immediately retreated to the furthest corner of the alley. At first Venell thought her eyes were deceiving her, for the second person to emerge looked well enough like a man, but he also looked like a beast. His skin was a dull red, and his stringy, black hair hung all around his head loosely. His yellow, lizard-like eyes bulged out from their sockets with a hellish fury as he bared a mouthful of needle-like teeth. He approached the woman, who cried out for mercy.

"Please! I didn't do anything, I swear! It wasn't me who killed them!" she sobbed as she sank down to her knees. The creature answered in a different language, its voice cruel and snake-like, but the woman understood whatever it was it said and began to cry and beg harder.

Nalahi averted her eyes from the scene. "This is what Bardon has become. It's always crawling with greth. Fucking greth. They make everything so goddamn revolting." She cursed.

"Greth?" Ash repeated, "Is that what that thing is?"

Nalahi looked embarrassed that she had forgotten that the Keoneos were new to the world after being isolated for so long. "Yes, they're mercenaries from Tuaega that Kras brought in by the thousands after half of Sireh's army either quit or mysteriously vanished. Kras cares nothing for conquering land and gaining power like his father. He hides in his castle and surrounds himself with soldiers he pays. He turned his power against his own people in some paranoid attempt to defend his throne. So now the numbers of greth in his army outnumber the men. But I suppose I relish killing those awful things, they spare me killing my own kind."

"We have to help her." Ash interrupted.

"Don't be a fool. We're here for a purpose, and that isn't it."

"So you expect us to just sit here and watch him kill her?" Ash hissed angrily. He began to stand, but Nalahi forcefully grabbed onto his shoulder and yanked him back onto the ground.

"If you try to save her, we will be captured and killed and we will never get to Kras, is that what you want? Don't you fucking ruin this!"

There was a loud slap as the greth forced his fist across the woman's face. She put her head to the filthy ground and grabbed his boots, begging him to stop. The greth seized her by her long, thick hair and forced her to sit upright so he could hit her again.

Venell placed her hand on Ash's shoulder, unable to wrench her eyes away from the scene. She could feel her brother ready to dash, but before he could, a dark shadow dropped down from the rooftops and into the alley. The greth slowly turned to meet his new enemy. In a flurry of movement, the greth was decapitated and the figure then swooped around the woman. Ash pushed Venell's hand away and bolted into the alley. Nalahi cursed and began to chase after him.

Venell watched helplessly as Ash threw the dark cloaked figure off the woman and tried to push him back against the brick wall. Her body started moving before she even willed it to. She shouted for her brother and grabbed onto his shoulder. Ash tried to shrug her off. His hands were grasping toward the figure's throat as he spewed a string of profanities.

As the hood fell back off the cloaked figure, she saw yet another monster. It was a pale-faced man covered in numerous, ugly scars. Blood was smeared over his lips and around his mouth, and there was a set of long fangs protruding obscenely from his mouth where his eyeteeth should be. She had never seen one of them before: he had the Red disease. Venell felt her entire body become paralyzed with fear as the Red man's eyes rested on her. His gaze made her feel like helpless prey staring into the eyes of a predator in its last moments. She felt her demise was imminent. The Red man once again swept up the young woman in his cloak. She threw her arms around him and in a single leap he returned to the roof top and disappeared.

Nalahi emerged from her hiding place behind the barrels and marched straight over to Ash. She landed a single good punch on the side of his face before picking him up and placing him back on his feet. Ash's head lolled around his neck as he faded in and out of consciousness.

"What the fuck did I tell you?" she said harshly in a lowered voice, though her fierce rage still burned through. She roughly grabbed his shoulder and slammed him against the wall.

Ash snapped out of his stupor and his icy, hateful look quickly returned. "You saw him! He was infected with the Red disease!" he hissed back.

Nalahi punched him again. "I could do this on my own! I have suffered as you have suffered. I felt sympathy for the two of you; I understood your need for vengeance. I could leave you here and you would be lost. YOU need ME. Don't forget that. One more slip like this and I'll let you rot in your own mistakes." She released Ash from her grip, though her enraged, golden gaze was enough to make anyone feel like they were still under her fist.

Venell was shocked to see Ash silent. He kept his gaze lowered, but she could still feel all the emotion radiating from his entire being. It was difficult for him to control his temper, but it seemed that his fear of Nalahi kept it from boiling over. When it was the two of them alone, Ash made all the decisions. With a new person in their closed world, Ash's role had to be different. He couldn't speak to Nalahi the way he spoke to her, or the wild woman would abandon them before he could finish his sentence. Nalahi began to walk away down the paved street that led to the heart of the city. Venell gently grasped her brother's hand, silently offering him comfort, as they followed.

Bardon reeked of garbage, smoke, and old booze. It was the middle of the night and the city was bursting with drunken energy. Loud parties and gatherings could be heard within every house, inn, and pub. Stray animals and homeless beggars took up the gutters, either sleeping or scrounging for food. Venell was shocked to see so many different people from all over Valehoutton and its neighboring nations: Tueagians with their thick, shiny black hair braided with golden decorative bells and their rich brown skin. There were even some people of the Godsmoors, native to Valehoutton before the Aejons invaded from the Northeast.

Most of the Godsmoorian people never left their reservation in Tiver, a mountainous region that covered much of the north of Valehoutton, for they still faced much prejudice and had such distinct features: pale, glittering freckles across their faces that mirrored constellations and other heavenly bodies. The people of the Godsmoors were distant cousins and religious counterparts to those that lived in Ellinhall; the Far East where it is said all life began.

Venell had been to Bardon once as a child, but it was a very different place. It had been home to only the upper class as it was the native seat of the Redals. Now she had to watch the pavement to avoid stepping in vomit. Many of the timber and plaster houses were decaying with age, and their roofs were thatched straw or wood shingles rather than stone.

Nalahi must have noticed how slowly the Keoneos were following her, as they were too preoccupied with their surroundings to keep up. "The Bardon you remember was home to Sireh's younger brother, Diar. He is the heir apparent of Valehoutton, as Kras remains childless. He and his family surrounded themselves with their allies and relatives until their settlement grew into the Bardon that you knew. When Kras came into power, Diar went into hiding with a close group of loyalists. Whether he's plotting or just protecting himself, no one seems to know. His estranged wife has been in Piaces, and I know he has a daughter, who would be queen after him." She paused to carefully step over a body, either unconscious or dead, lying across the pavement. "Without Diar, Bardon just kept deteriorating further and further."

The stench of the city nearly made Venell's eyes water. Rats squabbled over crumbs in the gutters. Venell stumbled as her foot fell into a brown puddle where bricks were missing from the cobblestone road. Her face scrunched up with disgust. The faint noise of a familiar and cruel laughter began to grow louder and louder. There was a well-lit building with large windows ahead, dozens of uniformed soldiers drank and gambled in a cloud of cigar smoke. Venell could see not just daggers and swords strapped to their sides, but guns. Guns had been outlawed since the Redals overthrew the previous reigning royal family, the Caeruleans. Now men of the royal army were carrying them.

More than one hundred years ago, a Caerulean king by the name of Hesshan fathered a bastard son through a common servant girl living in Star Palace. Though the girl's name had been lost somewhere in history, it was well-known that she married a rich man from the South named Rechaulle Redal. Upon learning of his new stepson's royal parentage, Rechaulle began to spread rumors of corruption around the capital and asserting that his stepson had better claim to the throne than the Caerulean's heir: Hesshan's niece, Bethell.

The bastard, Sireh, was the only child Hesshan had fathered. An industrialist, Rechaulle and his followers suffered few casualties storming Star Palace and killing the reigning Caeruleans with his mass-produced firearms. No retaliation ever occurred from the citizens of Valehoutton. In fear, they accepted their new teenaged king: Sireh Redal the first. Any that objected to his claim were quickly silenced. The rumor persisted, however, that Bethell and her betrothed husband, Raytara Caerulean, had escaped the sack of Star Palace, and were both hiding somewhere in the West. Both offspring bore the telling Caerulean trait of mismatched eyes, so it was likely they did not survive once their lineage was recognized.

"The inn before us is the most expensive one in the city and is very popular among the higher-ranking officers. I think it could be our best bet to find the king." She looked at each of them in turn, though Ash avoided her gaze. "Do either of you know what Kras looks like?"

Both shook their heads, ashamed. Venell had only ever seen a portrait of Kras and his older sister that had been made before she was even born, and she could barely recall what that one looked like.

"That's what I thought." Nalahi said.

Ash suddenly turned to his sister, "Venell, I don't think you should come."

Her brow furrowed, "You want me to wait out here alone?"

"If Kras is in there... this will all be over. But it will all be worth nothing if you aren't safe. So, I want you to stay out here. You've never faltered on your promise to me. This is the least I can do in return."

Nalahi began taking one step at a time up the stairs to the inn. She was growing impatient. Venell was floored. She couldn't believe the words she was hearing. Ash never shared tender words with her, not even before the quarantine. She was so touched she found herself speechless. She was barely able to stammer out a "yes." He followed Nalahi inside the inn and disappeared into the crowd of soldiers.

Venell stooped on the stone steps outside with her chin resting in her hand. The air was so humid that she could feel the water droplets in the air clinging to her throat as she inhaled. Now that she had a moment to think more about what Ash had said, she began to feel foolish. He didn't care about her safety. She should know that by now. He would have never held her to her promise for so long if he cared. He just wanted to keep her out of the way. She was weak. She was just a burden. Now that he had Nalahi he didn't need her anymore. She could do what Venell could not. She had always thought she felt alone even when Ash was with her, but this new sense of loneliness made her feel even more empty.

The knowledge that the Red diseased man that Ash had attacked was still out there lurking in the shadows began to throb in the back of her mind. She would try to push the fear aside, but just couldn't help feeling uncomfortable. The sight of those blood-stained fangs struck fear within her in some deep, untouched place. She finally began to grow more relaxed as the minutes ticked by. Her thoughts turned to what could be going on inside the inn. She had heard no sounds of a scuffle. Ash and Nalahi must be sizing up their foes. Maybe they couldn't even find Kras. It could be the wrong inn, or he could have left the entire city by now. Their fate was up in the air.

Everything around her seemed to suddenly slow down as her eyes focused on a single pair of black boots approaching the inn's steps. The boots paused for a second to crush the end of a cigarette into the damp stone, and then continued their course. All the noise of the crowds of Bardon disappeared as her eyes rose from the stranger's boots to his face. She could feel something surrounding him; an aura that she felt herself drawn to. She was utterly enthralled. Her mind still couldn't place what made him so different from the other travelers in the city.

Then it struck her: the Red man.

Without thinking, she bolted off the inn's steps and ran into the flooded street. She knew he was coming for her, and she had to get away. She hoped that she could lose him in the bustle of the crowd, but every time she dared to look behind, she saw him still following her. She silently cursed her brother for provoking the demon.

She turned off the main road and slipped into a narrow alley between two buildings. There was a maze of similar narrow paths throughout the entire city, but she couldn't waste a second to stop and figure out where she was. She just kept running from the monster behind her. She couldn't find her way back. She stopped at a corner to catch her breath. She didn't hear any footsteps behind her, so she risked a peek around the building. No one was there. She had finally escaped. Venell gasped for breath, her chest heaving up and down heavily. Just as she slumped against the brick wall behind her to rest for a moment, her eyes caught a flutter of cloth dart over her head. Footsteps pounded from on top of the building. They were coming in her direction. Red eyes glared down at her through the darkness.

She began to realize that there was no escaping him. He was the hunter and she was the prey; the weakest member of the herd, just waiting to be picked off. All her running had been futile. He was toying with her, but she still couldn't let herself surrender. She wouldn't give up on her life so easily after surviving the most horrific massacre that Valehoutton had ever seen. She ran again, darting down alleys and making quick, sharp turns.

Then she saw it: a dead end. She couldn't turn around; he had closed in too near behind her. She put her hands against the brick in disbelief. She had been caught. He had herded and corralled her like an animal. Now she had no other choice, she gathered what strength she had and turned to face her enemy. She nearly ran into him, he was so close. He lowered his head so that his face was even with hers. She became paralyzed with fear.

"Hello." He said as he grinned cruelly, revealing those awful fangs. "You didn't have to make me go through all the trouble of catching you, I just wanted to talk." He placed his hands on the wall on either side of her, using his arms to prevent her escape.

The misty rain that had been lightly drizzling the entire night finally formed droplets and began pouring down on them. She had to blink rapidly to see. She felt the water seeping into her clothes, making them stick to her skin. The man moved one of his hands around her throat and roughly pushed her against the brick. His long, black hair clung to his face and neck as small droplets of water began to run off the thick, twisted ends. The moonlight accentuated the white, jagged scars on his face, making him even more fearsome.

"Where did you come from?" he asked. His voice was calm, though his fingers began to squeeze.

"Cynn." She choked out.

"Don't lie." He said with a slight growl. "Cynn was wiped off the map over a decade ago."

"I know," was all she could reply.

He sighed, "And here I thought you might be at least slightly useful." He took his hand off her throat and instead he held both her wrists and wrenched them to one side while he used his other hand to grasp under her chin and pull her head to the side. She felt his lips press against her flesh. Instead of feeling fear she felt... hot.

    Her body temperature was rising, and her stomach felt flustered. His lips caressed her skin, kissing down her neck and over the swell of her breasts. He brought his hand up and ran it over her hips. She realized he wasn't even holding her arms anymore; they were just hanging limply at her sides. He smirked. She didn't feel any alarm as his eyes blazed red and she heard the slick noise of his fangs sliding out of his gums. One of his hands crept between her legs. The first noise she was able to make was a mere gasp. His mouth met with hers. Excitement rushed through her whole body as she felt one of his fangs graze her bottom lip and the taste of blood flowered on her tongue. A wild look crossed his face as he latched onto her lip, kissing her deeply and drawing her blood into his mouth. He pushed her wet hair away from her exposed throat and shoulders. He began to lower his head to her neck, but then stopped suddenly.

    "Oh, right, I forgot to ask your name."

She could only stare blankly into those red eyes for a few moments until she managed to find her voice. "Venell." She said finally.

"...What?"

"Venell Keoneo."

He stopped. His eyes returned to a pale grey color and his fangs retracted. He looked at her again with his human eyes. "Jet's daughter?"

She nodded, though she still didn't feel that her head was completely clear. It was raining so hard she could barely see his face anymore. She was confused as to why he stopped. She felt some deep longing within that made her yearn for him to touch her again. "Yes." She replied impatiently.

The man let go of her completely and took a step backward. "That boy that attacked me was your brother?" He said as though he was piecing together some great mystery in his head.

"Yes," she replied again. She could feel his spell beginning to lift off her.

"I'm so sorry. I didn't realize..." He stopped mid-sentence and took another step back in disbelief. "You were the only survivors of Cynn? Of all the people there, you two survived?"

She could only hear his voice now; she could no longer see him through the pouring rain. She felt herself becoming more and more alert with each passing second. She waited for him to say something else, but there was nothing but the sound of the rain hitting the pavement. She stood up straight, venturing away from her refuge against the brick wall. He was gone.

    She suddenly felt herself wake up from the trance she had fallen into. She felt disgusting. She felt soiled. She quickly fastened her pants and pulled her shirt down to cover herself. Her hands flew all over her body, trying to wipe off his touch. She couldn't believe herself. She couldn't believe she allowed him to have that kind of control over her. She would've completely bent to his will, and he wasn't even human. Her lip was still bleeding. She gently drew upon it with her tongue and spat out the blood left in her mouth. She couldn't stand the metallic, salty taste.

    She knew it was not safe out here. She had to get back to the inn and find Ash and Nalahi, they were her only chance of survival in Bardon. She had no idea how far she had run or even what direction the pub was in. She aimlessly wandered through the labyrinth of alleys, not knowing if she was just getting lost further. She finally found herself on a very busy road. People roughly shoved past her, trying to reach their destinations quickly to get out of the rain.

She heard a joyous roar building up within the crowd just ahead of her. "Hail your king! Hail King Kras Redal!" A group shouted in unison. The cheer spread throughout the crowd, repeating Kras' name over and over. She tried to catch up to the celebrating group. She felt her heart pounding. Was Kras in the crowd? Was she so close to him on her own? A swarm of greth surged passed her. Occasionally one of the creatures would turn to her with an approving hiss, but nothing more. She tried to keep her sights on the greth, but she could barely see over the crowd. She roughly pushed her way passed the endless flow of people, trying to catch up. It was possible they were going to wherever Kras was. To her disbelief, she recognized the steps of the inn she had been sitting on earlier that night.

She kept on the tail of the greth as they walked inside. The noise inside the inn was deafening. It was so crowded that she could barely press her way forward. The air was hot and thick with sweat and smoke. A man sitting at the bar laughed so hard that he fell backwards on his stool and crashed directly into her. He spilled his ale all over her already soaked clothes. He didn't apologize. He got to his feet and wobbled away. She pressed on, looking all over for her brother. She started calling out Ash's name, but she couldn't even hear her own voice over the clamor. She had been gone for some time while she was running from the man with the Red disease. She feared that Ash and Nalahi may have left the inn and gone looking elsewhere in the city. She felt like a lost child. She didn't know what to do next. All she could do was keep searching and keep fighting to hold back her tears.

An earsplitting crack brought a silence over the pub. As everyone recovered from the noise, all eyes looked up to see an older man with a jagged pink scar on his cheek, which left an empty patch in his beard, standing on top of the bar. He crushed glass underneath his boots as he walked across the tabletop, eyeing the crowd as he passed. He held a gun in his hand, which was aimed to the ceiling and smoking. His lips curled into an angry sneer, accentuating the deep lines on his face. "There's been an attack on the Bardon Royal Garrison." He boomed in an authoritative voice.

Venell tried to hide behind taller men in the crowd. She didn't want to risk standing out for one reason or another. The best thing to do was remain out of sight. She was fairly certain the man was not Kras, he was too old, but he definitely held a lot of power.

"I want all coherent officers to come with me to the Diar estate. We may have captured the perpetrator." He stepped down from the bar and exited the building, followed by a handful of shamed soldiers.

Venell's mind was racing. She hoped the officers were mistaken. She knew she had to follow them. If Ash was in their clutches, she had to reach him. She tried to push worse possibilities from her mind. She knew she could never carry out justice for Cynn on her own. She would fade away without Ash; she would have no meaning or purpose. She elbowed her way through the now-somber crowd and burst out the door.

It was still pouring outside, and the lighting ferociously crackled across the sky. She gathered the minimal courage left within her gut to push herself ahead, propelled only by her thoughts of Ash.

8: TRANCENDENCE

TIVER RESERVATION

At first it was just the sentries on the Northwest side, but then suddenly the entire west and north sides of the village's defense found themselves in battle. The chaos spread like a wave. Fire spread across the dead grass and licked at the tents on the outskirts of the village. Everything became doused in a red glow. Minortai had dropped his pipe and began running for the sick tent to find Siyah. He had yet to see a mercenary in the village, but the all too familiar panic was the only confirmation he needed. He cursed himself for leaving his short sword and bow in his tent. He was armed with nothing but his hunting knife.

"Siyah!" he shouted as he approached the sick tent. He threw open the flap to find the tent vacant. The bed where her brother had been lying for weeks was empty, the sheets covered in blood stains. Minortai felt panic rising in his chest. He left the sick tent, shouting Siyah's name. He decided to run back to the tent they shared to search for her, also thinking he could grab his weapons.

Before he could double back, he was caught by a blow to the stomach. Dazed, he fell back to the ground. A tall greth stood over him and grinned before it raised its double-sided axe. Minortai reacted quickly and rolled out of the way before the axe fell where he had just been laying. The greth struggled to pull the axe out of the soft earth, giving Minortai the opportunity to kick the creature over. It tumbled into the tent, becoming wrapped up in the canvas. Minortai picked up the axe and hacked away at the bulge in the canvas. Black blood soaked the material and the greth finally stopped struggling.

He carried the axe as he stepped away from the tent. It was cumbersome and unlikely that he could wield it proficiently, but he would have better reach with it than with his knife. He looked around helplessly for his wife, but all he could see was the growing fire in the distance. Hopefully the flame and smoke would draw the warriors back to the village if they hadn't journeyed too far already.

"Siyah!" He kept calling as he stumbled through the village. A group of women ran past him towards the South. He only occasionally saw other villagers; most tents were already deserted. He didn't know where else to look for her.

Some of the sick children were left abandoned on their cots; their families had fled for their lives. Minortai pushed the sight from his mind. He ducked behind a tent as he saw two greth lumber past him with stained swords. He waited until they had just passed before sneaking up behind them and burying the axe in one's back and then the others.

As he continued to stealthily make his way north, he finally began seeing the bodies. Corpses of everyone he knew scattered the ground. All three remaining elders had been hacked to pieces by their fire. The bodies of women and children lay with the sentries that had fled their posts.

A flash of lilac robe caught his attention from the corner of his eye. He turned and saw Siyah crouched and hidden behind a tent just across from him. He could barely believe his eyes and felt himself start to cry. The look of relief on her face suddenly turned to terror as a massive group of greth passed in front of the tents they were hidden behind. She held her hand over her mouth as though her breathing would betray her. There were more than twenty greth barking at each other in Tuaegian, about half of them were facing their direction.

His gaze locked with his wife's. He gripped the axe tightly, knowing he had to make a decision. Siyah didn't give him the chance. She crouched down and quickly hurried over to him, miraculously avoiding detection. She fell into his arms, both trying to be silent and contain their overwhelming emotions. He held her tightly and kissed her all over.

She buried her face in the crook of his neck and whispered to him. "I'm so sorry, we should've gone. We should've just gone. My brother had just passed before the greth came. He never even woke up for me to say goodbye and we should've just left." She sobbed into his shoulder. Then Siyah wiped her tears away and pulled a large dagger out from where she had it hidden in her boot. "We have to run now."

He kissed her again, told her he loved her, and then they ran. Minortai looked over his shoulder to see if they were being followed, but the greth weren't coming after them. Suddenly Siyah screamed, and Minortai turned to see six greth ahead of them. Before he could raise his axe, a greth with a huge hammer buried the head of his weapon into Minortai's ribs. He felt a crack and fell to his knees. He desperately gasped. The greth raised his hammer again, but Minortai blocked the blow with the axe handle. Siyah stabbed the greth in the throat and helped Minortai to his feet. Minortai struck the next greth in the neck with the axe, and then took off the arm of the next one. He had to get Siyah to safety, he had to keep fighting.

Suddenly his right leg gave out and white-hot pain seared into his brain. He heard agonized screaming and realized it was his own voice. A large spearhead was sticking out of the front of his thigh from where it entered at the back. He tried to rise, but his leg was not responding to his attempts. His vision was blurred. He still had the axe in his hand, and he struck the next greth that approached him in the leg. Siyah was knocked to the ground. A greth kicked her in the side and she cried out. Fury overtook Minortai, ignoring the searing pain of his wound he staggered forward and struck at the greth attacking his wife. His first blow landed, the next was deflected and he was knocked back.

A tall, lanky greth with black decorated armor pushed past the others, shouting something to them. It grabbed onto Siyah's hair from the back of her head. For Minortai, time seemed to slow to an excruciating pace; so slow that he couldn't miss a detail even if he wanted to. She wildly swung the knife toward the greth mercenary. It effortlessly plucked it from her hand, held it to her throat, and then cut deep into her neck. No sound came from Siyah's mouth, just blood poured out over her lips. Her eyes widened before her gaze froze. Her body went limp, but still the greth cruelly held her for him to see the gaping hole in his love's neck. Blood kept running from the wound and her beautiful dress became soaked crimson. Satisfied, the greth let go of her hair and she fell into the dirt.

He didn't have to fight anymore. Siyah was gone. He just had to run. He broke the wood of the spear off so just the head stuck in his leg was left. The lanky greth approached him suddenly. Minortai mustered all his strength and connected his fist with the greth's face. He felt teeth shatter against his knuckles and cut into his flesh. The lanky greth, the beast that slashed his wife's gorgeous throat, staggered backwards as black blood gushed from its mouth. Minortai brought the axe down over its head and kicked the body away with his good leg. He stumbled from the pain of shifting his balance. He went for his signature escape method and struck each of the two remaining greth in the knees. They fell to the ground and Minortai began to hobble south toward the Crags.

 He had to abandon the axe, as it was too much additional weight for his leg to bear. He thought about just falling, laying there until he either bled out or more mercenaries found him. He couldn't bear the thought of Siyah's mutilated body lay in the dirt surrounded by greth corpses. He didn't know what was propelling him forward still. He didn't understand his desire to survive. The flames of the village illuminated the peaks of the Crags. The mountains were the closest place he could hide. He would have to reach them first before he could safely dress his wound. He was incredibly light-headed. He might not make it even if he wanted to, and he didn't know if he wanted to. Siyah was gone.

 He could still hear voices in the distance. He didn't know if the greth would come after him or not, he was only one man, but he couldn't risk even a moment's rest. The terrain of southern Tiver was unforgiving; rocky, dry, and lifeless except for poisonous lizards and stickered plants. Even the slightest stumble over a stone or knotted root was agony.

He had nowhere to hide on the wide, flat land before the mountains. His only chance of survival was to take shelter within the tall, thick trees that lined the steps of the Crags. The image of Siyah held up by her hair kept stabbing into his heart and he began to cry tears of anguish. The peaks of the Crags grew bigger and darker as they loomed over him. He reached the forest that covered the mountain range just as the sun was beginning to rise. Any later and he might have been visible to the mercenaries, and his struggles would've all been for nothing.

His limbs shook with exhaustion and nausea began to set in. He collapsed onto a sloped ledge covered with layers of fallen leaves that were damp and beginning to rot. He couldn't see the sky from between the treetops, and his body was wracked with such pain that he couldn't feel the stars of Siyah fading into the morning above him.

He widened the hole in his breeches where his wound was. The skin around where the spear penetrated was turning black. The greth were such dirty creatures that infection was nearly certain in a wound caused by one of their weapons. Only the broken center of the wooden shaft remained in his leg. If he forced it out he risked bleeding to death, but leaving it in would only allow the infection to worsen. Minortai removed his outer coat and tightly tied the sleeves together around his thigh, just above the wound. He would have to play chance with his life today.

 Twice he gripped his fingers over the splintered rod obscenely protruding from his leg but could not bring himself to start pulling. He cursed at himself, tried to reposition his leg, but still hesitated to touch the damaged area. He couldn't even keep his hand still. He needed food and water, or he was going to die sooner than his injury would kill him. He kept his makeshift tourniquet around his leg and began to venture deeper into the woods. He could smell damp earth and knew there was a source of water nearby. He soon came upon a stream falling from a stone ledge and trickling down the steps of the growing mountain. He held his mouth under it, feeling it revive his body and mind. He then cleaned the wounds on his knuckles and leg.

 His side ached where he had been stuck with the hammer, but extraordinarily it seemed that none of his ribs had been broken. His hobbled gait was even becoming difficult to maintain as the infection around his gash continued to spread. He lay back under the stream, letting it pour onto his head and all down his body. It was too cold to be of comfort, but his body was already feeling numbed.

Minortai felt his body shake with a sudden start. It was bright all around him, he must have fallen asleep under the stream until midday. His body was stiff. Now that the adrenaline of the previous night had worn off, he was feeling every blow. The first thing he did was cleanse his leg under the water again. Fortunately, the blackness had begun to recede since the morning, but he knew the time to remove the shaft from his leg successfully was growing short.

He recognized some edible mushrooms growing at the base of a nearby tree. They weren't very appetizing, but he had to put something into his body. He fought the urge to vomit as he chewed a mouthful of the fleshy texture. He swallowed and then drank some more water. He retightened the tourniquet around his leg and firmly gripped the end of the spear shaft.

He inhaled. He exhaled. Again. Then again. He tried to think of Siyah when she smiled. Just as he exhaled the third time, he pulled as hard as he could on the wood shaft. Fresh blood spurted from the wound and he cried out in pain. He pushed past the urge to stop for a moment and compose himself and instead grabbed onto the slick, bloodstained wood and pulled again. He couldn't feel how much deeper the shaft was buried, for his leg was consumed with electrifying agony. He was able to grasp the shaft with his full fist now, and on a third attempt the shaft was released from his thigh.

    The pain still didn't stop when he threw the wood to the side. He gripped around the gaping hole and willed the excruciating torture to stop. The blood seemed brighter as it oozed from the hole. The color all around him suddenly began to shift as the world itself began tilting on its side.

    His face was suddenly lying against the mud as hues of bright green, magenta, and blue that he had never seen so vividly before danced across his eyes. He heard air rushing past his ears though he was sure that he was standing still. His eyes were open, but he kept seeing things in his head as though he was dreaming.

    Siyah was there, dancing through the purple flowers of the Godsmoors in late summer. The sun was setting and her skin glowed gold and lively as she disrobed and began to dance for him, naked. The stars were out in the middle of the day. Her celestial face smiled at him from above. Minortai the Matricider shone dully and alone. The nine stars of the Matricider began to drift apart. Some were bright, some faded, and then the lights began to rotate around each other. They spun faster and faster, forming different shapes and dazzling his mind.

"We all go to dust. We all go to dust." The stars told him.

He saw a desert of black sand. The grains glinted like dark glass under the hot sun. Clouds of shadowy dust filled the air. He felt his lungs fill with the heaviness. He had seen this desert before. The shadow of a palace glowered in the distance. Dark, dark eyes watched him.

"You will go to dust." The eyes whispered.

Suddenly the dust in the air disappeared. Dropping to the ground it bonded with the swirling sand. The sun beat down on him, stronger without the clouds blocking out its rays. The light became unbearable. It was so overwhelming that even when he shut his eyes it was still too bright. He found himself in a white void. He took a step, and his foot echoed in the emptiness. Suddenly, a pair of deep, grey eyes snapped open and stared right into his soul.

"Minortai!" It was a woman's voice behind the dark eyes. "Realign your fate. The future is not lost. You can still see your home again."

The void spun around in his head until he opened his eyes again. A young woman with black hair and ivory skin lay in his favorite meadow of the Godsmoors, the one covered with small, purple flowers. Her hands were raised above her head and he watched her chest rise and fall as she breathed. She smiled, and he felt his heart jump. Flowers of all different colors were laced into her short, softly waved hair. She brought her legs up and began to lift her skirts as she whispered his name.

Then he was among the stars, walking through the endless space of the cosmos. "Minortai, I gave my life so that you could live. Now live, my boy." He heard yet another voice whisper. He didn't recognize it, but at his core knew it through and through. He recognized it the way anyone would recognize their mother's voice. He felt a relief like he had never felt before. Tears fell from his eyes though he felt his mouth agape with wonder.

Then Siyah reached out and touched his cheek. He could feel her fingers upon his skin as he had so many times before. "You have so many more to love." She smiled and then disappeared into the Lover in the sky.

It was night when Minortai felt himself fall into his body. He felt so heavy he couldn't move. He was in the forest at the steps of the Crags. His wound was still slowly bleeding. His stomach rumbled with hunger and his mouth felt dry. He willed himself to open and close one hand. His fingers barely curled over despite his effort. Everything seemed so suddenly quiet. He must have been dreaming, though it felt more like had had gone on a long journey without his mortal husk.

He could remember it all so clearly. It had been so long since he had seen the Godsmoors, yet he could still picture that meadow vividly. He had seen that black desert before. It had to have been Snanka, where the sand was mostly obsidian and other volcanic rock. The palace he had seen in the distance wasn't Onyx Castle, Snanka's capital, though, it was somewhere else.

As the minutes ticked by while he reminisced, Minortai finally found the strength to sit up. Now that he felt fully conscious, all the gruesome details of reality were setting back in. Siyah wasn't in the Godsmoors, she was dead in they dry lands with her throat torn out. There were no flowers in bloom in that meadow, in all likeliness that meadow was also dead forever. He leaned himself against a tree and let exhaustion take hold of his mind. He drifted into a dreamless sleep, finally beginning to recover his wounds in both his body and heart.

He was awakened by the sound of an animal sniffing around him. It sounded big. He felt fear prickle up his spine when a large, wet snout warily investigated his maimed leg. He jerked his leg away, shooting pain throughout his entire body as he felt the newly healed skin in the hole tear apart again. He fell to the side, making himself an easy meal.

"I found him! Nehlas, he's here!" a woman's voice shouted.

He must have been hallucinating still. He had hoped his strange trip was at an end. Pain still wracked his body, and he felt his breathing becoming labored. He couldn't hope to lift his head to see if there was indeed a woman there. He slowly moved his eyes to look up. The world around him seemed to be within a dark tunnel that he could only see small parts of through a light at the end.

But there she was: a young woman with fiery hair and stars across her face. No, they weren't stars, they were freckles. Sharp green eyes grew closer to him as she studied his face. She wasn't one of his people. When he let his gaze fall back down to the earth, he saw the fresh prints of a large she-wolf in the mud. He tried to speak, to say anything, but he couldn't muster a voice. The ground vibrated with more feet approaching. The light at the end of the tunnel grew so narrow there was only blackness left.

9: THE MOON

BARDON

How could he have forgotten her? It had been so many years ago he had first seen those bright, blue eyes and felt them fully penetrate his heart. Venell Keoneo had been a small, skinny child that tightly grasped onto General Jet's pant leg as those eyes nervously darted about the room. Her father gently shooed her outside as he continued to discuss Snanka's line of succession with Ronnock's mother and uncle. He and Hellan were teenagers at the time, and Krisae was still a young child. Ronnock recalled being bored by the talk of politics and decided to follow the girl out to the gardens surrounding the tower.

The image of Venell's haunting eyes kept racing across his mind. They meddled with his plaguing dream of white flowers in a moonlit ancient forest; the forest breathing life as it savored an earlier rain. When he touched her in the Bardon alleyway, she gasped the same way he had heard over and over again every night. She had locked gazes with him through the pouring rain. Those pure, blue eyes, with unmarred color that pierced the iciest of hearts, had been staring straight into his.

His thoughts kept racing as he ran across the rooftops of Bardon and leapt to each one that lay before him. He had almost killed her. He had already begun to let the beast slip out and consume her; otherwise he would never have been so frightfully cruel to her. He interrogated her as if she was an enemy. He put his Red spell upon her. The taste of her blood lingered on his tongue and made the Red much more difficult to cage. He had almost torn into the sweet flesh of her throat before she told him her name. If she had said any other name, he would have.

He was brought back to reality when he caught a familiar scent in the air. He must have been getting close to her, as the scent was growing stronger. He stopped on the slanted tile roof of some travelers' lodgings and gazed down to the alley below. The trail he had been following had not been Venell's, but rather her brother's, though the boy's name continued to escape him. The boy's hands were behind his back and held by a royal soldier. A few greth hissed to each other while a fourth soldier struck the boy across the face.

"Yer better hope we catch you little blonde friend." A soldier loudly, and drunkenly, proclaimed to the Keoneo boy before spitting at him. The soldier took another drink from his flask. "The Viper Girl they been callin' her. Everyone dead 'fore they see her comin'. She's been giving us lots o' trouble out o' them Saltwoods. Fuckin' bitch."

The soldier holding the boy's bound hands forced him onto the ground and pressed his cheek to Bardon's filthy streets. He placed his boot on the back of his shaven head and pressed down slowly, grinding the boy's cheek against the pavement. The boy remained silent. The greth each took a turn kicking him in the ribs and stomach, but still he refused to give them the satisfaction of hearing him cry out. Ronnock rubbed his weary eyes and wrestled with his desire to leave the boy to his possibly deserved fate. From his rashness of risking to attack a Red stranger, to the sadness and fear he saw across Venell's eyes as she tried to hold him back, his gut gave him a bad feeling about the kid.

He was still Jet's son, and Ronnock at the very least owed his late commander the courtesy of keeping his children alive. Ronnock leapt down into the alley with his longsword drawn. He forced it though the gut of the soldier holding the Keoneo boy's hands and cut upwards into the man's torso, spilling his organs onto the cobblestone. The soldier beside him took a step back in surprise, giving Ronnock the chance to bring forth the dagger hidden up his sleeve and slash the soldier's throat. The man gagged on his own blood as he sank to his knees and grasped at the gaping hole in his neck. His eyes were wide with the realization that he was dying. Seeing that desolate look in someone's eyes never got any easier for Ronnock.

The two greth attacked him at once, completely ignoring the Keoneo boy. From the ground, the boy kicked out and tripped one of the greth. The creature smashed its pointed teeth on the bricks below, and Jet's son lifted his leg brought the back of his heel down on the greth's head to finish the job against the stone curb. The boy's icy blue eyes burned with white-hot fire and hatred. Ronnock stabbed the final greth through the chest as it lunged at him. He kept his eyes on what could be the real threat: Jet's boy.

He had yet to get to his feet; laying on his side and struggling to right himself without the use of his arms. He glared up harshly at Ronnock from the ground. "What!?" the Keoneo boy snapped at him. "What do you want!?" He ungracefully got to his knees and was able to rise to his feet. Small bits of gravel stuck to the scrapes on his cheek.

"You're welcome." Ronnock grunted back as he wiped off his blades.

The boy snarled in frustration. "Don't come around me again!" He started to stalk off with his hands still tied in ropes behind his back. The boy's stubbornness reminded him of that of his own sisters', perhaps even surpassed it.

"What happened? Where is Venell?"

The boy suddenly spun to face Ronnock, his eyes ablaze and his face twisted up in fury. "What do you want with her?" he fumed. His confusion only fueled his anger. Ronnock had a feeling he was always this impetuous, and he didn't like it.

"You don't know where she is," Ronnock said aloud as the realization occurred to him.

"You know where she is?! What have you done with her, you Red-disease ridden motherf—" He was cut off as Ronnock struck him on the side of the head. The boy lost consciousness and crumpled into a heap on the ground.

Ronnock slung Jet's boy over his shoulder and casually strolled back onto one of the main roads through Bardon. No one even gave Ronnock a second glance as he made his way through the busy streets. He could've been carrying out justice, collecting a bounty, or kidnapping; it didn't matter to the people of Bardon. It was none of their business as long as it wasn't happening to them.

The Green Roof was nearby, and he hoped Krisae would be awake by this time. He opened the rickety wooden door that led to the horse stalls of the Green Roof guests. Khazar stood attentively a few stalls in, looking strong and regal even though a homeless beggar slept behind the horse in a pile of hay and shit. Ronnock nudged the beggar awake. He looked around in a stupor, then finally began to drag himself out of the stall while scratching his ass and taking another swig from a brown bottle.

He let Ash slip off his shoulder and onto the ground. The boy was still out cold. Ronnock saddled and bridled Khazar, then lifted Ash over the stallion's back and bound the boy's tied wrists to Khazar's saddle. He noticed a flash of silver around the boy's neck. Ronnock tugged on the chain to reveal a blue and silver pendant. White shell was inlayed across the blue paint to form the shape of a waning moon. He unfastened the chain and slipped the necklace into his pocket. It might help him to gain Venell's trust if he could prove he knew her brother's whereabouts. He paused on his way toward the wooden steps that led up to the inn above. If the boy had been captured, there was no end to the possible danger his sister could be in. The boy would wake up soon, and the weak tie to the horse wouldn't be enough to keep him from running off and finding even more trouble.

Ronnock gritted his teeth and went upstairs to the room where he had left Krisae and Nai. Krisae stood directly in his path in the doorway. Her arms were crossed in front of her irritably, showing the rippling muscles of her arms from beneath the folds of her sleeves. Ronnock had no doubt she could send him flying across the room.

"How could you leave me to look after your new woman for you?" She took a threatening step toward him. "You're lucky I have some pity. It's been like looking after a child! The fool can barely feed herself!"

"I'm sorry, but that's exactly why I need to you take her to the base. I can't be bothered to watch her, and she keeps finding trouble." He rubbed the back of his neck, wondering to himself how much he should tell his sister.

Her brow furrowed. He should've known he couldn't hide anything from her. "What is it, Ron?"

"I have Jet Keoneo's son tied to Khazar in the stable."

Krisae's grey eyes flashed at him. "That's impossible. Jet was killed in Cynn, there's no way his son survived. How do you even know it's really him?"

"Because his daughter is also in Bardon. She told me who she was, and that the boy is her brother. I rescued him from some greth, but he's rather ornery, so he's unconscious at the moment. The girl is out there somewhere, and I intend to find her. I need you to make sure the boy is delivered to the Insurgo where he will be safe."

"I understand. That I entirely agree with, but on a side note..." She gestured to the room where Nai remained. "Why her?"

Ronnock chuckled slightly. "I was mistaken about her, but now I can't help but to feel slightly responsible for her well-being."

Krisae rolled her eyes, "I suppose having a pretty girl at the base will be good for morale. I'll need to take Khazar to get them both back. Kunzite can't carry all three of us. Will you be safe on foot?"

"I'm just worried about the Keoneo girl for now." He pulled his sister into an embrace and kissed her on the forehead. "Thank you."

She shoved him away and gave him a disgusted look, "Ugh, come on, Ron. Don't be all sappy." He saw her hide a smile.

Krisae liked to put forward a hard exterior, but she longed for praise and affection. She had always been the attention-seeker of the family, even before the three of them were exiled to Dust's Plateau with their mother. She took being sent away the hardest; Hellan and he were more than ready to escape their stepmother's abuse and their father's indifference by then. The only heartbreaking part was being separated from their sister, Rheena, who remained at court since her mother was the queen, not a mistress.

He could still vividly recall the day they were loaded into a carriage as if they were nothing more than luggage. They barely had any warning; most of their belongings were left behind. He sat beside little Krisae, holding her doll and sobbing "why," over and over. He kept an arm around her, but it did nothing to calm her.

Hellan and his mother sat across from him, looking like two sizes of the same person. They were both wore long-sleeved black dresses and cut their long, raven hair with heavy bangs, and now that Hellan had become a young woman, their mother allowed her to paint her lips red as she did.

The King and Queen stood on the black steps of Onyx Castle with their two children. His father's face was sullen and cross. Ronnock wondered if it was because he was losing his children, his mistress, or simply losing a battle to his wife. He crossly turned from the scene and went back inside his safe-hold, followed by a bawling teenaged Rheena tugging at his sleeve. As the carriage began to move, a satisfied sneer crossed Queen Cora's face. She had finally defeated her rival.

And he stood beside her. His soft, pallid face was just as smug as his mother's. The driver had to round the statue in the center of the courtyard and make a complete circle to exit to the Black Road. As they passed the staircase, Ronnock made sure to hold his middle finger up to the window, but low enough so his mother didn't see. The look of shock and offense across the Queen and Prince's faces was not satisfying enough to undo all their evils.

Ronnock returned to the streets, ignoring his urge to light up a cigarette. The air was damp and cold, the smell of rain finally overpowered the stink of the city. He allowed the Red to pulse within him, helping him to search the hive of streets for her smell or sound.

There.

The scent of white coastal flowers mixed with a salty breeze. He was relieved she was alone, he could tell by the footsteps around her. She had not been captured as her brother had. Where she was hurriedly walking uptown wasn't far from where he stood outside the tavern. She was panicked. She was either searching for her brother... or running from him.

He ran his hand over his hair again as he sighed heavily with regret. He could only hope she would listen to him after the grotesque display he had put on for her in the alley. He pressed his fingers against the cool metal of the pendant in his pocket. It was his second chance.

10: TRUST

BARDON

Lightning reached its wicked fingers much too close to the rooftops. The storm was fierce, like the earth itself was working to stop her. Venell felt the ground shake under her feet as they pounded heavily on the broken road. She tried to keep a distance between herself and the officers to avoid being noticed, but she couldn't fall too far behind and risk losing sight of them entirely in the storm.

Even through the heavy rain she could tell that she must have been coming upon the wealthier neighborhoods of Bardon. The bricks lay flat in the street, the holes were filled in, and the houses kept getting larger and more luxurious. The officers were ushered into a huge, red-bricked mansion on the right side of the road. They filed inside with their heads kept low, looking utterly ashamed of themselves for a reason Venell did not know.

The curtains at the front of the house were drawn so that she could not see inside. She quickly glanced around to make sure she was alone before scaling the short, brick wall that surrounded the mansion. Her heart was pounding so loudly she feared it would drown out all surrounding sounds. She had never been so reckless in all her life, but losing Ash was a thought she couldn't bear. Venell crept over to the side of the house, coming upon the first uncovered window. She cautiously peeked her head over the railing and looked through the window.

There was a roaring fire within the furnace of the mansion. It looked so warm and inviting inside. Everything was furnished with rich reds and golds, giving the entire dwelling a regal aura. Tapestries and gilded frames adorned the walls and fine fur rugs lay across the marble tile floor. The officers she had been following gathered in one of the further rooms. They were removing their rain-soaked jackets and throwing them carelessly in a pile on a highly glossed table.

She heard some sort of commotion begin to arise. Suddenly, three soldiers were knocked off their feet and onto the tile. The rest of the officers hurriedly regrouped to restrain whatever attacked the other three. Venell caught a flash of golden hair and dappled skin: Nalahi. She lashed out again, knocking several more officers off balance. The mass of officers practically piled themselves on top of her in an attempt to replace the broken ropes on her wrists and ankles with shackles instead. Nalahi sunk to the ground, breathing heavily, but there was a look on her face that denied her defeat. The officers regained their composure and exchanged a few words amongst themselves.

A heavy hand clapped onto Venell's shoulder and another covered her mouth. Purely on instinct, she screamed and drove her elbow back into her assailant's stomach. A man's voice grunted with pain, but he continued to hold her tightly, trying to overpower her. She managed to break an arm free from his grasp and sharply struck him across the face. He finally released his hold and she quickly spun around to face her enemy.

It was the Red man.

She almost screamed again, but the only people who would hear were Kras' men. She would rather die by this monster's fangs than by their hands. Venell felt her eyes widen as she fearfully waited for the slick noise of his fangs sliding out from his gums. She boldly raised her gaze to meet his. Only soft, grey eyes met hers. There was no monster, no creature of the night before her: it was just a man. A man, maybe in his early thirties, with a dreadfully scarred face and the most inviting eyes she had ever seen.

He grabbed onto both her wrists with a single hand and used the other to grasp the side of his face where she had hit him. "God damn, girl." He cursed under his breath. He grasped onto his chin, and with a loud pop he set his jaw back in its socket.

Venell forcefully pulled her arms away from him. "Please, leave me alone." She practically begged him. She fought the fear within her that any wrong move would suddenly transform him back into that red-eyed beast.

"Stop, I'm not going to hurt you. I'm so deeply sorry, before... I didn't realize who you were. We all assumed that everyone in Cynn was dead. I would've come if I had known, I'm so sorry."

Venell started to side-step away from him. He was crazy. He was a crazy Red-diseased man. "I have to save my brother. I don't know where he is."

"I do." He said.

She felt her entire body prickle. He was forcing her to listen to what he had to say by holding her brother out of her reach. If there were any truth to his words, she could not risk a chance to reunite with Ash. "Will you tell me?"

"In time. He's safe, I assure you."

"But Kras' men have him!"

He looked at her like she was the crazier one of the two of them. "No, I took him. He's with my allies. I can promise that no harm will befall him."

Venell found herself speechless. She wracked her brain considering all the possibilities. "You're lying!" She accused.

"What reason would I have to lie?" He replied coolly. He took something out of his pocket at extended his hand out toward her. She hesitantly accepted it. Cool, smooth metal pressed into her palm, and she felt her throat tighten with anxiety. It was Ash's pendant: the other half of their whole. There was no way Ash would've willingly given this treasure over.

"And how exactly were you planning to rescue him from all those officers, anyway? Punch them all like you did me?"

Her face burned with heat. She stumbled over words like a fool. "I saw our friend in there, she's been captured! And the last place I saw my brother was with her!"

The Red man's expression turned grim. He glanced into the window. Nalahi was on her knees, sitting back on her ankles and gnawing on a gag viciously. Iron links connected each of her limbs and fastened around her neck, forcing her to keep her head down. "Shit, why didn't you say that right away?!" he exclaimed.

He pushed Venell to the side, backed up a few paces, then slammed into the side of the mansion with his shoulder. The wood and brick gave way to his strength and he easily blew through it. Dust and debris flew everywhere. Everyone in the mansion stared at the explosion; dumbfounded.

The Red man's eyes blazed crimson-red and his mouth gaped widely to display his horrific fangs. "Everyone out!" he shouted in a deep, menacing voice as he stepped over the rubble.

The officers quickly obliged. They scattered like roaches, stumbling over each other in their panic and forgetting their royal coats, and then disappeared. In the meantime, Nalahi had managed to chew through her gag. "You better run, you fucking little maggots. I'm gonna get out here and tear your fucking heads off! Do you hear me?! I'm gonna fucking kill you!" Her pupils had narrowed to cat-like slits. Her face was fuming red and sweat was trickling down her forehead from the anger alone. As soon as they were all out of sight, she relaxed. She was just like a trapped animal.

The Red man popped the links of the chain, seemingly without much effort, and freed Nalahi. She got to her feet quietly, rubbing the red, irritated skin around her wrists and ankles where the metal had held her. She took a few more moments before she decided to speak, but she kept her gaze lowered in shame. "I saw him. Kras. I missed my chance... I could've stopped so much suffering...."

Venell had no response. She felt more pain from Nalahi's frustration than she had ever felt herself.

"I recognized his head officer; the one with the scarred right cheek. My father gave him that." She paused for a moment. She started to cry. "I let him get away. I didn't check the corners of the room. How could I have been so careless!? They were watching, waiting for me the whole time. I was stupid and he got away." She sobbed. "I was there when he gave the order to have my family murdered. I watched it happen. My older sister managed to push me through a window to get me out. I felt her die. I felt the tremor through her body when the axe struck her." She began to cry harder, hiding her face with her hands. "I don't know what happened to Ash. Venell, I'm so sorry. They pulled a bag over my head before I got a chance to look back."

The Red man tightly grasped her arm. "What happened with Kras?" he demanded.

Nalahi's feistiness sprung back into her eyes, even through her tears. She tore her arm away from his hold. "Who the fuck are you?"

"Ronnock Ukon, I'm with the Insurgo. Ash is safe with my allies."

She began to settle back down, but she continued to eye him distrustfully. "I spotted Kras in the inn. I didn't tell Ash; I didn't want him to break out in a blind rage again and make me miss my chance. I purposefully lost him in the crowd so I could get to Kras myself. Someone must have recognized me, because they caught me immediately." She closed her eyes and pressed her fingers to her forehead, looking utterly disappointed with herself. "Had Ash been captured also?" She asked the Red man.

He nodded, "I freed him from his captors and left him with one of the Insurgo's finest leaders. They should already be on their way to the base east of the city." He was obviously uninterested in Ash's safety, as he quickly began to demand what else Kras had said and if she knew if he was still in Bardon.

"He was well-guarded, and I'm sure they're rushing back to the capital." Nalahi chewed her lip as she looked from Venell to the Red man. "Bardon may face retaliation because of us. Kras takes every threat seriously. He may now believe there are more people hunting him than us."

"But there are more." Ronnock interrupted. "You are no different than any others we have taken in at the Insurgo. You've suffered in a torn, dying land and you wish to regain the country you once knew. Valehoutton has been falling into deeper despair ever since the Redals came into power. Kras is the final weight that the country cannot hold. Soon the levee will break, and the people must be ready."

Nalahi stood and rubbed the sores around her wrists as she thought. Venell fought the urge to demand more about Ash from the Red man. All she had was his assurances of her brother's safety, and those meant nothing to her. Having his pendant wasn't a promise of his safety. She felt it was more ominous. She wouldn't know anything for certain until she was reunited with Ash, and she silently prayed she would see him soon.

"You want us to go with you? Out of Bardon?" Nalahi asked. Her voice was laden with suspicion.

"I merely offered. I demand nothing." Ronnock replied. His casual tone made Venell uneasy. He was pretending as though they had a choice.

She, at least, did not if she ever wanted to see her brother again. She would give in to his coercion, and he knew it. What would she ever do without Ash? He terrified her at times, but she needed him. He hurt her sometimes, but she still loved him. He was her everything as she was his, even if he didn't always act like it.

Nalahi scowled at him before looping her arm around Venell's shoulders and leading her away from the Red man. They stepped through the remaining red brick dust that wafted through the air surrounding the man-sized hole in the mansion's wall. Nalahi pulled Venell's head to her and pressed her lips close to her ear. "I won't let you go alone with him, but I do fear that he lies. Sometimes it is the Red speaking and not their true mind. Ash may already be dead, or he may be in

Kras' grasp. You may never see him again. Consider your own life, Venell. Do you want to go with the Red man?"

She kept her face close to Venell's. Her expression was soft and patient. Venell felt warmth rise within her chest. She felt herself overcome with emotion and struggled to keep her watering eyes from forming tears. She gasped sharply as she fought back a sob. Nalahi kept a hand on Venell's cheek and wiped a tear away with her thumb. The tears weren't for Ash however; she was overwhelmed by the release of a tightness that had long sat in her heart. She had never had someone ask her feelings, nor ever been given a chance to chase her desires. The way this strange woman spoke to her was so drastically different from the way she spoke to Ash, and now to Ronnock. Venell didn't think it was pity, it felt like understanding.

Venell opened her eyes. Her brow was set hard with determination. "I want to go. Whether Ash is there or not, I think it is what we must do."

Nalahi grinned wickedly. "As do I." They turned back to the Red man, who stood with his arms folded and his scarred face set in a grotesque scowl. "Take us to Ash first." She demanded.

His arms remained folded, "It will take us well into tomorrow to reach the base on foot. My horse was taken back with your brother on it. I hope you don't need to rest."

"Just take us there, Red man." Nalahi snarled.

The Red man led them back into the reeking, swarming streets of lower Bardon. Luckily, he was tall enough to tower over most of the townsfolk, so Venell could still follow him even as she struggled to push past throngs of greth, whores, beggars, lost foreigners, and merchants pushing carts of their respective valuables. A heavy-set man with ale dripping off his beard grabbed Venell by both shoulders as she tried to slip past him. Nalahi wasted no time closing in on him before he could slur a single sentence, she wrapped her leg behind his ankle and struck him upwards on the chin. He stumbled and fell back into the hooting mass of his mates, mocking him for being bested by a woman.

The cracked and mottled stones of the paved street became further and further separated as the Red man led them down a stinking alley. Mud sloshed up onto Venell's boots as they sunk in further with each step she took. She exchanged a disgusted glance with Nalahi, who wore only rope and leather wrapped sparingly around her feet. She hoped that it was mud they were plodding through.

A bronze gate covered the end of the alley. It was sealed by a well-worn slab of wood slid through two metal slots: one on the gate and one on the city wall. The Red man slid the plank out of the slot on the wall and opened the thinly forged, unadorned passage. He didn't close it behind them.

The grasses of the Whispering Plains smelled heavily of rain, but fortunately the parched earth had soaked up the storm and left them with a minimally troublesome excursion across the plains. The clouds were beginning to clear. The air was brisk and refreshing. Venell felt a new strength spread throughout her body with each invigorating breath. She turned toward Nalahi, and the two women exchanged a glance. She felt empowered with the fierce heart beside her. She wondered if the woman with eyes like melted gold knew how important her words had been.

11: SUBSTITUTE

THE WHISPERING PLAINS, EAST OF BARDON

They had walked for nearly a full day in the same formation. Ronnock walked far ahead of the two women, and no matter what pace he kept they always remained the same distance from him. Their mistrust of him was well deserved, he knew, but it still made a knot in his heart to know that Venell feared him. Nalahi thought he hadn't noticed her fingering the bone hilt of her dagger every time he glanced over his shoulder to see if they were still following him.

They had left Bardon late into the night of the previous day, now the sun was beginning to set as a great dark shape in the distance began to grow before them. The base looked obscene placed upon the ocean of grass that was the Whispering Plains. All that could be seen even to the distant horizon was golden grasses blowing in the evening breeze silently. One could be lost in the sea forever if they could not read the sky. In every direction it all looked the same except for the ghastly stone block to the East that disturbed nature's curves.

The quiet of the plains was shattered by the clamor of the base's steel gates being drawn open. Sound carried far over the vast emptiness. The sentries must have seen them coming and were sending out riders. Sure enough, three riders came hurtling across the waves of grass towards them. Nalahi was instantly on guard, and Venell was also obviously on edge. Their suspicion was starting to get old.

"They're going to escort us in. You can ride with us or you can walk the rest of the way." Ronnock shouted back to them over the thunder of hooves. He flagged down Mayan on a red stallion and hoisted himself up behind his nephew.

"Where are you dragging in all these people from?" Mayan asked as he looked from each exhausted woman to the other. He must have been additionally referring to Jet's boy and Nai that Ronnock had sent back with Krisae the night before.

"Three are from Cynn."

He couldn't see Mayan's face as they rode, but he knew from the boy's lack of a quip that he was taken aback by the reply. Though he was not nearly as taken aback as Ronnock had been when he heard Venell's name while tasting her blood on his lips. He looked over his shoulder to see if the two had accepted the Insurgo's escort.

Venell had her head buried in Giness Anshee's back, and her clasped her arms around him as he rode for the base. Nalahi stubbornly held on the sides of the saddle on Hestys's steed. The seasoned warrior was much too prideful for Ronnock's liking; Hestys was probably irritable from being stuck with the inglorious task of escorting new arrivals.

Ronnock dismounted once they had passed through the gate. Khazar the Storm's lifeless eyes followed him as he walked. "Find Jet's boy and tell him his sister is here. That's probably the only way you'll get him to cooperate." He told Mayan. His nephew nodded and left.

Venell and Nalahi glanced around nervously. Some of the Insurgo stopped to get a look at them, but most just went about their business. It was nearly nightfall, and everyone was finishing dinner and readying to retire for the day. He approached the two, "My nephew is fetching Ash. I'm sure once he knows you're here he'll arrive quickly."

"Ronnock," Venell said. He felt a chill run down his spine and tingle throughout all his limbs. That was the first time she had called him by name. "Don't tell Ash that she saw Kras."

Before he could get another word in, Nai suddenly appeared out of the crowd and threw her arms around him. She shrilled about how happy she was that he was here, and that she was here, but he really wasn't listening. Venell gave him a slight smile and turned away, searching the crowd, as Nai continued to plant kisses all over his face and neck. Krisae approached and Nai finally relinquished her assault on him.

"I can't believe that of all people of Cynn to survive, it was Jet's son. Just look at him, there is absolutely no doubt. He looks just like the late commander." Krisae rambled breathlessly as Ash made his appearance following Mayan. She grasped Ronnock's hand and gave it a slight squeeze. "He doesn't talk much. How did you say you found him?"

"He tried to attack me in Bardon and cursed me for being Red."

Krisae looked back at him sternly, "Does he not know?"

"I'm not sure, but there was hate in his eyes." Ronnock nodded toward Venell, bringing the girl to his sister's attention. Venell was crying heavily as she fell into Ash's arms. He couldn't hear the words they were exchanging, but Venell just kept nodding and sobbing as Ash lifted her off the ground in a strong embrace.

Krisae's eyes went wide and she quickly turned back to Ronnock, "Yes, his daughter!" She exclaimed. She looked as though she might cry, and she covered her mouth with her hand. "And somehow they found their way to us. Maybe there is such a thing as fate."

"Don't get all romantic about it. You weren't the one that had to drag each of them here." Ronnock muttered. Krisae answered him again, but her voice and all the noises of the crowd began to fade into a distant, monotone sound. Everyone around him became a blur of background as he watched every movement she made.

She lifted a hand to wipe tears off her cheeks, but she was smiling. She gently pressed Ash's pendant back into his hand, then smiled as he fastened it around his neck. Her entire face lit up like a perfect, white flower opening to greet the morning sun. She lifted her chin as she laughed, he only wished he could have heard the sweet sound of it, but he could only watch as her eyes shone brightly, framed by long, heavy lashes. He could see himself right next to her. He pictured himself being the one to make her look like that. He could feel the warmth of her throat under his lips as he kissed her all over her wonderful flesh.

"Ronnock!" Nai said for what could've been the hundredth time. She grasped his chin and brought his face down to meet hers. Her mouth was set in a pout and she angrily tossed her long, black hair over her exposed shoulder. "Would you like to go to bed?" she asked coyly while twirling the end of his hair around one of her fingers.

"No," he said heartlessly and tugged her hands away from him. His annoyance with her was even more difficult to hide when it became mixed with his frustration of his spoiled interaction with Venell. He began to walk away toward the mess hall. Hopefully there was some food left, for his stomach had been tying itself in knots for hours. He put a cigarette in his mouth as he passed through the growing crowd, all eager to see Jet's children.

Nalahi rested a hand on his shoulder to stop him as he passed. He stopped for a moment as her eyes met with his. "Thank you," she said softly. Her mouth curled up in the corner like she was forcing the words out. "I'd heard of the Insurgo, but never ventured this far from the Saltwoods to see it for myself. I am relieved to see that it is a force to be reckoned with."

Ronnock assumed that was the best apology she could muster without actually admitting that she was wrong. While he appreciated her reconciliation with him, it was not who he wanted it from. He smiled back at her, though he was sure it looked as forced as it felt, and thanked her.

Luckily, there was a slab of meat that had not been cooked well enough to feed to any healthy human left in the kitchen, along with some cold potatoes and hard bread. He sat alone in the hall, everyone else had gone to their chambers. He chewed slowly as his thoughts turned dark. He didn't understand why he still put his heart into anything. He just couldn't learn his lesson.

After their mother's death, Hellan, Krisae and he were raised by her close friend, Khos Pilore. Khos was the first person Ronnock had ever known that was Red, but the older man had the disease well under control for years. It was before the blood cigarettes had been made a common luxury, so Khos would have to hunt more often than those presently infected did. He and Hellan were approaching their later teenage years when their mother died, but Krisae was still young and became very attached to their guardian for the remainder of his life. It wasn't long after Khos passed that Krisae left Snanka for the Insurgo.

He finished his meal and decided to just end his day by going to sleep. Not that he could escape from her in his dreams either. He took that western passage through the barracks of the recruits still in training. They were cramped, and the bunks were stacked two or three to a wall, barely leaving any room to sit up on one of the cots. He recalled the many sleepless nights he had spent in there as a young man, kept awake by the sounds of the other boys sniffling, coughing, crying, or fucking whatever girl they could persuade to bed with them. The bunks were soon replaced with the doors that led to all the officer's quarters. He had just turned the key in the old lock to his door when he heard someone say his name.

"I thought that was you," Venell said as she clasped her hands nervously behind her back. Ronnock watched her lips as she spoke; a perfect rosy color just begging to be touched by his own. "I just wanted to thank you for saving Ash and bringing us both here. You didn't have to help him, but you did. I know he's not an easy person to—"

He didn't know what he was thinking. He laced his fingers through her hair, holding each side of her face, and kissed her. He kissed her deeply, further intoxicating himself with the smell, feel, and taste of her. He didn't want the moment to end but she put a hand to his chest and pushed him away.

She just stared at him incredulously, but she didn't leave. Her eyes wavered as she waited for him to say something, and she took a step back. Her surprise faded into a hard frown. His actions began to set in and weigh heavy on him. "I'm sorry..." he couldn't think of anything else to say. He couldn't believe how bold he had just been, and he feared it would cost him.

"Why did you do that?" She asked quietly, still frowning.

"It's all I've been thinking about." He replied. He felt so foolish. All his thoughts of her were clouding his mind, yet he had to tell her the truth. He needed her to know.

She absently touched her lips while her eyes continued to study him. "Don't do it again." She said sternly, and then walked away. She didn't go hastily like she was embarrassed or disgusted. Her steps away from him almost seemed involuntary, like she had to think about each one. He watched her until she disappeared around a corner and out of his sight. Even then he still lingered, wishing she'd come back.

He may have just lost her forever by wanting her so badly. He placed his key back inside his breast-pocket and entered his room. Nothing had been moved since he had last been there. He had left the window ajar when he had last left for Bardon some two or three days ago, so the entire room smelled like the brisk night air. He lit a single lamp in the room but dimmed it, so everything was illuminated by a gentle, yellow haze.

He turned the mirror in the room to face toward the wall. He finally realized how exhausted he was when he allowed himself to relax on his bed. He took off his cloak and armor, laying them neatly on his sitting chair. He placed his belts of weapons on top of those and kicked his boots off under the chair. Everything he wore was black, as it always had been. He worked the leather wrap from the end of his ponytail and fastened it around his wrist, allowing his knotted hair to fall freely over his shoulders.

He lay back on the bed and rested a hand on his chest. He rubbed the sleep from his eyes and continued to stare at the ceiling. He thought about how Venell's feet shuffled when she walked. Her boots were too big, and obviously not made for her. None of her clothes were. She wore boys' brown breeches that fit too tightly and ended just below her knee instead of further down her calf. Her white tunic was of a common knit, and looked awkward beneath a fine, brown leather coat. She wore no jewelry or adornments, and she kept her black hair cropped to just below her shoulders. It hung heavy and straight but flowed gracefully with every turn of her head. Her light skin looked even more ghostly against the ebony strands about her head. Her full, dusky rose lips were usually pressed together in an anxious pout. It was true she looked very much like her older brother, especially since they both had Jet's piercing gaze, but her face was of a much softer contour, and her eyes had a narrow, almond-shaped curve that set his heart aflame when they looked at him.

There was a quiet knock on his door. It was so soft he almost missed it. He had to stop his mind from racing as he rose and grasped the knob. It creaked as he turned it. His breath caught in his throat as he slowly opened the timeworn wooden door. He saw bright orange-brown eyes under a furrowed brow on a flawless copper canvas. Nai cocked her head to the side playfully and placed one hand on her hip. She scanned the room behind him, looking to see if anyone else was with him.

"Why do you keep pushing me away, Ronnock? All I want is to see you. I do not ever ask for anything in return, I just ask for you, yet you still tell me no?" It was the first time he had ever heard some truth in her tone. She was hurt; she wasn't looking to use him this time.

He couldn't deny that she was beautiful, and her warm scent of spiced oils stirred at least a fraction of desire within him. But after the first time they made love, if it could even be called such, he had lost all feeling for her. He knew it would never return, especially not now that he had finally found what his heart had been searching for. After all those restless nights, lonely mornings, and cryptic dreams, he had found her.

But he couldn't have her, and there was no replacement.

Ronnock scratched his scalp as he pondered over what to say. His hair was matted into such thick locks that they would never loosen. He didn't want to hurt her, and the truth was not what she wanted to hear from him. "You can come in..." his voice trailed off as she took no spare moment to enter and pull her long, orange and pink silks over her head. She wore nothing underneath it. She held the end of her dress with one finger, and then let it slip off and pile onto the floor.

"You don't have to say anything else if you come here." She told him, her "o" sounds dragged out and accentuated with her Tuaegian accent.

He felt nothing stir in his loins and knew she would soon become offended if she saw him still flaccid. She grabbed his pant legs and pulled him closer to the bed as she sat down on it. Her hands slowly rubbed over his groin on the outside of his breeches. He tilted his head back and closed his eyes.

When he looked back down those haunting, sapphire eyes were upon him. It was her delicate, ivory hands that unfastened his pants. Her hands reached up and rested on his chest and abdomen as she took him in her mouth. He exhaled heavily with relief.

"I'm sorry I ever thought you didn't want me anymore." She gasped out in between the strokes she was making with her mouth. He didn't answer, but rather just turned her over so that she was lying on her stomach on the bed. Nai squealed with delight at his enthusiasm.

He closed his eyes again and pictured her sprawled out before him, waiting for him to make a move. His hands smoothed over her buttocks, gentle at first, then he pressed his fingers into the flesh more roughly. He heard that same gasp he heard in the alley echo throughout his bedchamber. He wanted nothing more than to hear that over and over.

Nai kept moaning, bringing him back to reality. He placed his fingers over her mouth, stifling her noises. He remembered how her skin felt against his, completely soaked in rainwater but radiating such a heat that he couldn't help but to let his fangs slide down from the sockets in his gums. Recalling the sweet, metallic taste of her blood on his lips was more than he could handle. He quickly pulled away from Nai before finishing. She looked back at him, full of distaste, but not nearly enough to compare to what he felt looking at her.

The incomparable guilt finally set in as he handed her a cloth and sat down on the bed with his face in his hand, still naked. She murmured something unintelligible, and then curled up to sleep. He looked over his shoulder at her disdainfully.

Ronnock quietly dressed himself and left the room. He didn't know where he would go, but he couldn't stand to wake up next to Nai.

12: THE ROTTING THRONE

JULY 1849:

STAR PALACE, THE CELESTIAL CAPITAL

Most of the palace was asleep, but not Delinda Redal. Her heeled boots announced her presence as she walked across the richly colored rugs lain across the stone floor of the castle. Her brother had summoned her to the throne room, or what used to be a throne room. Now it was Kras' cell. The room would surely also be his grave. Guards uniformed in scarlet and gold opened the throne room doors as she approached. The room stunk. It smelled of must and unwashed bodies. It was rare for Kras to ever be exposed to the outside air. The doors slammed heavily behind her as the guards stepped back outside.

Six more bodyguards stood around the king on his rotting seat. Cobwebs covered the ornate designs in the wood. The blue paint of the Caeruleans beneath had been slathered with the Redals' scarlet and gold, but the paint was chipping, revealing the ocean beneath. The large throne of old, dark wood leaned to the side where it was collapsing in upon itself. Kras rested his chin on his fist as he smugly watched Delinda approach.

The king's face was pale and sullen. He rarely ate for fear of being poisoned. His once vigorous frame had grown frail. His limbs were skeletal and his face looked drawn and sunken. His knuckles and elbows looked like obscene knobs growing under his skin, trying to burst through the paper-thin barrier. His golden hair had once shone like the new day but had long since turned white and brittle. He looked like a sickly child in an oversized chair instead of a man in his prime age. His eyes were always wide and squirrelly with apprehensions. Those apprehensions, however, were rightly placed.

After her great-grandfather, Rechaulle Redal, seized the throne from the Caeruleans in the name of his son, Sireh the First, Valehoutton remained in constant internal conflict. Many opposed Redal rule, but those voices soon fell silent. Political peril and bloodshed continued to spring to the surface through Sireh the First's reign, but then Valehoutton entered its first stage of peace under Sireh the Second's reign.

This was their father: King Sireh Redal the Second, a burly man with a burly soul. Their father had made a long-standing peace treaty with Tuaega after his army crushed the Tuaegian forces at the Last Battle of Neige Desert. Even the succession of Snanka was done on paper and not on the battlefield, granting King Aconite his own dominion over his lifeless kingdom. King Aconite thought he had won by getting a crown, but he had no knowledge of the crops and gold Valehoutton saved by cutting off his tumor of a country.

Delinda was the elder of Sireh's two children, born when he was still a teenaged prince. Even for the few years when she had been an only child, as her mother struggled to again conceive, she was underestimated due to her gender. Delinda seemed to be the only one to know what she was capable of. Once a son was born, Delinda was left by the wayside to teach and train herself for leadership, and so it had been since.

When she and Kras were both counting past their thirtieth birthdays, their father was still as strong and virile as he had been in his youth.

Though he kept his frustrations to himself, Delinda knew that her brother was lusting for the crown. He had been groomed for it his entire life; told that is was his birthright and destiny. Delinda couldn't help but to scoff at his entitlement.

She remembered the snowy night over twelve years ago when she was awakened by a clamor throughout the castle. It had been an unusually cold winter that year. Snow was uncommon in the South, and it continued to fall well into the early spring. She rose from her bed and tied her long, dark hair into a braid over her shoulder. She stepped out of her chambers and into the utter chaos. Servants, guards, diplomats, and numerous lords and ladies visiting the capital scuttled about the halls, all talking noisily and seemingly walking in no particular direction. She wandered towards the throne room, hoping her father would have answers. People ran about with jewels and other finery gripped in their arms, some holding as much as they could possible carry. Her bare feet grew cold against the stone flooring where rugs were missing. The throngs ebbed and flowed around her, but never consumed her.

She pushed open the heavy oak doors, with their hastily laid coat of red paint that covered the crest of the Caeruleans. The throne room was deathly silent. She clutched her woolen robe tighter around her as she approached the throne. Soldiers stood along the red carpet that marked the path to the king's chair. Their uniforms were crisply pressed and utterly unmarred. All stood facing the throne. Delinda slowly placed one foot in front of the other as she approached the chair. It was not her father seated there, it was Kras. Her brother's golden hair shone like a god's under his gold crown, ornamented with red stones. His head was raised high, and he looked down his face at her approaching. Their eyes met, and she knew what happened. Kras had killed Sireh, and no one knew but her.

"How dare you come before the king in your nightdress?" He had drawled that night.

Now Kras was only a shadow of the man he used to be. His sickly frame made him look much older than his thirties. When she had first seen him upon her father's throne that February night, he looked like he was meant to be on Valehoutton's highest seat. Now his madness was making the entire country ill. She could see the scene replaying over and over across his eyes. He had strangled their father in his sleep, the most intimate murder.

The guilt must have been eating him from the inside.

Tonight, Kras had called her to counsel. All gatherings were held in the throne room, seeing that Kras never left it except to retreat to his impregnable chambers in the South Tower. Usually the two of them would be alone, save his countless bodyguards, so she was surprised to see four councilors still seated at the table below the throne. Generally, none of Kras' other advisors were awake at the hours in which Delinda resided. For years she had been the night's captive.

Kras shifted his weight to the side and rested his taut face on a pale, bony hand. He blinked slowly as he watched her approach. She bowed curtly before him and waited for him to speak. He continued to glare down at her in silence.

"Why do you dress like that?" he motioned to her entire person with a sour look on his face.

She wore the same uniform that she demanded her men wore: a black linen shirt under a dark blue coachman coat with black breeches tucked into heavy riding boots. She had always felt more at home in men's clothes than in skirts. Perhaps it was because they made her feel more powerful, as if her attire would allow her to be taken more seriously by officers and councilmen, or perhaps she just felt more at home dressed that way. She never felt like herself in silks, lace, and taffeta; it made her feel like she was an actor in costume. She also found it easier to avoid courtship advances in her younger years every time she pulled on breeches and picked up a sword.

She made no response to the king, though she tugged at the sleeves of her collared tunic to make sure they fully covered her wrists. She clasped her hands behind her and waited for orders. He was just wind howling around a mountain. He would never topple her.

His voice was raspy and accompanied by taxing breaths. "Diar's only living child was still at his estate in Bardon. I proposed to our uncle to arrange a marriage between us and end any question of succession, but the imbecile refused. I sent men to collect her, but she had already vanished. I am certain she had help, she's young and stupid." He coughed heavily: a dry, hoarse cough. "She's likely heading east to Piaces, she has family from her mother's side there. I need you to intercept her before she reaches Piaces. Bring her here alive." He began to cough again and quickly waved her away in dismissal.

"What of the Tiver reservation? The mercenaries are chomping at the bit." One of the councilors questioned the king.

"Just finish off the dirt-worshippers." She heard Kras say as she passed.

Guards closed the throne room doors behind her as she exited. The paint was beginning to chip off here too, revealing the blue and white swirls beneath. She would have to leave the following night, for dawn was already too close and she dare not risk being outside when the sun rose. Living in the dark was a relentless reminder of the day she had tried to play god. She had meddled with the old ways of the Godsmoors and paid the price.

A second pair of footsteps fell in time behind her. Her colonel, Basaulte LaCera, had been loyally awaiting her. She allowed herself to smile with him by her side. She valued his strength as well as his devotion to her as his leader. His presence made her feel as though she could accomplish anything. Other women at court swooned about how strikingly handsome Basaulte was, but he was hers to command. His shoulder-length hair was as black as the night she thrived in, and his twisted beard accented his strong jaw. A leather patch was worn over his left eye and encircled the rest of his head, hiding the open orifice of an injury he had received years before. He towered over her, and his broad shoulders dwarfed her smaller frame.

"Dawn is approaching, my lady." His baritone voice told her. "Are you returning to your room?" She stopped at the foot of the stairs that led underground: her prison during the daylight hours.

He faced her. She stared up into his remaining eye. The color was so dark she couldn't see his pupil. "Should I prepare the elites for tomorrow night?" He asked her.

She nodded in response and held up six fingers.

"I will have them ready before nightfall." He confirmed to her. He turned to leave her to retire, then hesitated. "I wish I could hear your voice as before." He said, almost tenderly.

To that she didn't smile. She almost opened her mouth to reply; a habit she had only recently broken. She left him at the top of the stairs and retired to her room for the day. She latched the heavy iron lock and then rested on her bed. She would light candles if she had company, but she had been in the dark for so long she had already memorized where everything in her room was. She felt deprived of too many senses. She did miss the sun, and of course she missed her voice.

The next time she had found Kras alone after he murdered their father, she demanded he admit the truth to her. He continued to lie. She threatened to expose him. As she had turned to storm out of the room, he brought down a heavy iron candlestick over her head. She didn't awaken for two weeks and she had not been able to speak since.

Yet still she pressed on and worsened her fate. The silence made her alone. Not many of the men she commanded besides Basaulte could read or write. She was isolated even though she was surrounded. The world moved around her as she stood still. She felt the respect she had worked so hard to claim fade into pity. Delinda Redal was not one to be pitied.

After a year of utter loneliness, she traveled to the cavern of the Third Eye, in the far north of the Godsmoorian's land and overlooking the sea. It was the holiest site of the Godsmoors' people, long since abandoned after they were relocated to the Tiver reservation. Any Godsmoorian seeking to reach the Northern Shore would have to cross paths with the thousands of greth that settled across the valley.

It was said that the elders of the Godsmoors could speak to the earth, and that it was the old flow of life itself that was embodied in the cavern. It was an ancient place where the earth could hear its children speak. The cavern should have been pitch black, yet all the rock was illuminated by an eerie blue glow. Her men waited outside as she entered the holy site. She immediately noted the three openings in the ceiling of the cave, demonstrating its name. The center one was the largest and slightly elevated over the other two openings. Delinda could see the cloudy, grey sky typical of the coast through the eyes. After a short explorative walk, she found the cave empty of anything but saltwater dripping from stalactites. No life scurried upon the ground or crawled upon the walls like it did just outside the entrance to the cave.

Delinda sat and meditated for hours, maybe days, trying to gain some knowledge of her future. What path should she take? What would be the consequences if she rebelled against her patricidal brother? She prayed for her voice to return and give her the power to right the kingdom.

No answer ever came. Her desire began to turn to desperation. Her mind kept returning to what she had read of the Deep magic in an ancient book recovered from the Godsmoors' people years before. It indicated that sometimes a sacrifice must be given to receive, and the closer to human, the more powerful. She demanded an orphan be brought to her in the cave. She at least had enough heart not to tear a family apart. She'd relieve the country of one hungry, useless mouth to feed.

Her men soon captured a child left alone on the Godsmoors; a scared, starving little girl. She had the typical white-blonde hair and sea-green eyes of the native people, though she only had two stars on her face, as if her constellation was incomplete. Delinda knew nothing of the meaning of any stars and paid it no mind. The frightened youth seemed to calm for a moment when she was passed from Basaulte's rough, calloused hands into her own feminine ones. Perhaps she thought she was safe.

She spilled the child's blood on the sacred ground. Delinda did this herself, with her own hands and blade. The cave was deathly silent as the crimson pool began to spread across the glowing, blue floor. Delinda waited, but no vision or dream ever came. No sound manifested when she tried to speak. It was all for naught. The abysmal pit she felt in her gut was not for the regret of murdering an innocent, but also for her own failure and hopelessness. It seemed she would be doomed to silence for the rest of her life.

Thinking it was all futile after, Delinda rose from the small corpse on the ground and wiped her hands on her dark coat. She had thought no answer had come from the earth until the moment she stepped into the sunlight. Instantly, her skin began to burn and blister until Basaulte covered her with blankets and returned her to the darkness of the cave until night fell. The Deep had passed judgement upon her, and found the princess wanting.

And so she, Princess Delinda Redal of Star Palace, the Celestial Capital, became known as the Darkstar. The last time she had seen daylight it had nearly killed her.

13: THE VIPER

JULY 1849: THE INSURGO BASE

Ash ground his teeth together as he watched the Red man watch his sister. His fist tightened around his fork. He angrily shoveled a lump of mutton into his mouth and continued to glare over his shoulder as he chewed. He knew Venell well enough to recognize that her kindness toward the man Ronnock wasn't feigned. She genuinely enjoyed his company, and it burned Ash to the core. He would rather make Ronnock the villain and seducer, so he could intervene and keep Venell for himself. But the way she was blossoming during their weeks at the base... he felt as though he couldn't reach her anymore.

A dark-skinned boy, a few years younger than Ash, with wild hair that stuck out in all directions, took a seat next to him in the mess hall. "Hey, it's Ash, right?" He asked with a hurried, yet enthusiastic voice. Ash just nodded and kept his eyes on Venell as she gently laid a hand on the Red man's shoulder as they spoke. "My name is Mayan Ankatez. It's unbelievable to meet you. I mean, we met already, but we didn't really get to talk. Your father and my father are the ones that founded the Insurgo more than twenty years ago! And now we're both here to continue their legacies. It is truly amazing."

Krisae had also told him about his father's rebellious past. Ash had never heard even a whisper of the Insurgo before. He knew his parents must have purposefully keeping Jet's identity a secret from the world, while also sheltering both children from the truth. All those times his parents had traveled across the entire country to spend one or two nights on the Snankian border suddenly made sense. As did his father's quiet job as a blacksmith's assistant in Cynn, the newest colony and furthest place from the capital. Jet was hiding himself and his family from anyone that might recognize his face. The blue eyes and black hair he passed to both Ash and Venell would have been a dead giveaway to anyone looking for the old general.

It used to be that when Ash thought about his father, he pictured the time he saw him with Red eyes and a bloody mouth. The image was burned into his brain so deeply that he could never see Jet in any other light. That was until Ash saw his throat slit and his tall, lanky body dropped down into the dirt that coated the once pristinely white streets of Cynn. Now when he thought of his father, that was the image he saw. In that moment he couldn't help but to feel like it was a deserved fate. The soldiers were in Cynn looking for Red, but he hid from them like a coward. If he had turned himself over, Mother may still be alive.

Despite any physical resemblance Ash shared with his father, in no way was he planning to "continue his legacy," and he told Mayan so. The boy blinked at him blankly. He was stumbled over a few words, trying to find a way to express how utterly astounded he was. "Then... why are you here?"

"Nalahi, my sister, and I are going to kill Kras. This has been a diversion." Without finishing his food, Ash pushed his plate away and stalked off. He didn't necessarily dislike that boy Mayan, but Ash didn't want to discuss all the things Mayan seemed so keen on.

Nalahi stood with Krisae in the main yard. Both women had their arms folded as they watched fresh, young recruits wrestle each other to the ground and attempt to beat each other with their flailing, untrained hands. Krisae towered over Nalahi's petite frame, and probably still would have even without her well-shined, tall-heeled black riding boots that reflected every ray of sun that hit them. The two women had grown up in two different worlds, but their hardships made them just as equally deadly. Nalahi was lightning fast, dexterous, stealthy, and healed small wounds at an oddly increased rate. Krisae packed brute force in all her limbs and was both precise and inventive in a fight. That and she was Red.

Krisae noticed him first, or at least she acknowledged him first. "You could probably benefit from this." She said, nodding to the boys on the field. Nalahi smirked about something only she knew.

The boys training on the field didn't differ in age much from himself. Though as he watched them, he could help but to feel a weight sinking in his gut with the realization that he was very much unlike these boys. They all fought as though they had never felt true fear. None had ever had to fend off an enemy that had murder in their eyes. None had ever killed another human, and all felt as though they had something to lose. They were still so soft, so full of hope and dreams, like young men his age should be. The best fighter in the group could still be the first to fall in a real battle when his body froze in fear as thousands of greth swarmed before him, screaming and gnashing those horrible teeth.

A few men decorated with the Insurgo's jet-black symbol of Khazar the Storm barked out orders. The boys separated from their sparring partners. The sound of ragged breathing filled the silence between the officers' orders.

"Denyen!" Krisae shouted from behind Ash. She pointed at him and gave her comrade a knowing look. The dark-skinned officer had surprisingly light hair for his complexion. He raised his fist into the air and circled it around in a precise motion. All the boys swapped partners, and Ash found himself facing a lithe boy with sandy brown hair.

Ash raised his fists to guard his face. The other boy was younger than he was, though he was taller with a much longer reach. Those gangly limbs could give him some advantage over his own sturdier build. Ash could barely understand what any of the officers were bellowing; nor did any of their overly complicated hand-motions make sense to him.

Suddenly, everyone was on the move. The boy shifted his weight back and forth between his feet, staying light on his toes. He keenly watched Ash's hands. Ash watched the boy's eyes. He saw intent flicker across the hazel surface. Ash was already moving by the time the sandy-haired boy stuck out at him. There was no time lost on reaction. Ash knocked away the fist coming toward his right oblique with an open palm, then stepped into the boy's lunge with his elbow. The blow knocked the boy to the ground; his own force used against him. He noisily sucked in air and gaped at Ash incredulously. Ash smirked to himself, both at the boy's pain and surprise, but also because he was happy with his own performance. He hadn't been in a fight since he was a child in Cynn, but he had started numerous scuffles on those white pebble streets that only ended when an adult intervened. He liked to think he won all of those fights too.

Everyone began to shift again. Ash found his new opponent in a stocky, blonde young man with a darkly tanned neck and shoulders. His hands looked to be large enough to fit around Ash's head. He thumped his massive fist against his chest before extending his open hand out to Ash. Ash accepted the handshake, though he had to feign the camaraderie. He raised his fists again and shifted his balance to his toes in anticipation. Before Ash even realized the match had started, his opponent had already swung. His huge fist caught Ash on the left side of his ribs. He gasped involuntarily.

"You stand to side more, smaller target." His voice was deep and laden with an accent unfamiliar to Ash, but the common language was surely not his native tongue.

Ash gritted his teeth and ignored the comment. He raised his fists again, quickly swinging with his stronger right hand. He had been aiming for the face, but his opponent moved so Ash's fist glanced off his muscular shoulder. The blow sent pain shooting from Ash's hand and down his arm. He reeled back while grasping his hand.

"You fight with strong hand forward, you hit faster. Strong hand back, enemy see your next move. No good." He thumped his fist against his shoulder where Ash had hit him. "Must be fast, not very strong." He laughed loudly and deeply.

Ash felt caught in a blur of motion as opponents switched again. His ears were ringing with rage and his right hand was throbbing. The skin below his first two knuckles was raised and tender. He suddenly snapped out of his thoughts to find himself facing Mayan Ankatez. Mayan wore a scowl across his face. He was very unlike the annoying boy Ash had encountered at breakfast.

"You don't listen to anyone, and it makes you foolish." Mayan said under his breath. Ash could barely hear him over the sounds of other recruits struggling to subdue each other.

Ash raised his fists. He kept his throbbing right hand to the back, hoping Mayan would not notice his injury. Mayan kept his hands at his sides. Ash felt unnerved by his opponent's lack of readiness, but he couldn't wait any longer. He kicked out with his front leg in a sweeping move, but suddenly found himself hitting the ground belly first. He wheezed as the air was knocked from his lungs, and there was a sharp pain spreading from his shin. Then Mayan was on top of him with his arm locked around Ash's throat. He flailed his arms, trying to reach behind him and knock Mayan off his back, but the angle it was impossible to do so.

"Everyone here, absolutely everyone, not only wants to see the false king dead, but wants all the Redals removed from power. Look around you!

Everyone has suffered as much as you have! No one wants to join the Insurgo, they come because they've lost everything! Sireh the First killed the Caeruleans, Sireh the Second infested Valehoutton with greth and destroyed the Godsmoors, and Kras commits genocide trying to purge all the Red!"

Ash had black spots in his vision. His eyelids became heavy. Then Mayan released his hold. He didn't look so young anymore as he stood over Ash. His vibrant green eyes stood out even more against his dark, earthy skin. "You will never kill Kras. But we will. We will make this country right."

The room he woke up in was dimly lit and stuffy. His head was pounding, and his right arm felt heavy. He groaned when he saw it was covered in plaster from his knuckles to his elbow. He heard women's voices talking quietly. Suddenly, she was over him. Her ivory hand swept over his forehead, pushing his long bangs to the side and feeling for a fever. Her familiar scent was relaxing: a light scent of sea salt and flowers.

"Ronnock said you were knocked out in training." She said quietly.

Just the mention of that Red bastard's name was enough to put Ash back on edge. Hot embarrassment surged though his veins. He didn't answer her.

"It's late. The commander is letting you have this room until your hand heals more. You should get some more rest." She rose to her feet.

He grasped her wrist with his good hand, "Don't leave." He murmured.

She stopped, but she didn't sit back down. "Ash," her voice was quiet and apologetic. "I've been here for hours. Nalahi is staying now."

He hadn't even noticed Nalahi sitting on the other side of his bed. Her hair was down, and she wore a soft yellow nightdress that fell to her ankles. It was odd seeing her in real clothes; she looked like a completely different person. She sat with her bare feet on the chair and her knees under her chin. The mottled colors of her skin were visible under the sheer parts of the fabric. She said nothing, but her golden eyes went back and forth between the siblings.

He didn't want Venell to go. He wanted the comfort of her presence. He just wanted her near him, so he would know she wasn't off with that Red man, but he couldn't find the words to let her know. She left him alone with Nalahi, who kept her silence.

He settled back down into his bed. He tried to move the fingers on his right hand, but they were stiff and sore. "I'm losing her." He didn't even realize he said the words out loud.

Nalahi snorted, "You're like a spoiled child that only wants a toy when someone else wants to play with it." She drummed her fingers on the arm of the chair. Ash could tell it had been a fine piece of furniture before, but now it sported numerous holes in the leather that exposed the wooden frame beneath. By the way her eyes shifted, Ash could tell she was thinking before she spoke. "Keeping her the way you have been makes you feel strong, but you can't. You need to let her grow."

Ash didn't reply.

Nalahi looked around the room. It was windowless and the stone walls and floor were bare. She rubbed an eye sleepily. "I know it's strange for you to be around so many faces and personalities so suddenly. I hadn't left the Saltwoods for a long time before I met you two. Once my face was too well known around Bardon, I ventured there less. It has just been Aldrion and me." She rested a cheek on her forearms crossed over her knees. The skin on one was pink and ivory, while the other was dusky olive. "I miss him."

He didn't know why she was giving him this information. He couldn't tell if she was just trying to fill the silence, or if her words were a peace offering between them. She had never shown him any care before, not like she did with his sister.

Ash didn't say anything.

"You were still in the city when it flooded?" She asked him, lifting her head slightly. He had forgotten that while she was also from Cynn, she didn't have to experience the massacre or the flood.

Her question prompted the sound of rushing water to suddenly fill his senses. His heart fluttered with a moment of panic as he recalled bloodying his fingers against the cold, slick metal of the canal grate. He couldn't pry it off and the water was coming. He was underwater when he put the blade of his knife in the tiny slit between the wall and the grate. The second it was off, the current pulled him through the canal. It was dark, so dark. He still hadn't gotten a breath. His hands were in front of him. Every bump against the stone walls of the tunnel knocked a breath from his lungs. His shoes were gone.

Then he was in the sultry, suffocating room with Nalahi again. "Yes. The current carried me out to the Saltwoods. I caught onto a tree, climbed it above the water. I thought for sure the trees would fall just as the city did, but the current was not as strong with more ground to cover. Venell was there before me. We just waited there until it was over."

"The Saltwoods saved you."

"They saved you too."

"Yes. But they don't save everyone. I was the last one that woman pulled through the window... everyone else was dead. My older brother and sister, my parents, their two friends and their daughter; the whole room was slaughtered. Two neighbor boys, twins, and my baby sister were with me on the outside. We ran to the woods. One didn't make it. Viron. I had always liked him." She smiled sadly. "He was shot down. An eight-year-old boy running for his life, just shot down."

"We were starving. We had no idea how to survive out there. Baby Tyven was sick and I could not keep her clean. She died. I found her white and cold one morning. She looked so tiny..." She wiped a tear before it could roll down her cheek. "Shiron and I finally trapped a rabbit. When we went to take it, a bear appeared. Shiron tried to fight it off. But one swing and he was dead too."

Ash didn't like to hear any of this.

He didn't want to look at her as she pressed her wrists to her forehead and stifled heavy sobs. Her feet were rested but spread apart on the seat of the chair, her elbows resting on her knees. He kept his eyes forward; looking at nothing. Feeling nothing. His heart was already too burdened to feel sympathy.

But then he looked at her.

He didn't see her pain. He saw the gap between her legs where her nightdress did not cover her. She must not have noticed. She wore nothing underneath the shift, and through the opening between her uncrossed legs he could fully see her, as well as the curve of her buttocks. A ripple of pale skin flowed from her thigh to between her legs, making a patch of her hair there white. It was the first time he had looked upon Nalahi as a woman. The look of her womanhood seemed foreign too him, yet it was not off-putting. Despite her hard exterior, he could now see how delicate she really was. He knew now that she was nothing like the abrasive person she pretended to be.

His trance was broken as her eyes flashed at him angrily, but still she kept her knees up and did not close her legs. They just stared at each other; both knowing what he could see.

She suddenly stood, the shift falling around her calves, but the sheer form still left little to his imagination. "I opened my heart to you. You said nothing and just....!" She was so incredulous she could not even finish her thought. Not that she needed to.

He turned away and looked at nothing again. And he said nothing again.

She suddenly moved toward him with a furious hand outreached. Startled, he turned to face her as she grabbed him by the chin. She held him there with her golden eyes narrowed. The look of her fury was enough to make any man shake, though he was not entirely sure it was from fear alone. His mind suddenly flashed back to the first time they met, when she had him pinned to the forest floor between her thighs. How he wished to have his face there again, but under entirely different circumstances.

Her lips pursed with anger and she shoved his face away before straightening herself. "Fuck you." She muttered under her breath. "They call me the Viper, but you're the snake." She threw his casted arm back, slamming it against the brick wall.

His vision went white from the pain, and he heard his own voice cry out. When he could finally see, his body was covered with sweat and he found himself alone. For Ash, it was difficult to be alone with nothing but himself.

14: THE PRICE OF PRIDE

JUNE 1849: THE EASTERN CRAGS

Dream mixed with reality as Minortai continued to find himself in and out of consciousness. Every time he awoke to the jostling beneath him, he would suddenly remember Siyah was dead. He must've seen her blood spilled a hundred times now, and it was no less painful. Sometimes he would cry until he drifted back to his dreams. At first, he would see her alive there, smiling at him with flowers in her hair. He could feel her silken lilac dress beneath his fingers. Now he only dreamed of the black desert. Dying stars would start falling from the sky if he strayed from the path before him.

He kept hearing voices around him. They were kept hushed, but some were forceful. There was a woman. No, two women. When he would try to open his eyes, the world was just a blur of color. The light would shoot stabbing pains throughout his skull until he closed his eyes again. His body felt heavy and useless. He woke up once to vomit. The sensations were so strong that he felt his body waver and fall. Air rushed past him, and there was a man shouting.

He knew the voice. He knew the man's voice. The grip on his clothes was the same one he had felt as a child. A jolt shot through Minortai and he opened his eyes. He was truly awake this time. Much of his confusion lingered, but he could still recognize the mottled trees of the Eastern Crags. He lay sprawled out on a course fur with a roughly knitted blanket over him.

The forest was sparse and Minortai could see the clear night sky above him. The moon was not quite full, but its soft, white light was enough to grant him sight. Before he could fully take in his surroundings, the dull ache in his thigh overtook all his thoughts as the pain became searing. He cried out but resisted touching the wound. He felt dizzy again.

"He's going to die if we keep moving like this!" one of the women hissed.

"We're going to have to risk it, they're getting too close." Nehlas said.

"Nehlas," Minortai forced out. He had to let them know he was finally conscious.

Both the woman were crouched beside him, while his brother loomed over them all a few feet away. One was the freckled, red-headed woman he had seen before. She placed a pale hand against his forehead. "His fever finally broke."

"Nehlas," he said again, "we're in the East."

"Nearly." His brother replied. His voice was low, and Minortai could tell that he was exhausted.

"How did you find me?"

"I followed your tracks from where I found Siyah."

Minortai didn't want to cry, but he couldn't hold back a sob at the mention of her name. The mere sound of it turned the memory too real. He feared he already knew the answer to his next question: "Are you all that is left of your company?"

Nehlas didn't reply. Minortai sobbed again. All the men Nehlas had taken with him were dead. Everyone left on the reservation was killed. For all he knew, the Silverstars were the only people of the Godsmoors left alive. The greth had finally completed their genocide of his people.

"We were ambushed in the trees of the southern border. They knew we were coming. They saw us leave the reservation. They waited to raid until we were vulnerable." He finally said. His voice was cold and pragmatic. "I only escaped because Meras is so swift. The rest were run down. Our company now is a family from Ellinhall. We ride for Snanka." Minortai could hear the pain and guilt in his brother's voice, yet he could not find sympathy within his own heart. His brother blamed himself, but Minortai blamed him too.

Minortai finally opened his eyes again once his tears subsided. Nehlas had left. The red-headed woman remained. Her hands were stained with blood. She looked upon him worriedly. "Try to sleep." She told him. She gathered up bloodied bandages and left Minortai's short range of view. He didn't think he could sleep, but it soon took him.

He awoke at daybreak. A full-bodied blonde woman gathered her hair into a ponytail as she walked away from Nehlas' white mare, laden with supplies. Her legs were covered in blue tribal tattoos, the same patterns indicative of an Ellinhall native. It was said that Ellinhall once had a Godsmoors. It was the home of a sister clan to his people. As the human population grew, they encroached on the holy lands. Their short-sighted ways led to fire and destruction, thickening the veil between the Godsmoors and the Deep, leaving nothing but dead land. It was also said that beasts in Ellinhall walked in human skins whenever they wished. The woman saw Minortai looking at her, but she kept walking without paying him any mind.

A man with white-blonde hair suddenly approached him. Minortai was taken aback, thinking he was another survivor of his people, but the young man had no stars upon his face. The man smiled, obviously knowing what Minortai was thinking. "My mother was of the Godsmoors, but my father was not." He warmly clasped Minortai on the shoulder. "My name is Mordain Evening, it's good to finally meet you." Minortai smiled weakly at him. "My wife, Kajonne, is the one that has been caring for your wounds. Her sister, Wenn, is also with us. We head for the Insurgo headquarters in Snanka. Your brother agreed to accompany us there, and we found you not four days ago."

Minortai did not wish to be rude to his new acquaintance, but he found himself unable to muster any sort of response. He laid his arm over his eyes to hide the tears forming.

"I see you're not feeling well still." Mordain said kindly.

Minortai felt his teeth clench as flashes of Siyah's face continued to haunt him. The nightmare was over, but the reality that was beginning to settle in his gut was more than he could bear. It was true then that they were the last. The Godsmoors would never be reborn and they would die with Nehlas and him.

That night he could hear rustling in the distance accompanied by laden breathing and a woman's soft gasps. When he glanced around, he saw Kajonne and Mordain sleeping a few feet away from him, while his brother and the blonde woman were nowhere to be seen. They had both returned to their small camp by the time Minortai awoke as the sun rose.

"Are we still being hunted?" he asked Kajonne as she changed his bandages. A rotten scent suddenly filled his senses. He didn't dare to look at the wound, he knew exactly what that smell was. She only briefly looked him the eyes, but then quickly avoided his gaze. Her face was lightly freckled, but not with a constellation, and her eyes were a deep green. Tattoos of vines and flowers marked her hands in the same blue ink that decorated her sister. Her red hair was frizzy and unkept, cut bluntly just above her shoulders. She was not a striking woman, but something about her exuded warmth and beauty.

"We will always be hunted, your kind and ours: by greth, by men, by fools and bigots." She tied the dressings too tightly for his comfort, but he didn't say anything as he was sure it was necessary. "We need to find the kingsfoil weed. That may be the only thing to stop the rot."

She said something quietly to her husband before hurrying off. From the looks of how dry the trees around him were, Minortai knew there was no stream or river near. The kingsfoil weed only grew in moist soil, usually by a body of water. She must have known it too.

The sound of something large approaching through the brush turned his attention from Kajonne. Her sister, Wenn, suddenly appeared dragging the body of a huge buck. It seemed utterly impossible for a woman her size, or a man for that matter, to bring back such a large kill so easily. Mordain expressed his gratitude for the kill to her, but in no way treated it as something out of the ordinary. She began re-stoking the fire as he worked on cleaning the animal.

Minortai did not awaken again until night had fallen. He felt that he could no longer trust his senses. He was finding it difficult to distinguish between what he saw when he was asleep and when he was awake. The crackling fire was comforting. Mordain sat across from him enjoying his roasted venison.

"Where's Nehlas?" was all he could think to say to the man.

"He and Wenn have both retired for the night." He replied. "And Kajonne has yet to return from the creek." He did not seem overly concerned about his wife's whereabouts while the forest could easily be crawling with greth. Mordain must have taken note of his reaction. "Tiver is not the first land to overrun with greth. Much of Ellinhall is uninhabitable now because of the creatures. Once Tuaega agreed to peace with Valehoutton, they turned their attention to the East."

Mordain tossed the clean rib bone into the fire and leaned back onto his hands, looking up at the smoke rising toward the sky. "We've dealt with the greth for many years. The Wenn Dell sisters know how to avoid being seen if they wish."

While Minortai did not find his new acquaintance's company unpleasant, he found his patience running thin. "Why Snanka? Is this Nehlas' plan or yours?"

"We were first going to the Insurgo headquarters outside of Bardon. It was going to be a longer journey, but we didn't want to cross the black sands. Many refugees are flooding to the Insurgo from even outside of Valehoutton's borders. We will find safety and numbers, and the sisters look forward to putting their skills to use against the greth. However, we were nearly killed after stumbling into their eastern blockade of the Whispering Plains. We had to flee North and plan to backtrack to Snanka. We ran into your brother south of the Crags, and he led us to you." He slightly forced a smile. "So now you're all caught up."

He hadn't been putting it together all this time. He had been dreaming of Snanka. He kept seeing the desert. He didn't see the Insurgo Base, and it wasn't the country's capital in his vision either. It was an old palace. A wind-worn, solitary watch tower that overlooked the burning sands. His constellation waited for him over the tower like a constant beacon, twisting and spinning in upon itself.

"It's not the Insurgo." He said aloud without entirely realizing it. He tried to describe his vision of the abandoned palace to Mordain. He was either uninterested in Minortai's half-coherent ramblings or genuinely had no knowledge of Snanka's lands. He just kept shaking his head and shrugging in response.

Minortai awoke several times that night; cold, alone, and fighting back bitter tears. The fire had died out and particles of ash kept landing on him, but he was too weak to brush them off. Each time he drifted off he hoped it would be the last. He hoped he would not wake up to the throbbing pain in his body and the crippling memories in his heart.

The heat was boiling even within the stone walls. The black sands surrounding them made the palace more like an oven. He couldn't imagine how anyone could live in such a place. He sat in an old armchair, worn walnut with a dark stain, and moth-eaten upholstery. A long banquet table of the same dark stain extended before him. The other chairs tucked up to the table were crumbing and unusable. A layer of grey dust covered every surface, though marks and fingerprints let him know they had not gone completely untouched.

He looked up for the first time, to the other side of the stone dining room. A raven-haired woman sat across from him. The room seemed to stretch and the distance between them became greater. "Don't push me away, Minortai Silverstar, I'm the one that has been reaching out to you. Just be calm." The room began to stretch faster as he began to question his surroundings in a panic. Her voice was becoming more and more distant. "Minortai, my name is Hellan Lukifere. I'm in Dust's Plateau: the prison and final resting place of the king's first mistress."

Everything he had been seeing wasn't just a dream. This was too vivid. He could feel in it his bones that she was real, not just in his head. "Why me?" was all he could think to say. What could she possibly want of him?

"This part of the world, this plane, does not have many visitors. I saw you, a man of the Godsmoors, and I followed you into yourself. I've seen your life. I've seen your stars. All children to come that bear the constellation of Minortai will never again be remembered as the Matricider. You must come to me, to Snanka."

She wore a long-sleeved gown, even in the heat. It hung thick and heavy, just like her raven hair. Her steely grey eyes were unwavering but barely visible from behind her long bangs. She lifted a lit cigarette to her lips. They were full, but the same paper-white color as the rest of her skin. When she slowly exhaled a red cloud slowly encircled her and spread across her end of the table before dissipating. She looked at him again with her Red eyes. "Or do you fear me?"

Minortai had never met a person infected with the Red. He knew they were feared amongst the people of Valehoutton, but so were his own people. "We're going to the Insurgo base in Snanka." He didn't know why he offered up the information so freely. He may have nothing to lose, but that didn't mean he should put their company from Ellinhall at risk.

Hellan exhaled another cloud of red smoke. "Very well. You will pass through here on your journey. I will await your arrival." She put out the cigarette on the table, digging the burning end into the antique wood. Numerous other burned craters dotted the same corner of the table. She gave a slight smile when she noticed his surprise of her disregard of her historical abode. "Each time I hope it'll burn this place into the sand."

Then her look became grave. "Do not come into Snanka through Dry Canyon Pass. It may not be guarded, but that is because no one makes it though alive. Go north where the river still runs to cross into my country."

"Why? What happens in the canyon?"

She leaned forward onto her elbows. The ember from her cigarette was eating away at the heavy stain on the wood. "It's full of monsters. Monsters like me."

Minortai jolted awake to Kajonne's fingers inside his wound. He cried out and instinctively jerked to pull his leg from her, but she held him firmly and forced the crushed weed into his rotting flesh. His thigh muscles twitched, and then the skin around the wound tingled until it was numb.

"Sorry," Kajonne said quietly. "I tried to finish before you woke up."

"It's fine. It's not hurting." He almost felt empty without the pain. It kept his mind occupied so his heart wasn't in such agony. He turned his head to the side to avoid her gaze.

Mordain was sleeping nearby in a bundle of furs with no shelter over his head. In the distance he could see Nehlas' tent pitched. The noises he heard within it were all too familiar. It seemed no matter their circumstances, some things never changed.

1 : CONTROL

JULY 1849: THE INSURGO BASE

Commander Ankatez,

We've just returned from our meeting with Risa to find Cynn upside down. A drop of panic is in the water, and there may be little anyone can do to stop the ripples. There's talk of shutting the gates to make sure the disease doesn't spread to the rest of the coast. Celidian speaks of leaving, but there are few places I can go and remain anonymous. We'd be putting the children at risk.

This fresh hysteria has made me reflect on what I wrote to you before my retirement. I've thought all this time that the prejudice and fear were misplaced; as long as you made it through the change, you were still you. I've tried to build myself into a man that the lost could gather hope from, but, my friend, I may be wrong. The thought plagues me. It's been more than two decades since the disease first scarred my skin. I had such confidence that I could still thrive even with what I called my "supposed ailment" coursing through my veins. My prosperity never intruded on another's right to their own until that fateful day. I still don't know how I allowed it happen, but I am grateful every day that I awoke before I did more harm to my family. That boy's eyes have a different look now. How quickly we became strangers haunts me. I hope you never feel that distance with your own son.

Please be looking for more correspondence. I deeply hope that we will not require aid if the situation worsens, but we may.

Your friend,

Jet

Ronnock read over Venell's shoulder as she ran her fingers over the yellowed parchment that bore her father's hand. It had been over a week since he had first spoke to her about her father's time at the Insurgo, his role as a co-founder, but it was as though she still couldn't believe it. He watched her read through nearly a hundred letters as the morning grew old. Though the yard was noisy, the energy seemed to only increase her concentration.

After their awkward encounter outside his room, he had given her time and space out of both respect for her and embarrassment for himself. It seemed the more he tried to avoid her, the more they kept running into each other at every corner. She was usually with Ash, so he would grumble a "hello" and slip past the siblings. After a few days of their graceless happenings with each other, he came upon her leaving a room in the officer's quarters, just a few doors down from his own.

He hesitated at first, but then gathered the courage to call out to her. She turned at the sound of her name, but when she saw it was him, he saw worry cross her face. "Ronnock, hi." She said simply.

"You're, uh, is that your room?" he asked, though afterward he realized how creepy he probably sounded.

"No, it's Nalahi's. I was just visiting."

The seconds dragged on as they both seemed to be thinking of what to say next. "I'm sorry about the first night you were here, for what I did, I mean. It was unsolicited and I shouldn't have." He apologized to her. It was best to just get it out in the open than to keep up this excruciating feigned cordialness.

She paused before she responded. He felt his nerves waver as he waited for a reply. "It was unexpected." She said finally.

He inhaled slowly. "Well, I hope maybe we can start over."

She smiled, genuinely this time, "I'd like that too."

It was easy to talk to her about Jet, so that's where it began. The commander would be furious if he knew that his collection of correspondence with Jet had been borrowed without his permission, but Ronnock hoped he would be more forgiving since it was Jet's child who held the leatherbound book that the commander held so dear. Neither of them had said anything for hours, but he didn't care. He was perfectly happy sitting next to her, alternating between watching her facial expressions as she read and watching the young men spar in the training yard.

"It's not anger." She finally said.

He asked her what she meant.

"His letters to Iratez when they separated after the last war in Tuaega are the only time I can hear anger in his voice." She closed her eyes, picturing the words on the paper coming out of her father. "In those ones, it was personal. They had hurt him. And then it never surfaces again, even when discussing the genocide on the Godsmoors or the quarantine. It was bigger than him. He couldn't be angry, he had to be right."

Her hand framed Jet's signature at the bottom of the letter. "I'm angry. But not just for what the Redals did-" she was cut off by a sudden sob. She tried to stifle it, to pretend that it never happened. He moved to comfort her, but she waved him away. She was still trying to talk. "I don't get to be angry because Ash takes all of it. I don't get to be sad because I must be strong for him, but my heart hurts as if it all had happened yesterday. It feels like it all happened yesterday, yet at the same time I know how long it's been because the weight of this loneliness would not be so heavy."

She snapped the book closed and pressed her forehead to the spine. "He should've known! We should've left when mother begged him to and we didn't. He knew the evil they were capable of, yet he stayed to test it?!" She cried and held the pages tighter to her heart, not caring if he saw her tears anymore.

Ronnock didn't say anything. He didn't try to hold her. She had never allowed herself the relief of outpouring her feelings. It was a phenomenon he knew all too well, and he knew he had to just let her experience it. He was happy he could be that person for her. He would always be grateful for the man that listened to him in his time of need.

Her tears were gone, and instead words flowed from her. She began with her family's journey home from the border of Snanka, then the quarantine of the coast and the months of royal occupation the starvation, illness and despair of it. She was eerily calm when she spoke of the flood. Her left hand absently moved to gingerly hold just under her right ribs. "After we went back... nothing changed. We got older. The weeds started to overtake the ruins, but every day was very much the same."

Ronnock wanted to listen to her without any bias, but her words just made him fret over her brother even more. He knew the disturbed young man was trouble from the first time they had met, obviously, but had not realized how much his selfish behavior had shaped Venell.

Perhaps he shouldn't be around her either, for he was just as selfish. "Venell, tell me about the last time you were at the border." He didn't turn to look at her. He was looking forward, but his eyes weren't seeing anything.

"I don't know. We would travel that distance about once a year to meet some friends of my parents'. I didn't pay attention enough to know their names. I only thought about dreading the confinement of the carriage."

"You left the tower that last time. You went into the Orchane Forest alone." He allowed himself to glance at her from the side of his gaze.

After the look of concentration as she searched through her memories passed, she was incredulous. "Can you... see in my head?" she asked under her breath.

He held back a laugh, thinking it may offend her. "No," but he allowed himself a smile. "Venell, we were both there." She just stared at him. She didn't understand. "Your parents' friend. Their informant in Snanka was my mother, Risa Reven. King Aconite's First Mistress."

"Aconite," she repeated. They made eye contact for the first time since he had mistakenly kissed her three weeks ago. Her light blue eyes lacked the iciness of her brother's. She smiled at him. He saw the happiness spread across her face as she pieced together the recognition. "How did you get here?"

"Krisae came first. I gave in after I became Red."

"Had you already been... disregarded?"

"Yes." He replied. He didn't mean to sound so solemn. "I still went by Aconite even after a legitimate heir was born. I didn't change it until after we were sent away from the castle. He pressed his thumbs together nervously. "My mother said she had wanted to name me Ronnock, but the king insisted on me being named after him." He trailed off after finishing his sentence, feeling unsure if he wanted to unearth this box of tragedy with Venell.

"I had never known that Father was Red." She said, changing the subject for him. "I had only ever known about the... other side of it. That day he didn't pass the checkpoint, I thought it must've been a mistake. But the way he talked about peoples' fear and misunderstanding of it... It should've been obvious."

"I had only met Jet a handful of times, and none were very meaningful, just cordial and simple interactions. I could never tell him that I was grateful for what he had done for all of us, the Red. I, and I'm sure all others, thought life was over when Red began. He lived a life with it, beyond it, so I knew that I could too." He told her. She smiled at the notion.

That evening he had his dinner alone in the mess hall, late as usual. His mind was buzzing with all of Venell's words and expressions. It wasn't as difficult for him to contain himself around her anymore. She was becoming less of an idea, less of a memory and more of a person. Though he was falling for that person. He didn't dream of touching her anymore. He didn't dream at all, he finally slept through the night.

Mayan slid down the long bench to end up right next to Ronnock. He obviously has something to ask. Ronnock pushed his plate away and turned to face his nephew, who grinned awkwardly.

"There have been a few reports of a couple leaving Bardon tonight, cloaked and obviously trying not to be noticed. A man and a woman and they're heading south, away from the capital. There's whispers one could be some kind of informant." Mayan said to him in a hushed voice.

Ronnock raised an eyebrow, "You're acting as though this is a secret."

Mayan did not catch onto the tease in his voice, and his nephew's tone stayed just as serious. "Uncle, I never get to do anything exciting-"

"That's for the best."

"No, listen! Two people only! Father -erm- the commander hasn't assigned anyone yet. The Redals know we control the plains, so they won't leave them unaccompanied for long. We have to act now!"

"Mayan, are you asking me to go and take you with me? AND deceive my commander about your whereabouts?"

Mayan may have well been a toddler with a quivering lip. The lump in his throat stuttered his speech as he tried to find words to argue with.

"You're nearly a man, you don't need to ask me to help you sneak around your parents. It's time you learned how to do that on your own." Ronnock stood and began to leave. He hid the smirking look creeping across his face. If this boy didn't venture out from behind his mother's skirts, or father's cloak more accurately, he would never get out into the open world.

"Ash wants to come also." Mayan suddenly blurted out.

Ronnock stopped in his tracks. This move may be a little too bold for Mayan's first act of rebellion. "I did not hear that." Ronnock muttered and stormed out of the mess hall. He wasn't sure which of those boys leaving the safehold would upset the commander more.

As he returned to his quarters, he couldn't shake the feeling that he had just made a terrible mistake. They were just words, but he certainly feared their consequences. A knock on the door brought him out of his head. He was in the midst of his nightly rituals. he had already snuffed all lights in the room but one. He couldn't settle the annoyed feeling rising in his chest that it was Nai. She had been coming to his door nearly nightly to whine about how he didn't want to see her anymore. He'd always start out apologetic and understanding, but it'd end with the door slamming in her face. And that never made him feel any better. There were thousands of other men for her to fawn after here, younger and interested ones, and he honestly wished she would.

He irritably swung open the door, only to find Venell cringing from his forcefulness.

"I'm sorry, were you sleeping?" She stuttered out. She suddenly reminded him of the girl he had cornered in the alley during the rain. He hadn't seen that look in her eyes since that night.

"No," he answered quickly, rubbing his brow with his forefinger and thumb, feeling the valley on the bridge of his nose where part of the cartilage had been cut deeply many years before. He couldn't believe his own foolishness at times. "I thought you were someone I didn't want to see."

"I hope you never don't want to see me." She rocked back and forth on her feet from her heels to her toes as the corner of her mouth curved upwards.

She was teasing him. He had never thought he'd see the day when Venell would ever be playful with him. He allowed himself to laugh under his breath. "Did you want to come in?"

He closed the door behind him as she stepped into his room. She lingered in the doorway until he moved to relight all his lamps. Once the room was bright, she eased into her settings. They stood in silence for long moments as she looked around the room at his meager belongings. She began to trace the iron studs embedded into his boiled leathers draped over the back of the only sitting chair in his room. She drew her hand back at the sight of a dark red stain.

She was wearing different clothes that Krisae has scrounged up for her, though their stores didn't contain much for women. Her shirt was white linen with floral embroidery on the collar. It was a good shirt, but quite obviously worn by a previous owner. She had it tucked into a brown rough-spun skirt that flowed past her knees. The leather boots she had on actually fit her feet, unlike the pair she had arrived in. He wondered if she had realized that her clothing had likely come from someone who had died. She chose to remain standing to speak with him.

"May I ask you how it happened?" she murmured while clasping her hands together.

Ronnock released the lock on the smaller of his two windows and opened it to let in the night air. It was cool, but the noise below in the yard disturbed the peace. However, it was getting late and all those below should be turning in soon. The flint in his lighter sparked and he brought the flame to the red cigarette held firmly between his lips. He lengthily drew on it before settling on how to answer her.

He had to decide where in his story to begin. He knew the moment that began the chain of events leading to the Red consuming his family, but perhaps she didn't want to hear it. Like everyone else, she just wanted to hear about the violence that led him to becoming infected. She just wanted to hear it from him since she couldn't hear it from her father.

"My sisters and I were living with a caregiver until we came of age. He was one of my mother's friends. We knew he was Red, but it was not as widespread and feared then. We didn't fully understand it. It was also before someone thought to make blood cigarettes, so he had to hunt the old-fashioned way. I still don't know if he would kill someone when he left those nights, or if he had some method to not take it all." It wasn't completely a lie, but he didn't want her to know that the cigarettes were never enough on their own.

He cleared his throat and continued. "He didn't return for a few nights. We grew concerned, but we were very limited in our options. Hellan and I decided we would just carry on without him and not go searching for him like Krisae wanted." He nervously thought about lighting another one up before continuing but decided instead to just get the details over with.

"I had Krisae with me outside the tower just as the sun was setting. I still don't know how he had slipped so far into the Red... I haven't seen anything like it since either, not from someone that's been infected for so long. He went for Krisae first. I didn't even realize it was him. She was screaming and there was blood everywhere. I attacked him and managed to get him off her. Even then I knew it was too late for her; she was either going to die or become Red. I tried to strangle him as he kept spitting Krisae's blood at me. He went for my eyes but ended up giving me some of these scars instead." His fingertips touched some of the jagged scars across his cheek. He hadn't thought about that struggle with Khos for many years.

"I lost my grip and he bit into my shoulder. I don't know how I managed to find a large enough rock in all that black sand, but once my hand recognized the feeling, I grabbed it and brought it down on his head until... until I thought we were safe. I scooped up Krisae and rushed inside to Hellan. It was too late for both of us. We fought fevers for almost a week. I thought we would both die and reawaken as one of the animals that Khos had become. Hellan took care of us though. Once the fever began to fade, the change was gradual. Your body accepts the Red much faster than your mind."

Her hands were clasped in front of her; her eyes focused on the floor. She was processing his words. She was trying to make them fit into her own ideas and recollections. "Why..." She began but trailed off. She seemed to already know the answer was a mystery without any leads, but something in her just had to ask.

"No one, even the most brilliant scholars and doctors, have any idea why some keep themselves, and some are gone. For those ones, everything that made them who they were before the Red is dead. Only the monster remains." He felt a lump rising in his throat, but he wanted her to hear his next words.

"It's there in all of us. It was there in Jet, it's in Krisae, it's in me. It's always there, and it's always awake. Sometimes it's just... quiet." She was listening intently with a glimmer of fascination in her eyes. There was certainly fear. He could hear it in her pulse and smell it from her pores. But that other look was unfamiliar on her, and he thought it might be...

Excitement.

The thought made his skin prickle. It was almost too much. "Are you thinking about when I caught you in the rain?" His gums tingled as he recalled touching her wet skin.

"Yes." She answered quickly and breathily.

"Does it make you afraid?"

"Yes." She replied again with the same tone.

The back of his neck was aching. The tendons tightened all the way down his back as he clenched his jaw harder. "Then why are you here, alone, after seeing that? After I just told you that it's always awake?" She made no reply now. "If you want answers about you father from me, you can do it in the daylight around other people. Why did you come here?"

"I don't know."

"Yes, you do. What were you seeing in you mind when I asked about the rain in Bardon?"

"I can't say."

"Yes, you can. I can't say it for you. You are the only one that can ask for what you want. So, what do you see when you close your eyes?"

"I see your eyes red. It makes these sparks in me when I remember how afraid I was. But that made me feel these waves of... something. Of a freedom. Crashing waves that I want to be carried by. I know I'm not making any sense. Because I've liked our days together, but this other part of me is waiting to feel that rush again."

He could've melted into the floor. He drew his hand down his face. "Venell, I can never treat you like that again."

She suddenly looked so embarrassed. He had asked her to dig deep and show him her soul, and she did just that. She did it so well, but he couldn't give her what she wanted. She wasn't prey now, and never could be again. He took a step toward her, and she didn't recoil. He clasped both her small hands in one of his. Those blue pools of her eyes rose up to meet his. She lowered her lids as he lowered his head and pressed his lips against hers. He suddenly became very aware that he could smell her arousal. Perhaps they could meet in the middle.

He used his mouth to part hers and let his tongue slip inside. He held her face to his firmly with his free hand, keeping her wrists together with the other like he did during that storm in Bardon. The little gasp she let out against his mouth nearly drove him wild. He turned her head to the side and kissed down her neck and shoulder, pulling back her shirt collar as he went, inhaling her scent with every graze of his lips.

"Bend over and put you forearms on the bed." He told her. She stared at him blankly. He repeated himself. She tentatively moved away from him to the bed. She glanced back over at him, as if to make sure she was doing what he wanted. She put her hands palm down on the bed and leaned onto her forearms. He began lifting her skirt, balling up the material in his fists as he lifted it over her buttocks. Her breathing was getting louder. He fought back the urge to let his fangs slide down. The notion alarmed him. The Red was usually quiet when he was making love, if the hunt was not his intention. He didn't understand what was stirring it. And at the same time, he did.

She had on skin-tight black undergarments that covered from her belly to mid-thigh. His hand hovered over one cheek for a moment, then he placed it back on her hip. He exhaled slowly as he wrestled with what to do next. He felt her eyes on him and looked up to see her staring at him from over her shoulder.

"Is this what you want?" He asked her.

She nodded.

His loins stirred. He closed his eyes and tilted his head back. "I need you to say it."

"It's what I want."

"What is?"

Her bottom wiggled with frustration. "I want you to touch me." She whispered to him, shy to say her carnal thoughts aloud.

He didn't reply, but rolled down her undergarments until her buttocks were completely exposed. He drew a hand back and spanked her on the right cheek. She gasped and looked back at him over her shoulder. He squeezed the pink mark he had just made on her milky skin and inhaled sharply. He slapped her again in the same spot, but this time the noise she let out was husky and decadent.

"I want to see it." She said even more quietly, still looking back at him.

He gently turned her over onto her back. Her skirt was gathered up around her stomach. His lips must have been twitching as he felt his control slipping.

"Show me the Red again."

She was not talking about what he thought she was talking about. He staggered back, turning from her and pacing clear to the other side of the room. "I can't do that." He said, his voice laced with the Red. His gums hurt and his throat became dry. He heard her move on the bed. Afraid she would approach him, he shouted at her to stop. She froze. His heart sank with the weight of knowing he may lose her forever this very moment. He wished he had never given in to any of his desires in the first place. He should have never played into her fantasies. He should've known he wasn't strong enough to do battle with the Red like this.

"I need you to leave, Venell."

He had barely gotten the words out when he heard the door close. It wasn't the angry slam that he was used to from a spurned lover. The quiet click of the latch rang much louder in his ears than anything before. He stifled what felt like a sob welling up in his throat even though he was alone.

16: THE DARKSTAR

THE WHISPERING PLAINS, EAST OF BARDON

The cold winds that blew across the Whispering Plains were dry and biting upon Delinda's skin. Autumn was on its way. She pulled her woolen scarf over her mouth and nose. Puffs of heated air still wafted around her head each time she exhaled. Her knuckles were red and raw under her gloves from riding over the plains; not even her thick leather could fight off the wind.

She scanned the horizon for any figures leaving Bardon and heading East toward the next city of Piaces, a wealthy port town, but so far there was no suspicious movement. They were not far from where the Insurgo base stood amongst the yellow, blowing grass. The block-shaped fortress could faintly be seen against the indigo horizon. The rebels were Kras' enemy, but not hers. She and the Rhanian commander had come to an agreement earlier that year. They would be mutually independent and respected forces, and they wouldn't meddle in each other's affairs. They also agreed to keep this fact from their subordinates. To her men, she appeared fearless in her encroachment on the rebel lands. All the better that the Darkstar appeared invincible.

Her men continued to be the best part of herself. Four on her left and two to her right were mounted on horses as black as her own steed. Basaulte was the first rider on her right, as always, and on his other side was Young Tyr: her newest and most rash recruit. His skill alone was the only thing that earned the coveted position on her elite squad. His pride and attitude still required much molding.

On her left was Daven, an officer she had brought out of retirement, then Old Tyr, a reformed pirate that was of no relation to his younger namesake. Nanaba was on the outside of the formation, as he had the sharpest eyes. She had met the dark-skinned young man in a southern port, not far from where they now stood in Piaces. She knew being this close to such harsh memories made him uncomfortable, but Delinda trusted her men with her life.

The sixth and final man she had selected for her own was Gaillen, who had lost his family to Red Insurgo men. His eyes were steely and emotionless, but Delinda saw beneath that. He was not a broken man to mindlessly follow her, she would have many more than six men if that was the quality she wanted. He had nothing to lose, but he found purpose with Delinda, and that was the strongest loyalty she could ask for. Her purpose was his purpose.

Kras had summoned her to the throne room once more before she left the capital. For many long moments he only spoke loud enough for himself to hear. This practice was new, and Delinda wasn't sure if he was not aware of his own volume or if he was truly talking to himself. When she could finally hear him, he exploded about an assassination attempt. She at first began to think his mind was at last lost, but then he named his decoy, Rhodrick, as the victim of the would-be attack. Kras would often send his double to oversee the troops and lift morale. Rhodrick was at an in inn in Bardon when a fight broke out that threatened his life, and he only narrowly escaped murder.

"Diar... Diar is out there somewhere. Why else would his girl flee? He told her to flee after rejecting my offer. She may be going to him. We could follow her instead of capturing... no, too risky. Or just kill her. Her first, then Diar. No other heirs. Diar is too strong in Bardon still. If he's gone, all the whispers will stop." He swatted his hand past his ear as if to shoo a fly, but nothing was there. "The whispers must stop."

Delinda raised her eyebrows to her brother. Firstly, he couldn't seem to decide if he wanted to wed or to execute their cousin, and she also wanted him to retread on what happened with his double in Bardon, but he did not understand her gaze. Perhaps he was too preoccupied with the thoughts swirling in his head to even notice.

"Just bring the girl here." He said with finality. "She may draw out her father when he hears of our engagement. If not, we'll just eliminate her."

Delinda felt Nanaba stir in their formation. She woke from her memories and gazed across the plains. At first, she did not see what Nanaba had spotted, but soon three slow-moving figures came into view: two hooded travelers, one riding a small, slow mount, and the other leading it. She motioned to Basaulte to give the command.

"Just the one at the lead." He said in his baritone voice. Young Tyr knocked an arrow and aimed. He loosed it with near silence. The arrow's slight whistle could have easily been the wind. It found its target with a thud, and the lead figure fell. The person on the mule shrieked unconsolably, a young woman by the sound. She tried to spur her mount to run, but the animal was too spooked. Delinda motioned for her riders to move in.

They would surround the mule and lead it back to Star Palace in formation. Far outnumbered, the demure girl would surely come quietly. The sound of another loosed arrow finding its target made her whip her head around to find Young Tyr, furious he had fired without permission. Instead, she saw Gaillen falling from his horse.

His body loosely tumbled about the ground with a red feathered arrow sticking from his eye. None of her other men slowed or broke rank, as they were rightly disciplined. Delinda scanned the horizon for where the shot came from. Nanaba shouted to her, pointing across the plains to high, white grass in the distance. Fury boiled in her as she saw an arrow pass through Nanaba's neck, his arm still outstretched and pointing toward his killer. Her mouth moved as she mutely screamed and cursed.

She could not let their deaths be in vain. Fueled by her losses, she furiously kicked her steed's sides. Her eyes were focused on the flailing girl trying to dismount the stalled mule to flee into the grass sea. Basaulte was there first. He scooped up the squealing youth and flung her across Delinda's lap. He signaled for the men to retreat now they had their prize.

The girl was pleading to be released. She had not seen her cousin for years, but her resemblance to her red-headed whore of a mother was unmistakable: it was Apsonne, just as Kras had suspected. Her eyes looked hollow with worry, and her face was taunt and ashen for someone who couldn't be older than twenty. Unable to tell her to shut up, Delinda roughly shoved her head down into the horse's riding leathers to silence her. The whistle of arrows in the night air had not ceased. Their assailants could not have had more than two archers for the amount of time between shots.

Her horse suddenly jerked to the side, threatening to rear as Apsonne began screaming in agony. Delinda swore she had felt an impact. She looked down to see her stallion had been hit, but the shot had firstly gone through the back of Apsonne's thigh. She couldn't tell how long the shaft of the arrow was, but hopefully Apsonne's leg had spared the stallion. Kras had only asked for their cousin alive, not undamaged.

Perhaps the girl was too skinny, for her horse began to slow and stagger. As it knelt to the ground, Delinda saw the amount of blood he was losing. He wasn't going to make it. She grasped the bolt, trying to pull it from both the horse and the girl. Apsonne was doing her feeble best to attack her, slapping her hands across her chest and face. The idiot didn't realize that Delinda was trying to save her from dying alone on the plains. She placed her foot on the horse, pulling the bolt with all her might, when she saw someone approaching rapidly on the other side. She dropped to the ground, ducking under the swordsman's lunge and rolling to safety. She drew her own curved sword, waiting for the next attack.

The man was young, his head shaved on both sides to where just a shock of black hair ran down the middle. His teeth were gritted as he clenched the short sword in his left hand. The new moon allowed for little light across the grass sea, but she could still see the fire of hate in his ice blue eyes. He was not familiar with combat, she could tell by his stance. The Insurgo must have been sweeping up any gutter trash they found and arming them.

She heard movement behind her but couldn't react fast enough before a kick to the back of her leg brought her to her knees. She swung around to see a wild-haired, dark-skinned youth holding a spear. He had it aimed for her but didn't attack. He could've stabbed her in the back of the leg, but instead he had kicked her down.

Weak little boy.

She thrust her arm forward, hooking the curve of her sword around the back of his calf, and drew it back. Her sword cut through the tough leather wraps around his leg. He cried out and stumbled back, but the wound was not as deep as she had intended. She had meant to take his entire leg with her. She looked past the boy into the darkness of the vast plains behind him. Her eyes widened.

How could she not have heard? At least forty mounted riders were coming across the plains. She cursed and began looking around for her next move. Her teeth were gritted so hard she though they might crumble within her mouth. That fool.

They had an agreement, and he had utterly betrayed her. He would not live long enough to gloat of his victory against her. Generations to come would only speak of the crushing defeat the rebels faced at loyal Princess Delinda's command.

Before she could make a move to retaliate, she was scooped up by Old Tyr. The old pirate clicked his tongue against his brown, rotten teeth when he saw the anger across her face. She was no damsel in distress. "Blame Basaulte, your grace. I personally think you could've taken them all." She had never been so humiliated: leaving the mission empty-handed, slung over a horse like pillaged loot, with only four men remaining.

Basaulte came to her immediately upon their return. His attempts to soothe her only made her more furious. She could already feel Kras' loathsome, condescending gaze upon her, not to mention she had been fooled and betrayed by the Rhanian commander. He had reassured her of his unyielding support for her over her brother, regardless of her Redal name. He promised her that the Insurgo would ride with her should the time come. She would not be so gullible again, and he would pay for his disloyalty.

She roughly pulled away from her colonel and stormed off to her quarters. Perhaps the darkness she had grown so used to would bring her some peace. Basaulte was right on her heels, she couldn't even close the door behind her before he caught it. She turned to scream at him. Her mouth opened, but only empty air came out. She cursed at him in her head. She didn't want him to look at her. She failed her company as a leader. Nanaba and Gaillen were dead because of her ineptitude.

"Delinda..." He started.

She slapped him across the face. How dare he call her by her first name? Her hit had knocked his eye-patch askew. Instead of returning it to its proper position, he removed it. He threw the patch upon the ground and looked at her with his single eye. She refused to be drawn into the brilliant darkness of it. He touched the deep, scarred socket where his eye had once been. The skin was taunt and disfigured over the empty orifice.

He grabbed her hand and pressed her fingers to the pink ribbons of scar tissue. "Do you remember when I lost this? We were completely outnumbered at the Ellinhall border, but you were so confident they were nothing but dirt-worshippers armed with sticks that we rode to battle against better judgment. I was overpowered by one of their skin-changers. You blamed yourself for it then, too. But I didn't. I never will. I pledged my life to following you, and I will follow you until I die. And when I am finally struck down, it will be because I did not fight hard enough for you."

Basaulte knelt before her with her hands clasped in his. "We are all honored to serve you: our true queen."

17: THE HERO

THE WHISPERING PLAINS

Ash was becoming increasingly aware of his dislike for Mayan. They had arrived on White Hill, one of the few elevated areas of the Whispering Plains, a few hours past sundown. The hard soil under the white grass still retained some of the sun's heat into the first hours of the night, but as the moon rose, the cold from the coast began to blow in with the wind.

 They came from Bardon, backtracking to White Hill after spying the suspicious pair leaving the city. Ash didn't understand why they couldn't just approach them, it would've been two on two, but Mayan wanted to wait. Mayan was explaining his reasons, because it's what the Insurgo would want him to do, caution was key and other nonsense, but Ash didn't care. For hours they watched the two shadows cross the plains in the moonlight. Ash was getting restless.

He knew Mayan was trying to make peace with him after choking him unconscious in the training yard. Ash could've cared less about an apology; he was just interested in getting out of the base. He was beginning to feel confined there. He had a gnawing fear the he and Venell were unknowingly prisoners. Agreeing to accompany Mayan was his way of testing his hunch, which for the moment, was thankfully false.

Ash felt metal bump against his arm, awakening him from his thoughts, as Mayan again offered him their shared pair of binoculars. He accepted and held them up to his eyes, though he didn't understand Mayan's delusion that there would be something new to see. His right hand still felt weak from landing that poor punch in the training yard. He had argued with one of the medics about taking his plaster cast off the day after the injury, insisting that it wasn't broken. They finally complied, and Ash got to prove them wrong.

"We're going to have to move closer." He said to Ash.

"Or we could just confront them." Ash muttered, though loud enough to make sure Mayan heard him.

"I heard that tactic didn't do so well for you in Bardon." He said is so quickly, he must have been waiting for his chance to rub salt in the wound.

Ash was going to let it wash over him, as Mayan was quite clearly aiming for a rise, but the more the comment replayed in his head, the closer he felt his anger boiling to the surface. He felt the bite of cold wind across his skin and shuddered.

A sudden thud and subsequent scream jolted them into action. Mayan fumbled with his binoculars and they dropped to the ground. He left them and opted instead to knock an arrow on his time-worn bow. "Get me a shot!" he hissed at Ash through his teeth. "Where did that come from?"
Ash picked up the binoculars and scanned the gruesome scene before them. A skinny woman was trying to ungracefully dismount her mule, the other figure lay in a heap on the plains. He moved his gaze past them to further along the horizon. There was no movement save for the swaying strands of grass.

Then he saw shadows across the skyline: seven people on hulking, black mounts. He had almost missed them in the darkness of the moonless night. "There! They're on the move! They're coming for her!" Ash called to Mayan, pointing toward the approaching riders.

Mayan held his shot, measuring the movement and distance of his target. Ash had no idea how skilled an archer the boy was, but his hopes were not high. The riders were moving slowly. There was no chance of their target escaping, so they thought, so haste was not needed. Mayan exhaled slowly and released the arrow. Ash couldn't see it sail across the sky, he could only hear its whistle disappearing into the winds. He shook his head. The riders were too far, and the wind was too strong, and Mayan was just a...

A horse's shriek could be heard across the plains as it backed away from its rider's falling body. The remaining five wasted no time spurring their mounts to hurry. They knew they were under attack. Ash almost wished Mayan had missed. "We've got to get closer! We've got to get to her first!" he said forcefully. Mayan was knocking another arrow and gave him a judgmental look.

Mayan could not give him orders. He left him behind and took off running. He kept himself low in the grasses as not to be seen, though the night should have shrouded him well. He heard another whistle from above but did not know which direction the arrow was flying. He risked a peek of the stampede of hooves and saw a second horse was riderless. It didn't matter how fast he ran, they would reach the girl before him. He drew his short sword, prepared to take a stand against the remaining four. However, the riders split. Three went toward White Hill where Mayan remained hidden, and only two continued on toward the bawling girl. He smirked at his fortune and kept his pace.

The first rider to reach the girl scooped her up onto the smaller rider's saddle, then remounted his own steed. Both began to turn around and ride south, where they had appeared from. The girl's screams suddenly turned from fear to agony. The horse slowed from its gallop and began to waver. It knelt onto the grass and the rider dismounted. It was his chance. He was almost close enough to confront him, and he could taste the glory. The rider must have heard him approaching, even over the girl's wails, and as he turned his long, black ponytail whipped over his shoulder.

He then realized the rider was a woman, but it was no matter. Her teeth were clenched and her dark eyes furious. Their gazes met as he raised his sword. She drew a long, curved blade. It was light and thin enough to be wielded with one hand, and its guard was jewel-encrusted silver. He readied himself for an attack, stepping around her slowly so that her back was to White Hill. While he was disappointed his triumph would be over the weaker sex, he would take the victory regardless. He raised his armed left hand, only to feel his heart drop when he saw a flurry of wild, black hair appear behind her. She fell to her knees after Mayan kicked the back of her leg.

Ash cursed loudly. What was the point if there was two of them defeating a woman? He left her to Mayan and instead turned to the shrieking girl grasping desperately at her impaled leg. The bolt went through her thigh and into the dying black horse. She kept crying for Ash to save her after he already had his hand around the shaft. He yanked it out of both its victims. Her wound began gushing blood, and her cries faded as she lost consciousness. He grasped her under her arms and began to pull her from the scene, even as he saw Mayan knocked to the ground.

He hesitated and considered leaving the girl for the moment and helping the boy that dragged him out here. The female rider stood over Mayan, but she suddenly looked up and her eyes widened. Ash turned to see what she was looking at, and his gaze was met by at least forty mounted Insurgo soldiers tearing across the plains. A grey-bearded rider in a black coat identical to the one the woman wore snatched her up and placed her in front of him on his horse. Ash angrily watched the remaining five escape as the Insurgo soldiers encircled he and Mayan.

He knew he was scowling as he helped a skinny Insurgo man get the wounded, unconscious girl onto his horse and return to the base. Mayan's calf was bleeding as he mounted a spotted horse behind the big, dark-skinned recruit that Ash had sparred with previously. He refused an offer for a ride back to the base and chose to walk behind the hoard. He was hoping to be left alone to brood, but he had obviously gotten himself into trouble with the Insurgo's authority.

Back at the base, he found himself standing beside newly bandaged Mayan in the commander's office. Krisae stood behind Commander Iratez's desk with her arms folded. No one spoke, but the tension was thick. The door behind him opened and Venell and Nalahi were filed into the room, obviously roused from sleep. Nalahi avoided his gaze purposefully.

"I'll deal with you later." The commander bellowed and shooed Mayan from his presence. Mayan hung his head like a child caught red-handed and shuffled away. "Do you have any idea who you just confronted? Whose men you killed?" his round, dark face was turning purple with anger, even behind his black beard.

Ash shrugged. He wanted to reply that he didn't kill anyone, but he knew that it was not from lack of intent.

The commander was obviously annoyed with his casual attitude. "If you think Kras is the true despot, you know nothing of the Darkstar. Dangerous, ruthless, and cunning, she is. But more than anything she is UNFORGIVING. She won't forget this. You've made us more of a target than ever."

He and Venell remained quiet. Nalahi's furious gold eyes turned to him. He knew she was cursing at him in her head, but he couldn't help but recall the image of her from the other night in his room. She turned to the commander, "Not meaning to offend, but why are Venell and I here? We don't make stupid decisions."

Krisae laughed, but quickly covered her mouth and returned her face to a scowl when Iratez turned his gaze upon her.

"As far as I know, all you Cynn survivors are powder kegs waiting to blow up everything I've worked for." He pointed from Ash to Venell. "All your father worked for. All he died for."

"Our father was slaughtered like a helpless lamb. He didn't die for anything." Ash spoke up.

The commander rose suddenly and furiously swept his arm across his desk, knocking all the glass, ink, and papers onto the floor. He gripped the sides of the wood top and roared "You have NO IDEA who Jet was! Even if you are his blood, you don't mean SHIT to me if you disrespect his memory!" Spittle flew from his mouth as he shouted rabidly. "GET OUT OF MY FUCKING SIGHT."

Ash didn't need to be told twice. He was glad to be out of there and satisfied that his plan to get himself out of that abysmal situation worked. Nalahi and Venell remained behind. He had barely turned the corner of the hall when he ran into Mayan, who had obviously been eavesdropping.

"That girl we brought back here is Diar Redal's daughter." He said under his breath, as if someone around would hear. "He's been missing for months, and she was trying to sneak out of Bardon. She might know something about where her father is."

Ash stared at him blankly. None of that mattered to him.

"Diar is next in line for the throne after Kras. He's fair and of sound mind. He's the leader that Valehoutton needs, and he has a legitimate claim. Does that mean anything to you?"

"They're still Redals." He replied and pushed past Mayan. He wasn't sure if the Redal girl was being kept in her own chambers or in the sick ward, but either way he would find her. She was either the key to getting to Kras, or she would have to die too.

She was nowhere to be found among the rest of the sick and injured. He should've known. She was too valuable to be exposed to the general masses. He noticed a female nurse carrying a basket of wraps and ointments away from the ward. He stayed a distance away from her but followed her through the maze of identical hallways deep into the center of the base. She entered a room with a small, unremarkable door and closed it behind her. He waited around the corner as minutes ticked by. She finally left nearly an hour later.

As soon as the nurse turned to the far hall and was out of sight, he tried the door. It was unlocked, so he slipped inside. It was a small, cramped room with nothing but a bed and a lamp. The Redal girl lay with her eyes closed and breathing shallowly. Her eyes opened when the door clicked shut. She looked fearful at first, but she relaxed back into the bed when she saw him.

"You're the one who saved me." She smiled. Her teeth were straight and white. Her strawberry blonde hair had been in a complex updo but was now disheveled with wayward strands all over her head. When she spoke, her voice was soft and refined, like a lady that was raised in fortune. "I can't thank you enough. I'm sorry you must see me like this. My wound is still very painful."

Her pale green eyes flitted up toward him. They were tired and hurt. Her sockets seemed hollow and her cheeks taut. She had been lacking both food and sleep and was not used to being denied either. He wanted to hate her for her easy life of affluence but seeing her in her current state made it strange to muster the feelings.

"You're Kras' cousin." He stated abruptly.

Her face fell. "Yes. I assure you the king has no love for me and will not accept a ransom. My father..." she trailed off and hid her face behind her hands. "They already questioned me, I have nothing else to tell you!" She said with more force, but her voice was cracking. "If all you want is to ask me about things far out of my control, then please just leave!" Her chest heaved as she sobbed.

It was not that he was against strong-arming this girl and force her to tell him everything she knew, he just had the feeling that she was useless. He got up to leave, but then she spoke again.

"Wait! Please don't go. Can you tell me how long they're going to keep me alone in this room? It's like I'm being punished for my surname. It's cruel to keep me isolated like this." Her eyes were watery, and big, fat tears rolled down her blushing cheeks.

He stood by the door awkwardly. "I have no say over what goes on here. I haven't been here very long, and I'm not a part of the Insurgo."

"Are they keeping you prisoner too?"

He scoffed, "No, I can leave whenever I want. I'm just biding my time."

"I see." She said briefly. She fingered the worn, wool blanket covering her legs. "What's your name?"

"Ash."

"I'm Apsonne of Bardon. If you're not part of them... can you help me get to Piaces?"

"Why would I do that?" He had no desire to aide a Redal. He suddenly heard heavy footsteps approaching the room. Apsonne's eyes suddenly widened as she heard them too. Without thinking, he dove under the bed and made sure all his limbs were tucked cleanly underneath. He heard Apsonne quickly lay down above him, probably pretending to be asleep.

The door opened, and two pairs of shoes filed in. He was relieved not to see Krisae's heeled boots, as her Red senses could've easily detected him. "Lady Apsonne, we apologize for the condition of your quarters. We wanted to pass along the commander's assurance that it is for your own protection, and that it is only temporary." said a man's voice that Ash did not recognize. He sounded young.

"If you want to protect me, you need to take me to Piaces! I already told you I have arrangements there, they likely think that I'm dead by now!" she pleaded.

"The commander can assure you of your safety here. Our walls have never been breached." A second, deeper male voice said. "Kras and Delinda will expect you to flee to your maternal seat. A journey to Piaces would be unwise."

"Then he can tell me himself! You can't keep me here, once I can walk, I'll walk myself right out those gates and go myself!" Her speech was passionate, yet dignified and clearly formed at court. He couldn't help but to be slightly impressed by her boldness, especially since she was crippled. "I'll have no more words with you." She concluded. The bed shifted as she turned her body away from the pair at the door.

Without argument, and likely knowing her threats were empty, the two men turned and left him alone with Apsonne. He crawled out from his hiding place to meet eyes with her again. "I'll take you." He said before he considered his words. He wouldn't do it to help her, but rather to defy the commander. He'd see for himself what the Insurgo was hiding by preventing Apsonne from reaching her desired destination.

Her eyes lit up and she clasped his hand tightly with both of hers. She thanked him repeatedly. "I'll need a couple of days to plan, but I promise I'll get you there." He felt the corner of his mouth curl into a smile as he anticipated where this next journey would take him

18: NO WORDS

STAR PALACE

Delinda wasn't sure how long she had been standing outside the doors. Her timing was terrible; she'd have to interrupt the council meeting about the country's debt to Tuaega. Many of the greth soldiers on loan to the crown were on the Tuaegian government's payroll, and Delinda wasn't sure which of the two were more ruthless. Her father had begun to issue grants of land to the greth, inciting the first forced relocations on the Godsmoors, but now they were running out of this currency too. She lifted her hand to the door handle for what seemed like the hundredth time, only to drop it back to her side.

She hated this wavering, hesitant person she was behaving as. She needed to be rid of it. She needed to face the inevitable humiliation Kras would wreak upon her. She heard Basaulte approaching behind her. It was just the push she needed. She finally pulled open the massive door, and he softly closed it behind her. She knew he would wait for her outside to fall into place behind her steps the moment she left the throne room.

Things were different before she had lost her voice. Before she had lost part of her humanity. She used to have farfetched hopes of rising to outshine any Redal before her, and any to come after. She had grand dreams of finding love and a partner. She had once dismissed all of her guard, save for Basaulte, and made an advance upon him. He still had both of his eyes then, and he was so virile and dark she though he was the epitome of masculinity. It was there on the lawns behind the palace that she realized love wasn't in the cards for her. She felt some guilt for using her companion and subordinate for her self-discovery, but shedding that girlish, naïve hope helped her focus on her true goal: Valehoutton. She understood her worth now.

The council was small today, only two officials sat with Kras and his bodyguards. Kras did not like to have large groups sitting in when the talks were not of his triumphs. The room fell silent as all eyes moved upon her. She strode across the room, past the moth-eaten tapestries hanging from the wall, and approached her younger brother. She took the seat beside the skeletal royal treasurer.

He nodded to her, "Princess Darkstar." he greeted as he knowingly passed her a pen and parchment.

"Well?" Kras sneered at her.

She scribbled down what happened on the plains, then turned the paper towards Kras. She stared at him as he read, patiently awaiting the explosion.

His head snapped up, his eyes red with sleeplessness and hate. "You do realize..." he tittered something to himself, his fingers twitching angrily as he raised a hand. "That this was absolutely the WORST POSSIBLE OUTCOME!?" He threw his arms across the table, scattering all the papers about and sending every cup and plate crashing to the ground. Wine and ink sprayed onto Delinda's face and clothes.

"My loyal sister," he spat venomously, "has not only let Diar's sole heir slip through her fingers, but practically delivered her to the Insurgo!" The treasurer and other officer hurriedly voiced their disgust and agreement. "Is it your total incompetence that led to this, or is it perhaps treason? You may be a fool, but this is beyond my doubts of you, so you must have sent her off to our enemies on purpose! You wish to see my line end with me!"

She had to stop herself from rolling her eyes. "If that was my intention, why would I be here?" she thought to herself. She would have to write down her thought if she wished to communicate it to him, but it would lose its meaning in passing. If he could even grasp it in the first place, that is.

He straightened himself and readjusted his ruffled sleeves. Some of the gold buttons on his waistcoat were inserted into the wrong holes. He smoothed his long, stringy hair behind his ears before he spoke. "I suppose as king I must be benevolent and accept that you were bound to fail because of that smelly clam between your legs. You disgrace yourself and me wearing clothes meant for men; for capable commanders. You'd better serve me wearing a powdered wig and finding a suitable husband like the other women at court. You'd even serve me better working in the kitchens and emptying my chamber pot like a common maid."

Delinda sat there sternly and let his insults wash over her like waves breaking upon the rocks of the Northern Shore. He could not break her. They both knew she could strike him down from where she sat, and he would no longer be their family's only kinslayer.

Kras was annoyed he had yet to crack her stony disposition. He smirked before he delivered his next order: "Consider yourself relieved of your position. Your men will be reassigned to proper leaders. The council will begin searching to find you a suitor, though at your age and with your conditions, it will prove to be difficult. Then again, men love a silent wife. Perhaps Apsonne will suffer a blow to the head as well upon her arrival." He sneered.

He waved his hand to dismiss her. She could barely see straight. Her fury was burning so hot for a moment she could only see red. She didn't even realize she has risen to her feet. Her fists were clenched so tightly that her nails drew blood from her palms. "If you leave well, I'll consider keeping you on my council." He added for a final insult.

Taking her men was beyond any cruelty she imagined when she had entered the room. Insulting her was not enough for him anymore. He came between her and the only thing she truly loved. Her only source of pride. Her only joy. If only she could speak, she would tell him to go fuck himself. She'd tell him that he was nothing without her leadership. None of his efforts would have been successful if it wasn't for her battlefield tactics.

He would've been assassinated already if it weren't for her combat skill. A troupe of three Godsmoorian men had come to parlay less than four years into his reign under the pretense that they hoped his rule would be different that his father's. Delinda was standing in for one of his bodyguards that day, as fate would have it. She was immediately suspicious upon their entry, she could feel the deception in the air. They stood in a line before the throne, each one's hair whiter than the next.

They started by speaking praises to Kras. The king perked up and responded warmly. Delinda didn't believe a word. She saw every one of their movements slowed down and deliberate. The man furthest to the right was reaching behind his back. She didn't hesitate for a moment. Her blade slashed the white-haired man from groin to gullet before he could fully brandish the rusty blade behind his back. The other two backed away in fear. It mattered not to her if they had been aware of their associate's intentions. She ended them as well, cutting through them as easily as a hot knife through butter.

If only she could speak.

If only she had hesitated for a mere second that day, she would've been rid of her sore of a brother. She'd have never had to kiss his bony hand again. That smug face would've been ash in the wind.

But enough of regrets.

If only she could speak.

She turned hot on her heels and burst out of the throne room doors. She ignored Basaulte and marched past him vehemently. He called after her, but she kept up her furious pace. She felt as though flames were wafting up from under her boots.

He dared not call after her again as she stormed down the Long Hall back to her quarters. The sun was rising, she could already see streaks of orange light on the stone floor. She stepped though the beams hurriedly. Her legs covered by black breeches protected her from the rays, but she still didn't risk lingering. He followed her for a few paces down the hall before his footsteps halted.

Years ago, before their afternoon on the lawn, she may have secretly desired for him to pursue her, but she was a girl no more. She sought comfort in her companion's attention then, and she admittedly used him to try to fill the loneliness that had been there since her mother's death.

She thought she must have been wrong about him as she suddenly heard someone approach her. She rounded with fury, looking to stare him down in his good eye, but her gaze met with that of a strangers'. She studied the face for a moment, looking for a shred of familiarity. He was skinny and pale, his head shaved as bald as a baby's, with an ugly, hooked nose and red, sunken eyes. She would've remembered a face like that.

She was only caught off guard for a moment when he suddenly grabbed her by the wrist and neck. She pulled back hard, but he was stronger than his lean frame suggested. She reached down to her boot with her free hand and unsheathed a knife. It was her favorite little blade; no adornments or gaudiness, just reliable and sharp. She stabbed it deep into his side and twisted.

He howled with pain, releasing his grip on her throat. Her hand was slick where his blood spilled over it, making it more difficult for her to keep her grip on the knife. She switched it to her left hand and drew her curved saber with her right.

No one was coming from either end of the Long Hall. It was late, but she thought someone would've heard the scuffle and come to investigate. She wanted to knock him to the ground and interrogate him as she would've in the past. It seemed that he was specifically after her and trying to make quiet work of it. Like everyone else in her life, her would-be assassin had drastically underestimated her.

The cretin-looking man drew his own sword and attacked. Their blades clashed loudly, likely waking up the whole palace now. He parried her saber as she had anticipated, leaving him open to another stab from her knife. He staggered back, taking the blade with him within his body. She must have been over-confident for a moment, because she was suddenly taken aback by a blow to her cheek, and she felt her saber slip from her hand, she stumbled back a few steps. He first grabbed at her shirt, breaking away most of the buttons as she tried to wretch herself away while weaponless.

She landed a swift uppercut to his lower jaw, but it was not enough to break his grip, though she was sure she felt some of his teeth shatter within his mouth. He then grabbed a fistful of her hair and pulled back. She couldn't see as his head was wretched upward, and she couldn't reach him with her fists from where he now stood behind her. Holding tight to the base of her scalp, he walked her forward and slammed her against the window. The velvet red curtain smelled dusty, and she could feel the heat of the rising sun from behind its folds. Then he pulled the curtain back.

Her vision went white. She felt glass against her face for just a moment. She found herself senseless, except for the overwhelming smell of something burning.

19: LONELINESS

JULY 1849: THE EASTERN CRAGS

Minortai found some joy as he bit into a perfectly ripe peach that Mordain had collected that morning. He wiped the sweet juice from his chin and took another bite. It was the first thing he had eaten in days. He hoped he could keep in down, lest waste something so delicious. Time and Kaj's diligent care had done much to heal his leg. The infection had finally lifted, and the aches and fevers with it, but he would never walk the same again. He never thought of himself as a fighter or hunter, but those two options were more unattainable than ever.

  Their descent out of the Crags had placed them in warmer, pleasant weather, but they were still at a high enough elevation that Minortai could see for miles across the southern lands of Valehoutton. The rolling hills east of the Crags were lush and balmy. Nomadic groups of the Godsmoors people used to roam the lands, but they had long been turned over to Aejon invaders for farming and homesteads. Dry Pass Canyon, the Snankian border, was a blatant and jagged scar across the horizon. Beyond it the green of Valehoutton was traded for the obsidian sands, only marred by the mossy emeralds of the Orchane Forest near the southern border. Nearing the edge of his sight, black sands turned red, marking the beginning of the Southern Mesa. He had never seen the lands of southern Snanka, but he had been told many stories of its skinny mountains, almost like chimneys, and its layers of multi-colored rocks that resembled the lines of a painted sunset.

 Kajonne took a seat beside him, enjoying some fruit as well. She didn't look to him, but out to the distance as he was. Sucking the last bit of flesh from his peach, he then gripped the pit in his hand and hurled it over the cliff as far as he could. Kajonne laughed and flashed him a grin. She followed suite, though her pit fell so short it only made it a few feet away from where they sat. He chuckled slightly at her failure, and she shoved him playfully in return. Minortai enjoyed their little moments together. Mordain was a dull conversation keeper, Wenn was standoffish, and he took no pleasure in being in his brother's presence.

"It still feels so strange to be here. It seems that it was only yesterday my only worries were keeping our apothecary's books up to date and how long it was taking Mordain and I to conceive." He understood. Each dawn he thought he could roll over and pull Siyah closer to him in bed.

She absently took out her pair of herbal scissors, the handles mother of pearl, and trimmed the heads off a handful of spiky, purple flowers she had collected. She placed the heads in a pouch. She noticed he was watching her, "They're good for reducing inflammation and itching." She told him as she closed the pouch and returned it to her waist.

"Do you and Mordain keep the old ways?" he asked her. He was a half-blood Godsmoors, and she seemed in tune with the earth's flow, so it seemed likely to Minortai.

She shook her head as she began trimming thorns off a plant that had curled ends. "Mordain does not, he was raised by his father who had very little knowledge of the Deep. My family knows the truth, we were powerful in Ellinhall, but sometimes I feel as though we outstretched ourselves, and that is why we suffer now." She recoiled her thumb as she accidentally pricked herself on a thorn that she had overlooked. "One woman always bears the family name, that's why we call her Wenn. She was born Falerie Lena as I was born Kajonne Mahiel. I was so dedicated to learning, I thought I would receive the name after our mother passed, but Wenn was born with the Gift and I was not. So, the name went to her."

Minortai recalled seeing Wenn delivering that huge buck over her shoulder when he was still ill, and the mysterious she-wolf prints that kept appearing around camp each morning, no matter how far they had traveled the day before. While skin-changers were practically myth now, the remaining ones kept to tight family groups in the far east of Ellinhall. The Wenn Dell sisters had traveled far indeed.

"I understand your feeling that you're destined to be lesser." He told her softly.

She didn't seem to understand his statement. While the Ellinhall natives understood the Deep flow, she did not recognize his stars. It was refreshing to be around someone that had no concept of the ghastly fate splayed across his face for the world to judge him by.

It was the first time in his life he felt as though he was seen for who he was from the start. He didn't have to prove to her that he was a decent human despite how he came into the world, he was able to speak to her as any man would speak to any woman. She tucked a strand of her shoulder-length auburn hair behind her ear, and as he watched her, he felt something in his chest that he had not expected to ever feel again. The memory of Siyah's face immediately came to his mind, as did guilt and confusion.

"How?"

"It's believed that your stars are your absolute fate. You are compared to all that carried your stars before you. You can't change or fight what your stars give you."

"What are yours?"

"The Matricider."

She frowned, confused. "Well, is it true?"

"My mother died to give birth to me, so my stars were not wrong."

Kajonne looked angry. "They put you down for the rest of your life for something far out of your control?! For something that happened you were just coming into this world? What kind of shit is that?" She covered her mouth, seemingly ashamed of what had come out of it. "Sorry, I didn't mean to use that kind of language, but..." she looked off into the distance, still incredulous with what she had just heard. Then she laughed, at herself and at the institution his people kept. He couldn't help but to laugh with her.

"Kajonne is a constellation, isn't it? What do my stars say about me?"

"The Green Witch." He nearly chuckled to himself. He tried to keep a straight face. It seemed very fitting as he watched her peel back petals from a yellow, lily-like plant.

"Oh, you're kidding with me?" She said, smiling with realization.

He couldn't help but to laugh. "Yes, I'm sorry, Kajonne isn't a constellation." She laughed with him, but as it faded they found themselves in an awkward silence.

"Since we crossed the border, I've been having the strangest dreams. To the point that sometimes I'm not sure if I'm still sleeping."

"I have since I left Tiver as well." He told her. Kajonne clicked her thumb nail against her teeth as she thought. "I keep seeing a single tower in the Snankian desert."

"You see things?" She said, still clacking her teeth against her fingernails. "Has anyone spoken to you? Someone real?"

Minortai felt a chill run up his back as he thought of Hellan. He knew she was real, and he knew that they would soon meet. "Yes, as far as I know."

"Is it a man?"

"No, a raven-haired woman."

"It's a huge man, larger than any person I've ever seen, but I don't know if he's truly human. He hides his face behind a porcelain mask. He spoke to me of the old Caeruleans of Valehoutton. He told me to go to Snanka. I lied to Wenn, Mordain, and Nehlas about why I wanted to go there. I insisted it was for the Insurgo headquarters, but I honestly just need to know if that man is there to guide me to my next step. He knows something, if not everything, and I feel so deeply that I must find it."

Their peaceful moment was over as quickly as it had fallen into his hands. Wenn's cross voice was arguing sharply with Nehlas. Brought back to reality, both he and Kajonne avoided each other's gazes and stared intently forward. He could only hear every other word being spoken between the two, but he could tell the Wenn was the aggressor and Nehlas was on the defense.

Kajonne broke the serious air that had befallen them with a snort of laughter. She shook her head when Minortai looked to her. "He's a fool to think he can tell her what to do." She whispered to him.

"She's a fool for thinking he'll listen to reason." He smirked back at her. They exchanged smiles again, quietly mocking their older siblings' stubbornness.

"Then perhaps they deserve each other."

The lovers' quarrel was suddenly drowned out by Mordain's desperate shouts. He came running uphill from where he had been scavenging through more fruit trees. Minortai spied black greth blood on the blade of his knife and coating his right hand. Nehlas sprang into action before Minortai could even get to his feet. He donned no armor, but he rushed past Mordain with his longsword drawn.

"There's two more down there, they've seen us! I couldn't fight them off-" Mordain panted out as Kajonne took him in her arms.

After a quick clamor of metal, Nehlas reappeared cleaning off his blade. The displeased look that he shot Mordain was one that Minortai himself was all too familiar with. "How could a man be so incompetent on the battlefield?" he was surely thinking, or "Must I do everything for these weaklings?" He acted as though Mordain's brush with death was little more than an inconvenience, like killing a spider for your wife.

Kajonne continued to nurture her shaken husband as Minortai looked on. He turned to Nehlas, "Could there be more?"

"We should probably move to be safe." he muttered. He reunited with Wenn, who stood with her arms folded.

"You can't keep speaking to me as if I'm subservient. I don't know what your previous lovers were like, but I'm not your-" Nehlas continued past her, ignoring her expression completely. She clenched her teeth angrily and caught up to him. She grabbed him by the elbow. "This isn't over," she whispered harshly to him, thinking no one else could hear. "We'll continue this later."

Mordain put out their fire and quickly covered the ashes with rocks and dirt. Nehlas retraced their steps to cover their tracks in case there were still greth trailing them. Minortai helped the women pack their tent, sleeping blankets, and other supplies. They were on the move again within the hour. Minortai couldn't help but to feel some shame that he was the one on horseback while everyone else was on foot, but it was they only choice they had unless they wanted to move at a crawling pace.

As the party journeyed on, he noted that Nehlas kept near Minortai and the horse at the front, avoiding Wenn at the rear. His brother thought he could avoid their conversation if he just kept avoiding her. From his heightened position, he scanned the horizon. He had missed Mordain and Nehlas discussing which direction they were taking to the border, as he had been preoccupied at the time trying in vain to mount the horse without assistance. It eventually took both sisters hoisting him up and over, much to his shame.

Their hasty descent from the Crags seemed to have taken them too far north to access the only known bridge across the canyon and in to Snanka. He knew using the bridge would risk their exposure to a greth, or any other attack, but he had made the naive assumption that it was their route.

"It's full of monsters... monsters like me..." The grim warning from his vision echoed in his head ominously.

"Nehlas, we're heading away from the Southern Pass. Are we going all the way around to the North?"

"Don't be foolish, the bridge would only put us in danger and surpassing the canyon would take over a month. We're just going to find a way through. It's called Dry Canyon for a reason." His brother replied impatiently.

Minortai was all too familiar with the tone. The sound of it made him feel like a lonely orphan again. Back then, Nehlas was the only person he had, and his brother both disliked and resented him. Every word he spoke to him was short and irritated, as if Minortai's entire existence annoyed him. As if he was nothing more than a burden; a responsibility cast upon the young man that he never wanted after being robbed of his parents.

Minortai felt his voice catch in his tightening throat as the feelings that haunted his childhood rose up to take control of his heart. He felt small and helpless. His past self seemed more familiar than who he had grown up to be now that he was alone without Siyah. He wondered if he had ever really changed, and it was just her love that made him better.

Despite it all, he couldn't shake the voice repeating itself to him. He felt as though Hellan's steel grey eyes were watching him, urging him to convince his brother otherwise. The pressure to speak was rising up like a torrent building behind a dam that could no longer hold it back.

"I don't think we should go that way." he suddenly blurted out. He was as surprised by his objection as Nehlas was.

His brother's face graduated from annoyance to anger. Before he could put Minortai back into his lowly place, Wenn abruptly appeared on the other side of the horse.

"Why not?" she asked Minortai. Her voice was sharp and succinct, but he was beginning to understand that it wasn't personal. She simply wasn't one for pleasantries and would rather get straight to the point.

He wasn't sure how to reply. Would he sound like a lunatic if he told the truth? He wasn't sure if he could make up a lie fast enough. "Somehow I know there's danger lying there." He said, trying to find a middle ground between the truth and believability.

She seemed to consider his words for a moment, then said "That isn't enough for the two solid reasons we must avoid the other two options." He thought he sensed a bit of an apology in her voice.

She and Nehlas were probably right. He was embarrassed for even saying anything. He knew his brain was still a wreck, he couldn't be certain if everything he had been seeing in his odd limbo between dream and consciousness was real or a creeping insanity. For all he knew he was slipping into it deeper with each sleep.

His pathetic attempts to rationalize his feeling made no difference to the growing pit of dread within his stomach that the five of them were all heading straight to their deaths, and the eyes he felt on his back only made the weight heavier.

20: THE BUTTERFLY EFFECT

STAR PALACE

The scent of seared flesh still overwhelmed her senses. Her entire body was wracked with pain as she thrashed about in her bed. The soft silk of her sheets burned and stung against her skin. When the constant itch of it became unbearable, she felt the pain begin to melt away. She felt her body levitate off the feather mattress and become weightless in the air.

"Delinda, what is your fight against?" a deep voice rumbled through her head. The booming resonance was enough to make her head feel like splitting.

Suddenly, she found herself a decade younger. Her hair was in a thick braid down to her waist, it was before she started keeping it at a more practical length. Her throat felt raw from trying to scream the night before. She used to think that if she could just make a single noise, her hope that her voice would return would be renewed. But all her efforts had been in vain, and now she was left with a sore reminder of her naivety.

She was back in Cynn, just north of the city. It was late afternoon in early autumn. The sun's rays were golden and intense. Her younger self took the glow for granted. She paced outside the makeshift cells that had been hastily built to accommodate the newly found traitors to the crown. Kras had demanded she and her men round up the governor and all his councilors to question them about why they allowed the Red to spread unchecked in their city. He suspected they were Red as well. Delinda strongly opposed the imprisonment of the politicians' families, but her opinion was left unconsidered on a piece of parchment.

It had only been a few months since she had woken with a bandaged head and twenty people standing around her bed, wondering if she would die. Even the best of their doctors couldn't determine if her speech would ever return. The anger of her loss, and of her brother's wicked violence against her, was a deep, fresh wound. Regardless, Delinda knew her place at the lead of her company, and as princess of the country. In silence, she stood at her post.

The word "traitor" continued to bounce around in her head as she listened to a woman beg for her husband's life. The word just kept repeating itself to her. The following screams let Delinda know the wife's pleas went unanswered. Then she heard the cries of an infant. Her legs suddenly trembled underneath her body. *Traitor.* Could she really live with herself if she let something so cruel pass by her again? She could close her eyes and let it rush past her like the wind.

Or she could take the hammer from her side and smash it into the hollow iron bars of the cell. *Traitor.* The cheap metal bent easily and made an opening in the window large enough for her to pull a small person through. The noise of the bars cracking got the attention of the family in the cell, luckily, for she could not call to them.

The mother immediately recognized the opportunity and turned from the gruesome scene of her husband's brains upon the dirt floor to lifting her infant child up to Delinda's arms. The baby kept crying as Delinda tucked her small body into the crook of her arm, and suddenly she felt frozen.

What was she doing? What had she done? If word got out of her treachery, or her weakness...

Suddenly a young boy, perhaps eight or nine, had his arms outstretched as the mother boosted him through the opening in the stone to Delinda's arms. The boy was followed by his identical twin. Inside, Delinda saw that the eldest of the sons, no more than fourteen, was finally overpowered by the executioner with the axe. The mother shrieked again, forgetting the child with tears in her eyes at the base of the window as she fled to her dead son's body. The axe struck down the mother.

Delinda did not want to see the girl with the golden eyes staring up at her. The child's eyes were narrowed and twisted with anger beyond her years. A young teenaged woman, likely the eldest sister, stepped in where the mother failed. She grabbed the golden-eyed child and lifted her into Delinda's treacherous hands. The woman grasped the edges of the bricks and lifted herself up to the window. The golden-eyed child called out her name, "Miro," over and over as she pulled her sister's hand, trying to make her move faster.

A tremor moved through the teenaged girl's body and she vomited blood. Her eyes went wide with fear, then her head dropped to the ground and she was unresponsive. The child shrieked as she frantically tugged at her sister's limp hand, flailing around the dead weight of the arm and shaking more blood loose from the body. She screamed in protest as Delinda hurried her away from the tombs that held her family. Delinda knew she couldn't care for them. She couldn't take them. They would just be killed anyway, and she with them. She could not allow that. She was their savior, and that was where her mercy ended.

She roughly passed the squalling infant to the child's arms. Delinda frantically pointed away from the cells. She needed them to escape the encampment. She tried to utter a sound, to get the girl and the twin boys to understand, they had to run. They would not run. They couldn't fathom that the adult that had pulled them from certain death was not going to be their caretaker.

She pointed to the Saltwoods again and again, but they all just stared at her with hollow eyes. Finally, she picked up the hammer she had used to free them and swung it at one of the boys. He jumped back but did not flee. She swung at the girl holding the infant. She girl cursed at her and ran away as quickly as a laden child could. The twins followed. They only had to pass a small clearing before they reached the cover of the woods.

The pluck of a bow loosing broke through the air, followed by the heavy sound of the larger of the twins collapsing to the ground with a tail of feathers extending out his back. Delinda turned away as she heard more arrows loosing. She already did more than she should have for those children. She had committed treason. Her life could already be on the line if she was seen. She slipped away to the front of the barracks, never knowing if the other three survived.

Then she found herself a decade younger still. She had just had her first flowering, very late for her age, and had been proclaimed a woman and eligible to be courted by other highborn men. She sat in her mother's chambers as the queen applied makeup in her boudoir. Delinda's fists were on her knees, gripping the itchy fabric of her embroidered gown tightly as angry tears rolled down her cheeks. She knew her crying had made her eyes red and puffy, and she was sure she would be lectured about her appearance once her mother's tirade about Delinda's behavior during the previous night's banquet was over.

"Honestly, Delinda, you think you know everything," the queen began. She looked at her daughter sitting behind her through the mirror's reflection. She sighed and put down her brush. "You're still a child. Yes, you're clever and strong, but I can assure you your father and I know more than you. You need to secure an engagement. I did it, my mother did it, and you're going to."

She stood, still gracefully though she was laden with child, and crossed the room to face her eldest child. She placed a hand on Delinda's face, and the princess felt herself jump at the touch. Neither of her parents were often affectionate. She looked up at her mother through her tears. The queen was not remarkably beautiful, but she was graceful and keen. Delinda could only see their resemblance when she also wore jewels and dresses.

"I'm sure one day you'll know more than both of us." She said simply, and forced a smile with her red, painted lips.

She died in childbirth a month later. The sickly boy followed soon after.

Delinda felt herself falling. Then there was sand beneath her boots. It was brick-red sand that she had never seen before. It kept rising past her knees until she was buried up to her neck. Her struggling only made her sink further. Her eyes rose from the sand to meet mismatched eyes, one green and one brown, flecked with gold.

"Evil deeds cannot be buried forever. When that seed sprouts and the sapling grows, someone will recognize it and cut it down." A voice bellowed in her head. The sound made her brain feel like it was about to crack open.

The old, poorly lacquered doors of the throne room were gone. In their place stood an entirely new knotted, pine portal with blue embellishments. Panels were carved with images of the sun, moon, and other celestial bodies. As she lifted her hand to touch the wood, the doors opened, and light shone through. She could not see into the room for the brightness was too overpowering, yet the sun did not burn her. She took a step forward and felt the warmth of the light spread across her skin.

Then she was in the darkness again. She tried to scream as the memory of her flesh searing stabbed sharply into her mind. She jolted awake and was immediately overcome with the pain of her flesh. Cold, damp cloths were compressed over the right side of her face, chest and shoulder. Both her hands were also wrapped. Thick ointment was layered between the cloths and her peeling skin, making her entire body feel sticky and wet. Her wounds no longer burned, but the prickling of her open, blistered skin was hardly an improvement.

Visions of blue doors and mismatched eyes continued to plague her consciousness as she drifted in and out of sleep. Of all the wrong paths her ancestor took, his biggest mistake by far was not ensuring the complete end of the Caerulean line. Every few years a rumor would emerge of a child with mismatched eyes, but she and Kras were always quick to put an end to them. While the eyes were a common trait of that family, Delinda knew more than half of the Caeruleans alive at the time of their fall had normal eyes.

"...the sapling grows..." the voice said again.

"...cut it down..."

Those eyes. Over and over she kept seeing Caerulean eyes. One yellow like a cat's, the other mossy green flecked with brown. How many were still out there, wandering the world and biding their time?

Basaulte, Old Tyr, Young Tyr, and Daven all sat around her as she came to. She was in her own chambers, though they had to bring in seats for each of the four waiting on her. She was not accustomed to visitors.

"The assailant is dead, Princess Darkstar." Young Tyr spoke quickly. "We've been betrayed by the Rhanian once again. He feared retaliation so he sent his-" Young Tyr stopped as she motioned to him to hand her ink and the small book that she used to communicate messages.

She began to write, though the peeled skin on her right hand made every stroke agonizing, but what she had to say could not wait. She held the open page up to Basaulte, the only one of her company that was literate.

"I've seen the Caeruleans. I believe they are regaining strength." He read. He turned his eye upon her. She sensed doubt in him. Perhaps he thought the pain was disorienting her. He continued anyway. "My brother is not strong enough to deal with the threat of any true claimant. His power and sanity both wane with each passing day. Just writing these words could mean death for me, so I do not write them without cause."

She could see Basaulte's pulse beating faster in the veins of his arm that sat close to the surface of his skin. It wasn't fear. It was excitement. "Is it finally time?" He asked her.

Delinda sat up in her bed, trying her best to ignore the wet, taunt feeling of her bandaged, charred skin. She looked to each one of her men. This was not the first time they had had this discussion. Basaulte tore the page out of her book and set it aflame before throwing it into her empty fireplace to turn to ash. He fell to his knees at her bedside. The others followed suite.

"Never again shall we have to bear witness to abuse and malpractice. You deserve this. You were born for this." He said as gently as he could in his booming baritone.

"We have been praying for your ascension for many years, my queen." Daven said proudly. He held his right hand over his heart in a pledge. Her eyes went from Old Tyr, to Young Tyr, to Daven, and finally rested on Basaulte.

Delinda had never been handed anything. Her skill, her intellect, her power: she had made them all herself. She had been neglected, shunned, and abused her entire life. She had been humiliated and ridiculed in council. Her brother thought he could take her men from her, but he never would. He would never understand honor or loyalty. Her men were hers until the end.

It was time for Delinda Redal to build her empire.

21: A MARRED NAME

THE INSURGO BASE

Nalahi was quartered in an unused officer villa, the only one of their company to be so well accommodated. Ash and Venell at least had their own rooms, but they were only big enough for a bed, and his didn't even have a window, though it was preferable to the first few weeks that he spent sleeping int he barracks. He was supposed to only be in his stuffy, brick room temporarily but no one had asked him to relocate yet.

Much to Ash's discomfort, this meant her room was near both the Red Ukons'. He felt anger and envy every time he saw that Red scum look at Venell, undressing her with his soulless grey eyes. Still, he did not wish to be seen near Nalahi's room. He didn't want to explain to anyone why he was going there, least of all Venell. He didn't know what she would think about his intention.

He sipped a mug of ale just down the hall from Nalahi's quarters. He knew she was in there. She had retired quite early in the evening, just after supper. He wondered if it was because she was avoiding running into him. The ale was lifting his courage, though fear and doubt remained loud at the back of his mind. This time it had nothing to do with anyone finding them out, not even Venell, he was only afraid of her. She could turn him away, and all his stirred feelings would be for naught.

He kept picturing how she angrily stood up from the chair in his room, her slip nearly sheer so that he could see every curve of her form. Emotion and passion radiated from her being, swathing her in a golden aura. When he thought about her like that, he couldn't think of anything else. Not of Kras, not of death, not of Venell. It was the only peace he had known for ages, though it was too fiery and carnal to be called peace. She made him feel like an animal, but animals had no thoughts of hate.

He set his empty mug down on a windowsill and approached her room. The air seemed to be growing heavy around him. He had no words planned for her, and he certainly couldn't think of any now as he knocked on her door. She opened it almost immediately. She was wearing the same men's tunic and breeches that she had been wearing earlier that day, as well as her leather belt that held multiple knives. Ash had yet to see her wear shoes since their first night at the base. She had tossed out her rope and leather sandals after their arrival, claiming they smelled like Bardon.

"What?" She demanded.

He didn't say anything.

"What have you been doing? I heard you come up the stairs an hour ago." That hot fury was rising in her. It filled him with desire.

"You're still angry with me?" he asked her. He felt courage from the ale lifting him higher than he should venture.

She hit him in the chest. It was certainly not as hard as she could have, but it still caught him off guard. "I can't stop being angry with you." She said, roughly grabbing his shirt in her fist. Her lips parted as she prepared to say something else, but no words came out. She just gripped the material of his shirt tighter.

He stepped forward, making her fist touch his chest. She pushed him back. "You cannot come in!"

"You wouldn't have answered the door if you did not want me to."

Her molten eyes flashed at him. She yanked him into the room. Her arms were folded as she leaned against the door to close it. "You disgust me. You give people worth based on their value to you, and now you think you've found a new value in me." She shook her head in distaste. "I'd tell you to go prey on someone else, but I fear you'll just try to put your poor sister back under your thumb." The white streak through her dark eyebrows was more pronounced when she was scowling.

"There's no way I could feel this fire and... you feel nothing." His face was so close to hers he could feel the heat of her skin. "You can't end it before it could begin."

Ash reached out toward her cheek. He did not see it happen, but she unsheathed one of her knives and held it against his throat, close to his left collarbone. "Oh, I'm ending it." She said through gritted teeth.

Ash had anticipated that familiar icy feeling to take over him as it did the last time she held a blade to him, but he had only felt fire since the day he had seen all of her. He leaned his head forward and kissed her. He felt the blade bite into his flesh and blood trickle down his chest. She drew his soul in though her mouth. He knew she felt what he did. It was impossible for this burning to be one sided. Nalahi dropped her dagger. She lifted a hand up to run it over the stubble growing on the one of the shaved sides of his head.

Then she suddenly broke their kiss and shoved him away. She was silent for a few moments as she stared at the wall. "Get out." She said sternly.

He blinked as he looked down at her. He heard her, but her words did not settle in.

"I'm being foolish. Get out, I want to be alone." She repeated.

"Nalahi-"

Her golden eyes flashed at him. Her anger only lighted his passion further. "Do not speak my name, get out of this room! We're only connecting over shared trauma. This isn't real. It's not what you think. It's just a release from all the fucked-up shit we saw and did when we were children. It's just a way to cradle our past selves. It does nothing conducive for us now." She opened the door and waited for him to exit. "I won't be your bandage."

"I can be yours, then."

She scoffed, "You would rot me."

He didn't go quickly, but he left her to stew alone. He mulled over Nalahi's words as he made his way to the stables later that evening. With Apsonne's injured leg, they would need a horse to get her east. He planned on observing the daily comings and goings of the stables so he could properly plot their escape. As he sat there, he began to realize that the getting of a horse was not the problem, but going through the single, always-manned gate was. He stared across the courtyard at his black ore foe, fuming.

Mayan was able to get them both out for their escapade across the plains, but he doubted any of the Insurgo would trust him on his own, especially not now the commander was livid with him. Not to mention how he would smuggle Apsonne out too. He walked in circles around the compound, but the gate was truly the only way out and in.

At the eastern-most corner of the base, he was again disappointed to see there was no other gate. In dismay, he turned to make his way back to the main hall to find Venell for a late supper. He was surprised to cross paths with Krisae, who had been following the commander's entourage a few paces ahead of her.

With her heels she was taller than Ash, and her arms were larger around than his own. She wasn't particularly heavily built or broad shouldered, he was mostly just caught off guard since he was used to Venell and Nalahi's small statures and slight frames. Her face was very young, and he couldn't deny that she was pretty. His dislike of the Red was not stirred with her as it was with her brother.

She nodded to acknowledge him, then broke off from the commander's group. "Keoneo." She said simply. She lingered, waiting for a response. She raised an eyebrow at his silence, then decided to continue regardless. "I've been meaning to catch you alone. Ronnock told me something that disturbed me the first night you were here, and then that fit in the commander's office-"

"I don't have anything to say." Ash said, turning to leave.

She grabbed onto his shirt near his shoulder. He pulled away, but she became more forceful. With just her single hand she slammed him up against the stone barrier and pinned him there. He gripped her hand to tear it away, but she was ridiculously strong. When he looked back to her face, she was grinning, and her eyes were crimson red.

"You're going to have something to say to me." She said, her voice nearly a growl.

Ash found himself searching for familiar faces behind her, desperately wanting out of her grasp. "No one here will choose you over me, Keoneo," she said, noticing that he was looking for help. Her eyes receded to their regular shimmering silver. Her seraphic face turned pouty, "So you might as well give me what I want."

"Okay," he stammered out. He didn't mean to say anything.

"Oh, good." She said, smiling innocently. "I only wanted to ask you if you had always known that your father was Red."

"As long as I can remember." He responded through gritted teeth.

"Then why do the Red make you so angry?" She dragged two fingers down the side of his face gently, and it was then that Ash realized that she wasn't even holding him down anymore. "Why would you speak so ill of your own father? Tell me what he did to you." Her voice sounded so angelic that he wanted to give her everything she wanted, and yet at the same time it was reminiscent of his mother's comfort. He couldn't decide if he wanted to fuck her or cry in her arms.

He was suddenly back in his childhood home in Rinoll. He had loved it like he had never loved their home in Cynn. They had a yard where his mother gardened vegetables and flowers. He would often sit with her outside while she worked. The two of them were alone a lot. The house always felt different when his father was home; like there was a stranger invading upon him and his mother. Ash tolerated his presence, however, as his mother always seemed to be relieved when he returned home. She would encourage him to play with the children they could hear playing across the way, but he just wanted to be in her company.

That was until he met Watkin. The red-haired boy was a year younger than him, but they quickly became inseparable. While he was quiet and shy in front of his parents, as soon as the two of them were alone, Waddy would come up with the best adventures for the two of them to act out. He knew all the best stories, but some he just made up them as he went.

It was twilight, almost time for Waddy to go home, when Ash returned to the garden from fetching freshly peeled pomegranate seeds from the house. When he came upon the scene in the yard, the bowl slipped from his hands and shattered. The seeds spread everywhere, camouflaging themselves amongst the spreading vermillion upon the ground. The monster hovering above Waddy's torn body turned its evil eyes upon him.

He was frozen under that red gaze. His legs trembled as he stared back at death. He felt hands upon his shoulders as his mother suddenly appeared. She grabbed him and flung him backwards, screaming at him to get into the house. Then she ran to the monster. She grabbed each side of his face, smothered in Waddy's blood, and called his name out to him. Ash thought for sure the monster would rip her apart too.

The fear he felt then paralyzed him even now. That evening he had stood there helplessly and allowed his mother to endanger herself. He swore he would never be so weak again. He would be a fighter. He would be brave and heroic.

Ash felt like the words were being drug out of his mouth against his will. "He killed my friend when I was a child. The only one I had. We were five, maybe. I saw him tear out his throat to satisfy the Red."

"Oh, yes, baby boy, that is hard." She said as she put her thumb on his bottom lip. "Was it just the one time, or did he hurt you like that more than once?"

"Just the one time. My mother had to interfere. I don't know how he recognized her in that state, but he did. They covered it up, and then we moved Cynn. They both acted like it never happened. Venell has no idea and I never told her." He said nothing of his father's cowardice causing the death of his mother and the people of Cynn. Krisae's voice was as seductive as it was comforting, and it was distracting him and pulling him out of his memories and into the present.

"Yes, that is such a burden." Krisae purred to him. Then her tone suddenly changed, and her gaze turned steely, "But we've all had to deal with shit. Dragging an inspiring name through the dirt isn't going to help anyone out, so you best keep you little problems to yourself." She kissed him on the cheek and walked away.

He was speechless and breathless. He felt like he had just suffered a hit that knocked the wind out of him, though in a way he had been.

22: THE THIRD EYE

JULY 1849: THE NORTHERN SHORE, VALE-HOUTTON

Jayen Rillo knew she was dying. The wound to her side was leaking so much that her legs were becoming slick with blood. She cursed the greth with every stumble from one rock to the next. Angry waves slapped against the jagged shore, spraying saltwater across the rocks and into the air. It was cold and the sky was grey, as it always was here. The mist of violence, the sea versus the earth, hung in the air here for all eternity.

She had fled the reservation in Southern Tiver four days ago, and she had finally made it to the Northern Shore, clutching her wound tightly, as if her hand could hold in all her insides. She no longer cried, but the memories of Haylle and Keetan being struck down played over and over in her mind.

Jayen had been fleeing the greth raid with her young daughter's hand held tightly, when Haylle was struck in the head with a hammer. She had been pulling the girl along to force her to keep up, and suddenly the body became much lighter. Jayen turned to see Haylle's skull spread across the plains, though she still held her hand. She had to let her go to escape. Her hand slipped from Haylle's, and the six year old's body collapsed. Jayen knocked a single arrow to her bow and loosed it into the head of Haylle's murderer.

As she did, she heard her husband cry out. She turned to see Keetan's innards spilling onto the yellow grass, slipping through his fingers as he tried to hold them in. She loosed another arrow into that greth and cried in anguish. She should just let the evil things kill her so she wouldn't have to go on with the memories, but for all she knew she was the last of her people. She had to reach the Third Eye.

Another greth got too close to her. She reached back to her quiver and panicked as she found it empty. It slashed at her with its rusty scythe. She tried to dodge, but the blade opened her flesh from rib to thigh. She had lost her dagger in the skull of greth from a previous invasion, and now she was not nearly strong enough for hand-to-hand combat. She narrowly avoided its second lunge at her and forgot about revenge. She had to escape. She clasped her side closely as she sprinted into the Crags.

Now every small slip upon the wet, rocky cliff nearly blinded her with pain, but she had made it. Her pilgrimage was complete. She only had to lift her body past one final boulder to reach the Third Eye. She didn't know what to expect, but the remaining dash of hope in her heart depended on it. She needed some sort of answer, another survivor, anything…

The Third Eye was empty. There was no blue, glowing light from within as she had been told. It was just a dark, wet seaside cave. High above her head, three gaping holes in the ceiling of the cave amongst all the dripping stalactites demonstrated how the cave gained its name. Water slowly leaked in through each of the eye-shaped openings, making the floor damp and slick. No life grew upon the walls and none scurried upon the ground. It was completely barren, just like her hope.

She abandoned her faith and walked back onto the cliff just outside of the cavern. Exasperated, she turned to face the sea and sky. The tide was rising, and the waves now crashed upon the rocks she had just crossed on, washing away her stains. Her numb toes crept to the edge of the cliff. Below, she could see the crabs her body would feed scuttling upon the shore. She could no longer keep the creeping darkness at bay. Instead of falling forward as she intended, she fell backward. The floor hummed and vibrated. She could barely open her eyes, though through her lids she saw the faint glow of a blue light.

She was in her home in Southern Ellinhall. Her belly was swollen as Haylle grew within her. The autumn leaves swept up the stone steps of her doorway. The air was damp and cold mists hung low over the land. She meticulously pricked blue and red ink in swirling patterns around Keetan's wrist and forearm as he touched her belly and spoke to their unborn child. He told her of his childhood Godsmoors and his journey of self-discovery to Ellinhall he began in his late hundreds. His white, blond hair was unruly and uncut. Light stubble covered his strong jawline. His green eyes looked up and met hers, seeing into her very being with his ancient knowledge. Jayen had only just turned two-hundred when she discovered she was pregnant, while Keetan was nearing his fourth century.

Then she held a child in her arms, but it was not Haylle, and the arms were not her own. The baby, a squalling boy, opened his eyes just long enough for Jayen to see that one was shockingly green while the other was brown and flecked with gold. Someone threw a blanket over the babe and snatched it from her arms. "We must hide them both." A man whispered harshly to her.

She cried out for the child, but then found herself standing alone in the Godsmoors. The land had strangely always been home to her, though it was far from where she had been born. She knew all her people felt the same resonance. Everything was silent. The constellation of the Matricider was high in the sky, shining like a beacon to her. Instead of feeling apprehensive and off-put as she should, she felt drawn to it. Those adverse stars held all the answers. She was Jayen, The Virgin Huntress, and she had already broken her stars. The Matricider could break his too.

The land seemed to shrink before her, and she was pulled across the vastness of Valehoutton, seeing valleys, mountains, forests and rivers rush past her, until she found herself before Star Palace. The Matricider watched her from above. She pushed open the heavy oaken doors, decorated with fresh carvings that told both recent history and ancient lore. Her fingers brushed over a relief of the sun.

She expected to be attacked as she entered the castle, for none of her kind would possibly be welcome since an assassination attempt by three Godmoorians. She was standing in the throne room. It gleamed with new life. Beautiful cerulean and cream draped the room. Kras' rotting throne was replaced with one of ivory and ocean blue. The glory of the throne room faded as the moon began to fall from the sky. Its white glow faded to black and it crashed to the earth just above a single white flower. The small thing looked as though it would never survive, but as the sun rose, the flower reached up to greet it and shone with such brilliance it rivaled the sun itself.

Then she was in complete darkness. The deafening sound of the waves had faded into a murmur. The night had brought calm. Her head was swimming with confusion of what was memory and what she had imagined. She wrapped her arms around her stomach to find that her blood had thickened and slowed. She felt like weeping, but the tears wouldn't come.

She didn't feel the raw pain of her insides anymore. Perhaps her time was near. She stared up to the stars. The constellation of the Matricider was rising in the East. She had forgotten that it was so visible this time of year. She wished to see Keetan or Haylle's stars one last time, but Haylle's would be hidden until the end of winter, and Keetan's would be far into the southern sky. She willed herself to roll to her side, seeking Keetan. Her body followed her attempt with ease.

Jayen sat up. She pulled up her shirt incredulously. Underneath all the dried blood, her skin was intact. Her wound was gone. The Third Eye had chosen her. The Deep had chosen for her to live. Now she found herself able to weep. She thought of Haylle. She thought of all her people that had perished. She could very well be the only person of the Godsmoors still alive. Her land would not have chosen for her to go on if it didn't want something in return. She just had to listen. She had to listen to what it needed from her.

Her focus was again caught by the Matricider, brighter and higher in the sky than she had ever seen. She had to go east. After all the evil that had befallen her people, an archaically malevolent constellation was nothing to be feared. It mirrored the brilliance of the white flower she had seen in her dream, as if both reflected the sun itself. The sound of the waves below her made her feel as though she was enveloped in the endless blue. Time had become misaligned in her mind. And the child she saw... Had the Third Eye shown her the past? Or was it the future? She was still trying to piece everything together.

She knelt back onto the rock, laying her hand gently upon the ground. "I'll do all that I can with this gift." She whispered. She would not allow the memory of her land or people to be silently erased from Valehoutton's history. She would fight to her last breath. Jayen Rillo rose a new woman.

23: THE SUN

THE INSURGO BASE

Venell had been fretting over her foolishness for more than two days. She was so embarrassed by the things she said to Ronnock that night in his chambers that she wished she could just disappear into nothing. She had ruined the blossoming feelings between them with her stupid fantasies. She knew she had hurt his feelings too, and that was even more unbearable than her shame.

She and Nalahi leaned over the edge of the southern turret as the sun was setting. They quietly gazed out over the vast expanse of the Whispering Plains. The distant horizon was turning indigo, making a beautiful contrast against the golden blowing grasses of the plains. The smell of smoke blew up from the chimneys of the kitchens and the pits of the yard. If she squinted, she could see the dark shadow of the Crags to the East.

Venell couldn't help but feel that they both had something to say to the other, but neither could seem to find where to start. She wanted to blurt out to her only friend what she had done, and how she was feeling for Ronnock, but the words kept sticking in her throat.

Nalahi drummed her fingers on the railing apprehensively, and she kept looking over to Venell, then back out to the plains. Her dark brows were furrowed in thought, making them stand out even more against the gold of her hair. A ripple of ivory swept across her tawny skin near the end of her right brow, and the hairs there were white. Venell had grown used to the woman saying whatever came to her mind. It was unnerving for her to be so silent.

She was brought out of her head by footsteps approaching. She turned to see Ash coming up the stairs, his hands folded over his chest. Nalahi made an audible scoff, then turned heel and left haughtily. Venell looked from Nalahi's departing figure to Ash's sullen face, and back. She puzzled herself on what the two were having differences about. Perhaps that was what Nalahi was trying to bring up with her.

"I'm going to have to leave for a while." He whispered to her. "I'm taking the Redal girl to Piaces. You can't tell anyone."

"What? Why?" Venell suddenly snapped at him. Her voice was heavy with displeasure and disapproval. Once the words left her mouth, she found herself more surprised at her response than Ash was. Taken aback, he took a moment to regain himself and continue. Neither of them were used to her questioning him.

"She needs to reunite with the rest of her family, not be kept prisoner here."

"Since when do you care about anything like that?" She almost felt as though her body was rising above the brick floor that she stood on. She felt anger stirring in her stomach, but also disgust. She heard the lie in his voice for the first time, yet now she was sure it had always been there. "What's the real reason? Do you even know?"

"She's a Redal, it could get me closer to Kras."

She couldn't stand to listen to him a moment longer. How could he have such little self-awareness? "No, don't use that like you always do.

You just want to get out of here. You don't like anyone here because they don't kiss the ground you walk on. You want recognition, and you're trying to get it from that girl. You don't care about helping her, you only care about yourself." She pushed past him and began to storm off.

She turned over her shoulder before she took a step down the stairs. Ash didn't look ashamed of himself as she would've if someone had told her a difficult truth about herself. He was surprised, but still indignant, and that incited her outrage further. "What would you even do if you got to him?" She added brusquely, putting the final cherry on top of her tirade.

As she descended, that floating feeling began to fade, and her steps fell back into her body. She felt so liberated. She felt invincible, but also that she needed to keep telling the world all her feelings to keep this rush going. She had to go to Ronnock and apologize to him. She had to make things right and tell him of her growing affection.

She was almost in a panic searching for him. It felt as though she had a time limit, before her boldness wore off, to reach him. She tore through the halls of the base, scanning the courtyard from the third story windows as she passed.

She burst into the mess hall in her near-frantic search, startling Mayan and the Redal girl during their dinner.

She didn't want to look for him in his quarters. Perhaps the timid part of her was apprehensive about invading his personal space, or perhaps it was her association she had with that room to the bitter end of the other night. However, her body was moving independent of her misgivings. She hastened down the officers' hall until she reached his familiar door. This new intrepid woman didn't knock, she just opened the door, though a little too forcefully. The metal knob banged noisily against the stone wall behind it, and she unwittingly recoiled from the sound. Her hands awkwardly flung about until she clasped them behind her back, but not so awkward as the position she had just put Ronnock Ukon in.

Alone in his chambers, his clothes were lain across his sitting chair and he held a wet cloth in front of his wash basin. He froze, and the cloth slipped from his hands to make a wet splat on the floor. His hands flew between his legs to cover his private parts. "Venell," he said, obviously surprised. "I... I'm sorry, I didn't lock the door."

She was admittedly also taken aback and couldn't help but let her eyes wander over his true self. The scars that covered his body were as extensive as the ones across his face. The jagged, pink flesh looked alien against his otherwise smooth, pale skin. His chest was covered in black hair, with a trail leading to where his hands lay across his groin. He looked taller, yet lankier, without all his heavy, black clothes on. His hair was tied behind his neck, but cascaded down his shoulder in its thick locks, decorated with three exotic, colored beads. The surprise across his face made him look even more vulnerable.

"I like you," she blurted out, otherwise ignoring his nakedness. "You've done more for me than you know, and that makes me like you." She shut the door behind her and took a half-step forward. "But even more than that, I like you for all that you are. I like that parts of you that you don't like. I like the parts that you hate. You think they make you something else, but they just make you human. I'm sorry for how I acted, and I hate this distance between us. I've hated not seeing you the last two days. I don't want it to be like that. I want to see you every day."

Silence thumped between them for multiple heartbeats. She hurriedly tried to think of something else to say, but the harder she tried, the further she seemed to get from anything articulate. The rush was finally gone and her feet were flat on the floor. She considered reaching for the door and running back to her own quarters to escape his response, or lack of one, because he wasn't saying anything.

He was just staring at her, almost as though he was wondering who she was, or if this moment was real. He slowly rose to his full height from his embarrassed, hunched position. He crossed the room and closed the distance between them. She watched his every movement breathlessly. Her eyes rose to meet his steely grey ones as he towered over her.

He lifted his hands to either side of her face, no longer hiding himself. He dipped his head down to meet his lips with hers. The sweetness of it wrapped her whole body. She could easily find herself addicted to this feeling of getting what she desired. His fingers laced though her hair, then firmly, yet gently, gripped the back of her neck and pulled her closer to him.

She could feel the heat of his naked body through her clothes. They momentarily broke their kiss, and she opened her eyes to look at him. Their gazes met, and it was the most intimate thing she had ever experienced. He was already so vulnerable before her, allowing her to see all his physical self, but now as she looked into those swimming, slate pools, she could see even deeper within him. Ronnock pulled her into an embrace and held her there. His face was nestled into the crook of her neck as he sighed heavily.

She ran her hands over his shoulders and chest, appreciating every rise and fall. His touches were firm, yet restrained, as he undressed her. Her borrowed clothes lay scattered across his floor as he laid her down on his bed, leaving her wearing nothing but her pendant. She was expectant, wanting him inside of her, but Ronnock made no move to do so.

Instead he gently caressed between her legs. The texture of his coarse hands on her soft skin there drove her wild. The decadent feeling he was building within her almost made her feel guilty. It was rich and delicious, and those same waves that she felt undulate under her bellybutton every time he looked at her were growing stronger than she had ever felt before. He held her chin with his other hand, keeping her face to his. The waves were crashing within her now, but she kept feeling that she had to hold them at bay.

"Let it go," he murmured to her.

She tried to let the wall down, but still felt something in the way. A block within her mind made her feel like she had to keep caging that feeling.

"It's ok, let it go," he said again as his hand kept its luscious momentum against her.

Then it happened. Her vision went white for a moment. Her body was tensing and releasing simultaneously. The vibration of the waves was reaching every cell in her body. He held her face to his as she shuddered, as though he was guiding her through her inner journey. The saccharine taste of pleasure coated her mouth as she felt herself begin to tremble. She closed her eyes for a moment, seeing rainbows behind her eyelids.

He wrapped her up in his arms strongly and kissed gently all over her forehead, eyes, cheeks and neck before coming back to her mouth. "Good girl, you did it." He smiled widely at her in between his kisses.

Her chest was heaving as she placed a hand on one of his cheeks. He turned his head slightly to press his lips to her palm. His face was coarse as though it was coated in sand, as he had let his facial hair grow scruffy in the past few days. No hair grew on the white scars crossing his face. The deepest cut went from eyebrow to upper lip, running diagonal across his nose. The bridge of his nose had a small dip where the cartilage had been slashed away. Her heart swelled as she took in the sight of him, thinking to herself how beautiful he was. She began to part her legs beneath him.

"We don't have to do that." He told her quietly as he laced his fingers into her hair.

"I want to sleep with you." She replied. "I want to feel what it's really like." She felt that he was going to renew her. She wouldn't be confused about what it meant anymore if he could show her the way.

Ronnock gently kissed and bit on her neck as he adjusted himself to enter her. The feeling engulfed her. Though he was within her, it felt as though he was all around her. She couldn't tell if it was truly his hands upon her, or just the feeling of all of him submerging all of her. Every inch of her skin was alive. Every part inside her was electric. It felt as though she couldn't hold him close enough to let him know how good he felt inside of her. She wrapped both her arms around the back of his neck. His breath hit her earlobes. He whispered to her that she felt so good.

Each thrust felt so wonderful she could die. Her mind wandered in the throes of pleasure. She could feel the texture of memories. She could taste feelings from childhood. He lifted her legs up so that each was over one of his shoulders, practically bending her in half. He penetrated her so deeply, she swore their souls were touching. She had no control over how her face was contorting. His hands gripped her strongly, they made her feel owned, wanted, and loved.

She looked into his eyes as the intensity between them grew. He met her gaze, and they were the only two people in the world. The bliss of it brought tears to her eyes. She saw the same shimmer cross his.

"I love you." He breathed to her.

His words intensified the sensations within and without her. She loved him. She loved how he made her feel. She loved being wanted this desperately by him. His affection made her feel powerful in ways she never knew existed. The other night when he made her bend over with her undergarments down, she thought she would feel ashamed. She thought she would feel put down by his dominating behavior, but it was rather the opposite. She had never felt so alive. She had never been so in control, in her own way. He was stronger, he was telling her what to do, but he did it all for her. He did it all because he wanted her. In that way, it was her that retained dominance. That was their trade; their give and take. They both knew it, and it was beautiful.

After he reached his peak, he lay beside her breathlessly. They pressed their foreheads together, tears in the corners of both their eyes. Hours had passed and the cool night air of autumn was drifting in from his window. Her perception of eternity was more skewed than ever as she lay in his arms. Time had always seemed to drag on for her life, but now she finally got to enjoy each moment. She absently slipped her hand between her legs, feeling his seed settled inside of her, warm and satisfying.

She nearly jumped out of her skin, out of her entire peaceful stupor, when his fingers brushed across the purple skin on her side. Parts of the wound were still nearly translucent, never fully healed, and the flesh still felt tender and electrically painful when touched. It seemed unfair to her that she could run her fingers down any one of his scars, but the second he touched her imperfection she recoiled.

"Sorry" she apologized quietly.

He chuckled slightly and moved his hand to instead rest on her waist, just below her wound. He found no seriousness in the thing that she had taken so seriously her whole life. The thing that she thought would allow no one else to love her.

Venell found herself boggled by the sound of the door opening. She couldn't quite place what it was, and it took Ronnock looking to it and tightening his grip on her arm until she put it all together. He pulled her to the side, away from the door, as thought it would protect her from what was coming.

"Shit," he muttered under his breath as the Tueagian girl Venell had seen hugging him the first night sauntered into the room.

"Ronnock?" She exclaimed, gesturing wildly at the two of them abed. Venell quickly pulled his dark sheets up to cover her naked body. "What is this? You do not love me, then?" Big tears began to roll down her cheeks from her shimmering, dark blue eyes that stood out sharply against her copper skin. She seemed to make a point to look at Venell directly with her crocodile tears. The "o" sounds in her speech were so attractively drawn out, Venell couldn't help but to feel a twinge of jealousy.

"Get out, Nai! Get out!" Ronnock shouted at her. The Tueagian girl still stared at him empty-headedly, until he finally got out of bed to shoo her out. Then she smiled wickedly, as though she had won. Her eyes suddenly appeared more green than blue, but perhaps it was just the light.

He just held a thin sheet across his groin as he took her to the door. To Venell's anger, she tried to press her body against his. Her face transformed from a devilish grin back to that of a sad, spurned damsel. "What about all the times we make love? It's no good? Did I not make you happy?" she blubbered to him.

"I've been telling you no for weeks, but you keep acting like you don't understand." He opened the door and began ushering her out. "Leave me alone, Nai. Leave us both alone."

Her arched brows narrowed and her eyes flashed an angry auburn. "You'll regret this." She spat venomously.

Ronnock shut the door and remembered to turn the lock this time. He drew his hand down his face in exasperation. "I am so sorry." He said to her. His voice was laden with shame.

"Who is she?" Venell asked him, deciding not to just let it go. She wasn't going to swallow her feelings down with Ronnock. She was going to do it right with him, and if he wanted her, he was going to have to do the same.

"Someone I should've never involved myself with, firstly," He sighed. "That's Nai, I rescued her and others from a slaver in Bardon. We we're involved for a while, but I found I didn't like a lot of things about her. She isn't taking the rejection well."

"She has feelings for you."

Ronnock sighed as he fingered the purple bead in his hair. "No, I think it's a hit to her ego." He looked over at her and place a hand on her naked thigh. "I'm sorry, it won't happen again. You're the one for me, you always have been. I just hadn't found you yet."

She accepted his words. She was glad that she had pried instead of wondering in silence and jumping to conclusions. His touch comforted her as he held her against his body. However, Venell couldn't shake the feeling that this wasn't the end of Nai's meddling in their love.

24: THE NOBLE WARRIOR

DRY PASS CANYON, THE SNANKIAN BORDER
Nehlas stared down the gorge of the canyon as though it was a foe he could intimidate. Minortai could watch each thought cross his brother's mind: he frowned as he considered walking nearly fifty miles south to an intact bridge, both losing time and risking an unwanted encounter. His brows twisted further as he considered traveling all the way north around Dry Canyon entirely. His expression softened, and his eyes darted quickly from side to side as he concluded that he needed to convince the rest of the party to scale the walls to reach the stairs carved into the far side of the cliff about a mile back north.

Party members would argue that they'd be too vulnerable, or could easily be caught in an ambush, or even a flash flood, but his patience would not allow another option. Everyone would just have to see it his way or go off on their own. He turned back to the group and presented his decision. Kajonne showed some apprehension, but after looking from her husband to her sister and sensing no fight, she stayed silent.

Minortai stayed silent too. He had been at the impasse with Nehlas many times before and each had the same outcome. It was no different now, even with his warnings and pleads. He had nothing concrete to prove his suspicions, so to Nehlas his words were mad ramblings from a dream. If he continued to argue, would Nehlas really persuade the party to abandon him? He couldn't be certain, but he had no desire to be alone, and would likely not survive given his physical state. His wound began to burn as he thought of Siyah's death and the arrogant look on Nehlas' face the day he led away the last of the reservation's defenses. Maybe this time it would be Minortai that lost his life. It would be the best-case scenario for Nehlas, as he would finally be rid of his burdensome brother.

The trail down the cliff was not difficult, Minortai knew as he trailed far behind the rest of the group, but his strength had not yet returned.

He felt short of breath with little effort, and his skin felt sweaty yet cold. He was careful not to disturb his wound, firstly because of the pain, and secondly not to undo all Kajonne's hard work. He looked up to canyon's peak, about thirty feet above his head now. The horse, Meras, had stayed for a while, unsure of where to go, but it had finally begun to wander home. Yet another reason to disagree with Nehlas' impatient choice: now they would all be on foot through the black sands of Snanka; Including one member of the party with severe difficulty walking.

Minortai pathetically scooted himself down a steep run of rock, glad the others were paying no attention. There were roots, some as thick around as his forearm, creeping through the rock, though there seemed to be no tree nor brush in sight. Nor did any birds sing or creatures scurry. Besides the conversation below him, and the sounds of his soles and buttocks scraping across the gravel trail, everything was silent and lifeless.

He stopped to listen harder. He couldn't possibly delay them any more than he already has, so it was no matter. It wasn't a peaceful silence. It was the kind the kind of silence that was hiding something. Secretive and only heard when someone was themselves silent enough to identify it. Not everyone could be that silent.

He didn't panic, but he didn't like it. Being cautious made no difference to his own safety, as he was even more useless than usual in his present state. He could see the shadows of Kaj's eyelashes cast upon her cheeks. Her freckles blended into her face with the light of the late afternoon sun. He felt sick thinking that his inability to stand up for himself may have put her in danger.

"It's full of monsters. Monsters like me." Hellan's grim warning echoed in his ears. How much a fool she would think he was if she could see him now.

Shadows were falling over the canyon as the sun began to sink over the walls, though it was still light on the ground above. He finally reunited with the party at the base. Nehlas and Wenn cast him impatient and irritable stares. Mordain and Kaj had taken the time to eat and rest themselves.

There came a sound that Minortai hadn't heard in years. A guttural mix between a growl of hunger and a cry of pain: something not animal, but not quite human. His skin prickled, and he felt his heart jolt in fear. One of them was near. He'd only heard it once before, but it was enough to remember forever. Sometimes he still heard it in his dreams.

He turned toward the South, and someone stood there that he not been there the moment before. It was difficult to make out through the spreading nightfall, but he could see that it was a young woman. She was bloodied and naked with a black, festering wound that stretched from her navel to her chest. Fresh, red blood was smeared around her face and neck and coated each of her hands like crimson gloves. Kaj gasped and called to her, taking a step forward and offering help. Minortai didn't even think, he was just reacting. He grabbed Kaj and forced her behind him. She started to object, but then that sound came again.

Then it shrieked: a piercing, painful, hungry cry. It was so quiet after it faded that he could hear Kaj's heartbeat beside him. It started running, ungracefully, as best it could with its rotting limbs, toward them. Nehlas finally realized it was not a woman anymore and approached it with his sword drawn. Kaj cried out and hid her face in his shoulder as Nehlas skillfully swung and removed its head from its neck. It kept shrieking that bloodthirsty sound until Nehlas stabbed it through the eye socket.

It was in that moment that Minortai became painfully aware that both Kaj and Wenn were unarmed, and that he and Mordain only had close-combat knives to defend themselves. He also saw unbridled fear on Mordain's face, and his pale skin and thin arms. Then himself, hobbling with stained dressings on his leg.

It was like watching roaches appear from the woodworks. Their movements and synchronicity were a storm of bloodlust. Their little party was quickly on the move, desperate to escape before the terrifying threat could get any closer. In the growing darkness, he feared they would miss the stairs. They had to be close. He would see them at any moment.

He didn't hear Mordain fall, but he heard Kaj and Wenn screaming his name. He either tripped or was grabbed and brought down, a male Red with burning eyes grasped onto both his legs and pulled the half-blood further into his grasp. Sensing blood in the water, more turned their attention to Mordain. They could smell the excitement crackling in the air. Nehlas slashed through two emaciated Red to get to the sisters. Wenn reached out to him, leaving behind her sister and brother-in-law.

Kaj was still holding onto Mordain's hand with both of hers, trying to pull him up, telling him to walk, when one of the Red ones opened his stomach and began feasting upon his entrails. His body shook as he screamed, his brain gone from the pain. Some of the Red thought they could steal their share away from the others, grabbing handfuls of Mordain's innards and running off with them, jerking his body in every direction. As one of the Red grabbed onto Kaj's wrist, Minortai smashed a rock onto its face. He put himself between Kaj and the stain that was once her husband. He could barely direct her away from the scene. She was gone inside too.

He held her face in his hands and forced her to look at him with those deep green eyes. "He's gone. I know, Kaj. I see Siyah everywhere. But they're gone and we're here. You must listen to what I say so you get out of here alive. That's what Mordain would have wanted? He would've wanted you to live, right?"

She nodded, and suddenly a look of cold focus and determination crossed her face. Her eyes looked sharp as she looked for Wenn. "Can you run?" she asked him. He shook his head. "Try to keep up as best you can."

She led the way now. Ahead of them, he could hear Nehlas' sword clashing with hordes of Red. They barely noticed as he and Kaj came up behind them. They were too focused on the commotion Nehlas was causing. Minortai saw the stairs rising out of the deathtrap behind the masses of gnashing teeth. Nehlas and Wenn must have thought they were moments from freedom before they were cut off by more Red. Minortai bitterly wondered that if the couple had escaped, would they even have looked back to see if he or Kaj had made it?

His eyes scanned for an opening between the grasping hands and gnashing teeth, but Kaj was focused on the center of the hoard. She clasped her herb scissors in her hand and began her assault. She threw a Red to the ground, stabbing it in the eye socket before moving to the next one. She kept shouting for her sister. The blood and the noise began to turn the attention of the Red. Minortai could feel the shift.

He caught a glimpse of white blonde hair and Nehlas' blade reflecting the moonlight. The hoard was thinning around Nehlas and Wenn now that they had more targets. The sun had finally sunk below the canyon, shrouding them in darkness. The next time Minortai caught a glimpse of the pair through the bloodied bodies, he saw his brother fighting alongside a silver and white she-wolf. Wenn's clothes lay scattered across the rocks. She gnashed her teeth and leapt onto a Red blocking her escape to the stairs, tearing out his throat and nearly decapitating him. Wenn spotted her chance and went first, dodging any grasping Red hands and escaping to the stairs.

Kaj saw her sister reach safety, so she quickly spun around looking for... him. She was looking for him. Her brows were furrowed, and blood flecked her cheeks and chin like her freckles did, but those green eyes were looking for him. Even with the flurry of blood and danger around him, he could help but to feel a rise of emotion deep in his chest knowing that she was looking for him. Their eyes met, and she dashed forward swiftly grabbed him by the elbow, trying to support his desperate attempt to run with her body pressed against his side. She'd stop to kick or stab at any Red that got too close. Minortai hadn't even realized they had reached the stairs until he had to swing his injured leg up the first step.

Nehlas' back was to him, below him on the stairs, effectively cutting down any Red attempting to follow them. The further up they rose, the less Nehlas had to swing. Minortai watched in disbelief as the Red piled on top of one another at the base of the steps, unable to grasp the motor concept of lifting their feet to climb a stair. They growled and cried and shrieked at their escaping meals.

In the darkness, the moving sea of bodies below them may have been swarming rats or insects. From above, they looked so pitiful. Their fevered, rotting bodies unable to think of anything but blood. Their arms outreached, thinking that if they could just stretch a little further, they could reach thirty feet above to snatch their prey. Their teeth clacked together in excitement and anticipation.

He turned away from the sea of death below. Kaj and Nehlas were breathing heavily next to him. Both slowly turned to see Wenn, who had skin-changed back to her human form. Dirt and blood streaked her face, and her silver hair was awry and sticking to her sweaty skin. She was far from the collected demeanor that she normally cast. She made no attempt to cover her nakedness, though in the night air she must have been cold. The skin from her right forearm looked as though it had been peeled away. She held the open wound out and away from the rest of her body, as though if she didn't acknowledge it, it didn't exist.

Kaj knelt in front of her sister, fumbling with the supplies she still had on her person, as if she could help the grievous injury. Even Minortai knew that surface area damage was more difficult to recover than depth. Especially out on the road, and especially in Snanka with its whipping winds and coarse, black sands.

Nehlas stood above the sisters with no emotion crossing his face. His sword was sheathed, but his hand remained on the hilt. "Was that done by their hands or with their teeth?" he asked Wenn.

She looked up at her lover, seemingly annoyed rather than suffering from the skin missing from her limb. "How would I know? All I remember is how much it fucking hurt, and what damn difference does it make?"

Nehlas pushed Kaj aside to take a closer look at the arm. "All the difference." Wenn tried to snatch her arm away but winced in pain. It was her first real reaction to the wound that Minortai had seen. Nehlas looked to him, "What do you think?"

Minortai could feel the daggers Wenn was staring at him as he approached. As he gently held her elbow to bring the edge of the wound close enough to see in the moonlight, he realized he had never been within a foot of her before. He then saw the impressions on the edge: teeth. One, or more, of the Red had scraped off her flesh with a bite, likely as she jerked her hand away while attempting to escape. Exchanging glances with Nehlas, he didn't have to give a vocalized answer.

Nehlas stood and drew his blade, then the sisters panicked. They angrily demanded what he thought he was doing. "It's a bite. We don't know how long until she becomes one of them. She'll kill each of us if given the chance."

"You don't know if it's the same for her kind, you've never-" Kaj pleaded, but Nehlas cut her off.

"It's the same. She'll become ill, then she'll wake up Red."

Wenn stared up at her lover with her steely blue eyes. "You were just using me to keep warm then?" She spat at his feet. "I sensed cruelty in you, but I was too infatuated to acknowledge it. Now I see you."

Nehlas was entirely unfazed by her stinging words. Perhaps because he already knew they were true. His hand remained on his weapon, ready for the change or a strike.

"Not everyone infected becomes like those Red." Minortai was surprised by the sound of his own voice. He hadn't meant to speak up, but his heart had made his decision before his head could say no. "Jet of the Insurgo was Red and retained his sanity. You'd deny her a chance to live and make Kaj the last person left alive in her family because you're afraid?" He felt his anger returning. Siyah's violet eyes flashed across his mind. He could almost smell lilacs over the thick scent of blood in the air.

Nehlas had to quickly retaliate, less be branded the villain in the matter. "You blame me for this, when if you hadn't been slowing us down, we would've been out of the gorge long before those things even knew we were there! You're weak, and weaker still that you thrust your ineptitude upon me. I'm the reason any of us made it out alive at all!"

Minortai took the bait, foolishly, "You won't escape the consequences of your decisions! You demanded the warriors leave the reservation, the rest of our people are slaughtered. You refused to lose time and decided we should all take the canyon trail when we were inexplicably warned not to! Maybe this time, the decision is not yours to make!"

"I am not at fault for any of this!" Nehlas seethed through a clenched jaw. "If I hadn't led, no one would've decided on any action. We would've waited until the end of time. The greth would've found them before they even took their first step! You and the others would've been wandering sheep without me to guide you." He did not acknowledge either Kaj or Wenn. "And now the wolves will come for you."

Nehlas stormed off toward the North, away from both the Insurgo and Dust's Plateau. Minortai's first thought was that Nehlas was making a spectacle, hoping that either sister or Minortai would coming fawning after him and beg him to stay, but he had burned his last bridge. No one watched him go. If it had been a show, perhaps he was too prideful to return when he realized he was unwanted. Minortai quietly wondered if he would ever see his brother again. Despite everything, that notion gave him no joy.

There was no rest to be had as the Red fever burned through Wenn. She lay wrapped in a makeshift outfit of Minortai's coat and Kaj's shawl as her body shook and sweat. She whispered apologies for every wrong in her life to Kaj, who kept shaking her head and assuring her all was forgiven.

Even all Kaj's herbal and medicinal knowledge could do nothing to slow the rage of the Red. "Stop talking like it's the end, it isn't." Kaj said through her tears.

"I'm so sorry for all the times I made you feel like you weren't one of us because you can't change your skin. See all it helped me now." Wenn's voice was becoming weaker. Minortai could only wait in silence as the two made their peace. He could taste the bitter irony of his brother's absence as he listened.

Wenn lost consciousness a few apologies later, but Kaj refused to leave her side. Both the Wenn Dell sisters clung to a thread of hope, so he would too. He offered Kaj his water skin, which she drank from gratefully. She didn't try to press it to Wenn's fevered mouth. Minortai realized that Kaj's thread was fraying.

The wound on Wenn's arm was bubbling with blisters and black rot. He watched her chest rise and fall with each breath of her turbulent sleep. He and Kaj sat there, still not speaking, only waiting. He heard the change in Wenn's breathing, her exhales became the quick, panicky pace of an infected Red, though she still did not wake up. He and Kaj exchanged glances. She was making him nervous still sitting so close to her sister. He feared that if Wenn awoke and attacked, Kaj would be bitten as well.

"Wenn," Kaj said, gently shaking her by the shoulder. There was no response. "Falerie, are you there? Wake up."

Wenn's eyes snapped open. They were burning red, and they locked onto Kaj. A long groan escaped the blonde woman's throat as she slowly began to bring the hand on her injured arm up toward Kaj. "Tell me you're there." Kaj repeated through tears and gritted teeth. The groan from Wenn began to sound more like a growl. Minortai stirred, his dagger drawn, prepared to kill the Red that possessed Wenn's body before it could take Kaj from him too.

With a cry, Kaj pierced Wenn's temple with her scissors, burying them up to the handles. The creature that was once Wenn fell back and died, its mouth open to reveal elongated eyeteeth. Kaj removed the scissors from her sister's skull and embraced her limp body. She sobbed as she rocked back and forth, holding her tightly and apologizing over and over. Minortai quietly took a seat on the ground next to her. He placed a single hand on her shoulder and looked up to the sky.

Through the gaps between the trees, he could see Siyah peeking through the leaves. He tried to think of what she would say if she were here, but he was not as strong nor as articulate as she had been. As he held Kaj there under the stars, he knew he wanted to be strong for her.

2 : CHAOS

AUGUST 1849: THE INSURGO BASE

Venell held the commander's collection of correspondence with her father in one hand and rested her chin on the other. She was nearing the end of the compilation, though she wished it could've gone on forever. For each letter she read, she could hear either her father's or the commander's voice in her head saying the words aloud.

  She still hadn't spoken to Ash since their argument on the turret. She had seen him from afar a few times, once getting a dinner plate and once whispering with the Redal girl, but she ignored him and left before he could say anything to her. She wasn't trying to punish him, but she still couldn't stand to speak with him. She knew if she did, his words would just infuriate her all over again.

She had stayed with Ronnock in his quarters the last two nights, perhaps that was part of why Ash hadn't sought her out more adamantly. To her relief, she hadn't had any more run-ins with Nai. She would be grateful to have that woman out of her and Ronnock's lives. She felt a stab of jealousy at the mere thought of her.

Ronnock had bid her farewell that morning before he and Krisae had left for Bardon. The commander had asked them to investigate the Diar Estate, where Apsonne claimed she had been hiding, and capture anyone they found alive.

"Did you tell him that the estate has a giant hole in the wall now? It seemed like it was under the control of Kras' men when we were there, how could she have possibly stayed hidden?" She inquired after he told her of the commander's request.

He was pacing around the room with his arms crossed in front of him. He had lost his hair tie somewhere in the midst of their earlier lovemaking, so his knotted locks flowed loosely over his shoulders and down his back. He too seemed perturbed at their mission. "I did, he would have none of it." Krisae even seemed confused. "I mean, he's usually stubborn, but not so unreasonable."

His lighter crackled as lit a cigarette. He paused his incessant pacing to blow the red smoke out his open window. "In the past month he's sent Krisae and I out twice together, that's more dual missions than we've shared in the past ten years." His fingers drummed on the windowsill nervously. "Maybe it's nothing, but I feel like it isn't."

"You're still going."

"Krisae is going."

She could respect that. It comforted her to see the love and respect between the two siblings. It was healthy and genuine. She wasn't sure if that kind of relationship would ever be possible to manifest between her and Ash, but she certainly hoped it was.

He said he'd return by the following morning. Their last kiss was sweet and long, and she absently touched her lips as she recalled it. Her heart fluttered within her chest when she thought about his face. Distracted by her daydreams, she shut the book of letters and tucked it under her arm. The sun had set over the horizon, and the dim lanterns were not enough light for her to read by anyway. She rose from the bench overlooking the yard from the second story. She considered seeking out Ash to try to reconcile but opted instead to make her way to Nalahi's room to see if she was available to talk. During the past few days that she had dedicated most of her time to Ronnock, she hadn't been nurturing her connection with her friend.

Something seemed off as she descended the stairs back into the inner base. She couldn't quite place the feeling of unrest in the air, until she heard an alarm sounding. The banging noise cut through the air. She didn't know for certain what it meant. Were they under attack?

The halls became crowded as she continued upon her destined path. The scents of sweat and panic flashed her back to Cynn. Her mother was telling her to stay hidden on that wooden merchant cart as everything around them swirled and collided. This was not a drill. Something was terribly wrong. The same uncertainty and fear that she felt filling her body was the same that was taking over everyone around her. The unknown was the most dangerous ingredient in a panic. People will react without thinking, like sheep being herded for the slaughter.

She couldn't tell if any the faces around her were familiar. Had she seen him before? Had they been completely invaded? The clamor of swords meeting deafened her. A couple taken in only a few days earlier were cut down in front of her by a greybearded man in a black and navy uniform coat. She could barely hear their final cries over the growing chaos as their blood spilled across the thirsty stone floor. She sprang back and took a different path, but she kept seeing the same uniforms.

So far she had gone unnoticed. Was it a coup? What was happening? They weren't Redal uniforms, so who was killing them? Venell was incredulous as she spotted a familiar shock of gold among the dark cloaks and spilled blood. Nalahi was breathing hard, both her daggers drawn and stained, her tanned face splattered with black blood.

"It's the Darkstar's men, they're everywhere in the base, them and hundreds of greth and other Redal men. It's not safe here, we're on our own again. It's time to go." Nalahi said to her. Her voice was calm, but it wavered as she spoke.

Venell disagreed. They had found a family here: a family that had been broken as they had.

"I know you have feelings for Ukon. You'll never see him again if you're dead. We have to get out of the base or we'll be trapped." Nalahi said with more force behind her voice. She held Venell's hand tenderly. "Please, you're my friend and I can't leave you."

A hand clapped on Venell's shoulder. She quickly tore herself away and readied her fists to defend herself. It was Mayan, the commander's son, supporting the weight of the captured Redal girl on his shoulder. The girl was crying and clinging to Mayan desperately while clutching her injured thigh. Nalahi repeated her speech to Mayan that they needed to escape the base if they were to have a chance of survival.

"They've already breached the inner wall. We'll never make it across the yard. Hestys and the other seniors are barely holding the line. It's only a matter of time before they capture or kill us all." Mayan said, exasperated. Venell saw that his calf was bandaged and he was avoiding putting weight on his right leg.

Nalahi searched his face desperately for another answer. "There has to be a way... we can't die here. Not after what we've survived."

Mayan exchanged a glance with the bawling princess. Venell could see they had a plan they had yet to share with Nalahi and herself. "Alright, for Cynn." He agreed. "We have to get to my father's office in the West wing. There's a hidden passage out. I'm taking Apsonne there, she's Diar's only heir. We must get her out. That's our mission. You came to the Insurgo, and now you're in it. This is your first and final task."

The young man's speech swelled in Venell's chest. The inspiration grabbed her heart, she was ready. She could do this for this place and these people that showed her that the world still held beautiful, vivid colors. She nodded and agreed fervently. She wanted Ronnock in this new world. She wanted Ash in it too, she'd love her brother no matter what. Everyone she had met here, even just in passing, was part of it now. Mayan was right, this was bigger than her and the men she loved. Nalahi agreed as well.

Mayan held a sabre in his hand but he could hardly wield it as he bore the princess's weight. Venell was unarmed, not that she would've been much help with a weapon, which left the group's defense to Nalahi. Mayan shouted out directions to Nalahi from behind Venell and she in turn successfully led them from one hall of the Insurgo's labyrinth to the next. As the golden-eyed survivor cut down a black-haired attacker, a bulky metal object went spinning out of his hand. It skidded heavily across the floor and stopped at Venell's feet.

She picked it up tentatively. Mayan exchanged glances with her. Nalahi cut down a foe ahead of them. Mayan held out his hand and Venell placed the revolver and her trust in it. For a moment she didn't hear anything and the flurry around her slowed. Mayan turned the barrel, looked to her to make sure she was watching, clicked back the hammer on the top of the weapon, and showed her how to aim. He handed it back to her. She held it close to her torso as they continued deeper into the bowels of the base.

As Nalahi rounded a corner before looking she was suddenly knocked to the ground by an armored greth. Venell clumsily aimed the revolver how Mayan showed her but hesitated. Luckily, Nalahi tripped the greth from her place on the ground and his hulking body came crashing down. He lashed out at Nalahi, and his sharp, black nails cut into flesh of her cheek. She let out a guttural roar as she drove one of her daggers into the gap between its breastplate and helm, stabbing it deep into the creature's neck. She got to her feet, bloodied and breathless.

"Let's go," she urged, taking no time to recover. Venell stared wildly at the dripping wound on her face. The cut she had received in the Saltwoods healed in a matter of seconds, but it seemed as though Nalahi's mysterious power was waning. Despite the mayhem around them, Venell couldn't ignore the knot of worry forming for her friend.

Mayan was shouting something and Venell spun around to see. He desperately pointed his sabre at a greth fighting a sandy-haired Insurgo soldier, the greth was clearly dominating. "Giness!" he called to his comrade.

Venell fumbled with her weapon again. She held it out with both hands and pointed it at the greth's unarmored chest. She pulled the trigger as she exhaled. A spray of black blood showered the Insurgo man as the greth's head exploded out the back. He looked around him in utter shock, looking lost until he saw Mayan. They embraced briefly, Mayan spoke to him hurriedly and then shifted the burden of the princess over to the skinny, sandy-haired Giness. Mayan gave his sabre a quick test swing, and they all continued on.

Venell wouldn't have recognized the door to the commander's office on her own, even though she has been there only days prior. It was unremarkable and did not appear particularly sturdy. As the five of them slipped inside, Venell noticed metal plates covering the back of the door.

The princess had a look of disbelief on her face. "We made it!" she declared.

Mayan muttered something about "not being free yet," as he approached the commander's desk. He suddenly recoiled and leapt away from where he had been kneeling on the ground. His body shook as he retched, the contents of his stomach bubbling up. Nalahi ducked under the desk to investigate. She slowly rose, a saddened look upon her face. Mayan, still visibly shaken, stifled a sob and tried to look strong.

"The commander." She mouthed to Venell.

With creaking and a plume of dust, Mayan revealed the trapdoor. It was too dark to see anything below. Nalahi, already thinking ahead, had lit the lamp from the commander's desk and held it into the chasm before them. Cobweb-covered stone steps led further down into the mysterious darkness. It was eerily quiet below, especially in comparison to the screams and clamor echoing from the other side of the office door.

"I'll lead the way," Mayan said, and Nalahi handed him the lamp. She again held a dagger in each hand. Giness and the princess followed Mayan.

Nalahi lingered at the threshold, eyeing Venell. Their first encounter seemed so strange to think back on now. It seemed it had been ages since she had first met eyes with the fur-and-leather clad wild woman, though it had been mere weeks. She admired her fellow survivor so much. She knew much of her change, her ability to find her voice, was gained from watching Nalahi live her life. She wanted to follow her down that trapdoor and continue their journey together, but her past was still too heavy.

"You're not coming." Nalahi stated. Her brows were furrowed with worry, not with anger.

"I love you, my friend." Venell said as she embraced her. Tears sprung to her eyes. She felt something damp spread across her shoulder. She thought it was blood from Nalahi's wound, but as they broke off their embrace, she saw that her golden-eyed friend was crying as well.

"Get Ash, don't be too far behind." Nalahi said, trying to force a smile. They both knew this could be the last time they saw each other.

Venell slowly lowered the trapdoor as Nalahi disappeared into the darkness. She replaced the rug to its home covering the outline of the secret route, doing her best to avoid glancing at the commander's mangled body. The sharp, metallic scent of his blood was more difficult to ignore.

She stood beside the door while listening intently for a break in the commotion. Her pulse was pounding in her ears as she cautiously turned the knob. She had barely pulled the door open when it crashed into her forcefully. She wheezed and doubled over as the knob slammed into her gut. Her head was spinning as she felt herself being gathered up in someone's arms and forced to walk. He tightly bound her wrists behind her back as he spoke to her, but she couldn't make out the words.

The banging of weapons no longer rang through the halls, but the screams had not stopped. Her captor had to lead her over the hundreds of bodies that littered the floor of the base. She could barely take a step without accidentally feeling a limb under her foot. Her stomach churned with horror and she felt tears behind her eyes. It all happened again. She had reached too close to the sun and she was coming crashing down. It all happened again just as she was learning to hope.

26: MOTHER

THE WHISPERING PLAINS, UNDERGROUND

Mayan knew the lingering wound her received from the Darkstar herself was nothing compared to the gaping hole Apsonne sustained through her thigh. It made him feel that much weaker that the pain was getting to him so fiercely. He had no choice but to press on, yet the image of his father's eyes frozen open in death kept flashing across his mind as he tried to squint through the dark tunnel. It was all too much. He had not realized how blessed his life had been in comparison to all the wayward souls the Insurgo took in. Now he was truly one of them. Now he truly felt the plague of the Redals.

    He felt some fortune in his party, at least. The Viper Girl of the Saltwoods, a formidable foe of the crown, without whom they may not have made it this far. Prince Diar's heir, Apsonne, and his longtime friend Giness Anshee. Giness was as seasoned as he was kindhearted, and Mayan trusted him with his life. Mayan led their small troupe, the lamp in one hand and his sabre in the other, followed by Giness and the princess, with Nalahi guarding their tail.

"Where does this lead?" Nalahi hissed at him from the rear of the group.

"I don't know, Father never told me where it went, only that it existed for crises. Maybe he thought it best that no one knew?" His father's plans had always a mystery to him.

He wished his last conversation with him hadn't been regarding his act of defiance. He had just wanted the opportunity to prove to his father that he was as worthy a comrade as all the Insurgo, in strength and in loyalty, but the commander would hear none of it. Disobedience was a pestilence and Mayan had brought it into the base. Father had always been hard on him but it had only made Mayan want to work harder for his approval.

Even with the oil lamp at full capacity, Mayan could barely see a few feet ahead of him. He tried to check all angles of the tunnel as they shuffled through, just as he had been taught, but he had a hard time looking up from his feet to make sure he wouldn't trip. As they pressed on, the hard-packed dirt path became sticky with mud. Roots of trees snaked like vines above their head. Mayan wondered if they were being led west to the Saltwoods or east to Piaces or the foot of the Crags. Beneath the muck, he could see there were stones paved below.

"Wherever it leads, we should seek refuge in Snanka. My mother remains at the Insurgo Headquarters across the border. Apsonne will be safe there and the rest of us can pick up where we left off."

"Great, more Ukons." Nalahi muttered to herself. He heard Giness chuckle from behind him, a welcome sound after the hell they had just escaped. Perhaps everything would be all right after all.

"I trust you, Mayan, thank you." The princess said sweetly.

Mayan couldn't help but to smile. He had been growing fond of Apsonne, whom was not much older than himself, and had enjoyed their time at the base the past couple of weeks. He would help her get around, and she would introduce him to books that she recognized in the base's meager library. Her pale green eyes reminded him of a meadow. They shared almost all of their meals, usually discussing how far he had gotten through her favorite titles. He never thought he would be grateful for all the boring reading lessons he used to have to sit through. Apsonne would playfully call him her savior. It was only yesterday she touched his hand for the first time, he still felt his stomach flutter thinking of it.

The group began to cough and gag as a rank smell began to fill the tunnel. It had begun as a wafting, unpleasant odor, but the stench rapidly grew unbearable. It seemed to only get worse the further they went into the tunnel, but there was no possibility to go back. Only death awaited them there. For all he knew, the passage had already been compromised, and greth and Redal soldiers were pouring in the other end.

The lamp light shifted as it bounced off a slanted wall of earth before them. "A dead end." He grumbled aloud. He lifted the lamp, investigating all the walls around them, but found nothing. They were trapped in this stinking tunnel. Why would his father even build the escape route if it went nowhere?

"Wait, let me see that." Nalahi said, relieving him of the lamp. She examined the dirt walls, even digging her fingers into them as she looked for a hidden passage. Drops of water landed on her bare shoulder, arresting her attention. She lifted it as high as she could and pointed to the ceiling. "There's another trapdoor, we just have to get up to it." She stated. Mayan looked up and saw that she was right. Water dripped from a rotting wooden square surrounded by muddy soil.

Nalahi sheathed her daggers. The jagged wounds across her face had finally stopped bleeding and were beginning to scab. Giness shifted Apsonne to Nalahi's arms. She held the princess up with one arm and lifted the lamp high with the other. Giness hoisted Mayan up onto his shoulders. They agreed Mayan would be the one to climb up, even though he was larger than Giness, because he could barely hold his own weight on his injured leg, much less another man's.

He and Apsonne exchanged a coy glance before he ascended, and he felt that flutter in his stomach again. He hoped she was seeing that he was a capable leader and that she could trust him with her safety. He would protect her at all costs.

Giness hoisted him up. They teetered around for a few moments, trying to gain their balance. He felt around the perimeter of the soaked wood as he tried to find which side was loosest. When it didn't budge, he opted instead to wrap his coat around his fist and punch through the soft, wet slats. The wood gave way easily, and he peeled back broken pieces to make an opening big enough for him to fit through.

He carefully stood on Giness' shoulders, the skinny soldier wavering slightly to keep steady. Mayan peered out of the hole he made and was surprised to see the manicured Southern foliage that indicated they were approaching the Capital. Night had fallen and the air was wet and cold. He shouted down to Giness that the tunnel had led them south.

He thought that this is what it felt like to be one of the senior Insurgo; to have adventure and solve mysteries. He was succeeding too. His team was special, he knew, they would be the ones that would help rebuild what was lost once they reached Snanka. It would be their names going down in the history annals at the capital after the Redals were finally overthrown.

When he looked back up, he only saw the long, needle-like points of a greth's teeth. He couldn't fit his arms out of the hole, only his head. He had trapped himself. He could only look into the creature's bulging yellow eyes as it grabbed a fistful of his hair with one hand and held its long, saw-like sword to his throat with the other. He felt the point of it pierce his skin, but nothing else. The feeling of liquid filling his throat overwhelmed his other senses. He tried to shout to Giness to lower him down, but he only sputtered out blood. The greth stared straight into his eyes, smiling and laughing as Mayan choked. He couldn't breathe. He tried to inhale, only to feel hot bubbling in his throat.

The creature's terrible face finally disappeared as Giness must have sensed something was wrong. Mayan found himself on his back in the mud, looking up to three faces surrounding him. Nalahi pressed fabric onto his throat. He knew it was no use. Apsonne sobbed, it hurt him to see those pale, green eyes weeping on his account. He only wanted to make her smile. The blur of movement behind her was Giness jumping to the group's defenses.

"Mayan, it's just as important to pay attention to your lessons is as it is to be a fighter." His mother told him as he fidgeted in his chair. "The best soldiers are the smart ones." She always knew what to say to keep his attention. He itched to play swords with the other boys so he could be a great warrior like his father, but mother insisted on book lessons.

He felt the warm sun on his skin as he sat with his mother on the terrace at Onyx Castle. He had never much liked the stuffy place except the upper promenade, covered with flowering vines to provide shade from the hot, Snankian sun, so that's where his mother chose to teach him to read, write and count.

He looked up into her dark, green eyes, wondering to himself how someone could be so beautiful. He could only hope that one day his wife would be as beautiful and smart as her. He thought he might be crying as he thought of those long afternoons with her. It had been years since he had seen her and much too long since he felt himself comforted in her arms. How foolish he was to ever think he had outgrown her embraces. He held her flaxen hair between her fingers just as he used to do as a child. It was so different from his own coarse black hair that it fascinated him. "I'm sorry, Mom."

"I love you, Mayan. You did well, and I'm so proud of you. Just rest, my little boy."

Mayan closed his eyes.

27: BROTHER

THE INSURGO BASE

Venell was led down an unfamiliar hall within the base. The Redal soldier shoved her roughly from behind as he held her bound hands painfully against her back. He was clad in typical Redal red and gold, while the Darkstar's men that swirled around here were adorned in navy and black. Greth stalked the halls with their vicious teeth bared and their weapons stained. Many carried treasures and any other loot they thought might be of value. Her captor stopped her at the end of a line-up, where soldiers were holding other captured Insurgo in a similar fashion. Her left her unattended there, sensing no fight from her.

She saw Ash held just few feet from her. Their eyes met, just like they had the night they clung to life in the trees. She wanted to run to him.

She knew he could feel her reaching out to him with her soul since she could not with her arms. She wished she could take back the harsh words she spoke to him the last time they were together. Black greth blood soaked his clothes and had splattered across his face, blended with the fresh red from a wound across his brow. Although he must have been standing still for some time, his breathing was still heavy from battle.

A tall woman with braided, dark brown hair and a masculine build strutted down the line-up. The way she carried herself made it clear she was in charge. Venell thought to herself that she must be the Darkstar. A long, navy blue waistcoat hid most of her skin, but Venell could see that her hands were covered in bandages, as was the right side of her face. One hand was placed behind her and the other on the hilt of her curved sword. She stopped just before Ash and examined him. Her eyes narrowed with hatred.

She turned on her heels and made her way out of the hall, waving her hand to gesture at the officer at the corner, standing at attention for her signal. She disappeared from sight, though Venell could still hear her heeled boots clacking against the floor from a distance.

The short, thick-chested officer walked alongside a long-haired greth wielding a hammer. Two other young men, new Insurgo recruits, were captured and held to Ash's right. One more, an older man, to his left. The officer and greth stood before the first Insurgo recruit. The officer sneered and the greth flashed its long, needle-like teeth. The young man recoiled from the red-skinned creature, closing his eyes and turning his head.

His face wrinkled up as he held back tears. She heard a cruel laugh uttered from the officer, but she couldn't tell what he was saying to the recruit to make him shake his head so vehemently. The young man looked up to meet the officer's gaze, tears and mucus streaming down his reddened face as he pleaded for what Venell could only assume was his life.

With a shrug the officer waved his fat hand nonchalantly before meandering down the lineup. The long-haired greth lifted its hammer above its head and brought it down on the young recruit. His head split and his body hurtled to the floor. Venell could feel her heartbeat in her throat. She watched as Ash avoided both the sight of the man's broken skull and Venell's eyes. He kept his head down and forward.

The second recruit in line jolted forward, trying to escape his captors. He lost all composure just as the first did. A pool of blood was quickly spreading across the stone, seemingly following the officer's heels as he stopped in front of the second recruit. This one was angrier and more adamant in his pleas to live. Venell heard him say "I don't know!" over and over. "I never saw her!"

She knew they were going to kill him too. And Ash...

She found herself trying to rush to her brother, but someone suddenly grabbed her bound hands behind her back. "Whoa, don't do anything stupid now." The soldier said to her quietly. She could tell he meant it; asking her to preserve her own safety.

She couldn't turn enough to see her captor but she did her best to get a glimpse of the black waterfall of hair behind her. "That's my brother, the next is my brother." She whispered harshly to him. She wasn't sure if her admission would save or condemn them, but she had to try.

"Then I hope he knows where Diar's daughter is. Or that you do."

Venell heard the disgusting crunch and thud as the greth's hammer broke apart the second recruit's skull. The pair then stopped in front of Ash. A burning sense in her stomach bubbled upwards, so high that she could feel the churning in her throat. Ash was saying something to the officer. She wasn't sure if he was speaking too quietly for her to hear, or if the panic in her head was drowning out all other sound.

"And what makes you think you're more important than those two sacks of meat, there?" the officer loudly said to Ash as he gestured to the two dead recruits. Ash kept eye contact with the officer as he responded. The officer was silent for a moment as he seemed to be studying Ash's face. "Intriguing, but it won't make any difference if you can't help me."

It was too close, much too close. She turned back as far as she could to look at her captor. His eye was so black she couldn't see his pupil, yet she could tell he was looking at her. "In the commander's office. Behind the desk there's a trapdoor to a passageway." She said. She hoped Ash couldn't hear her.

Her captor loosened his grip on her. "What of it?" He asked, leaning down toward her face. His other eye was covered with a black leather patch.

"Diar's daughter escaped through that passage. I don't know where it leads, but that's where she went." The weight of her betrayal was unbearable. Nalahi would never have done what she just did. She would've taken it to the grave with defiance on her face.

Her captor didn't miss a beat. He whistled and gestured to the other officer. "Hamden, got it."

The officer looked incredulous. Soldiers began to align around her captor as she was handed off to someone else. "Well, looks like it's you are more important, Keoneo." He sneered at Ash. He stepped away, calling to others to fall behind the one-eyed man that had held her.

"I want her with my men and taken back to my chambers, not with the other prisoners. Do not make me ask twice." He said to another soldier, resting his unnerving gaze upon her. He was a tall, handsome man in a rugged way. His olive skin was complimented by waves of raven-black hair and a scruffy beard to match.

Ash and the only other remaining Insurgo man were being taken with the officer instead. Worse than imprisonment, they were going to be separated. "My brother..." she said to the one-eyed man.

"He shouldn't have been foolish enough to toss around a famous name. I'll never be able to get him away from Kras' men." He held her chin and looked into her eyes. "But you're not foolish. You're a good girl. A smart girl. I can protect you, but you must do as I say. I can assure you the only way for you to ever see him alive again is for you to be quiet now."

She was quiet, but her eyes were on Ash. He was trying to look back at her over his shoulder. It seemed as though for a moment everyone's back was to Ash but her. No one was watching him, and the hammer-bearing greth was suddenly looming behind him. The short, auburn-haired soldier holding Ash's bindings stopped to speak to a comrade. The greth shoved soldiers out of his way until only Ash and the auburn-haired soldier were in his path. The soldier argued, but a hammer to his ribs was stronger than his words.

Ash tried to dodge the hammer coming down from above him, but the blow caught him heavily in his shoulder. He cried out and fell to the ground, his right arm hanging loosely from his torso where the impact had shattered his bones. Chaos began to swirl amongst the troops. Shouts to stop, orders and threats were being barked as they rushed to stop the greth's hands from coming down again. The creature was too big and too strong.

"Fuck Jet Keoneo!" the greth roared out.

"Fuck you!" Ash screamed at the greth, his teeth stained red from his bloody mouth.

The greth roared, knocking a soldier off his arm and bringing its hammer down. For a moment, in that hideous creature, Venell saw something very familiar in its face. The world slowed and became silent. The crimson pool on the stone ground was spreading beyond the circle of men still trying to detain the hammer-wielding greth. Lights trailed in her eyes every time she turned her head to either side. She felt herself losing her footing, but her captor held her up by her underarms. She felt the chain of her pendant snap as his finger got caught beneath it.

Everything went dark as a thick, black material was wrapped around her eyes. "You'll be glad you didn't see." Her captor said to her in his quiet, yet deep, voice.

"Let me see him." Venell demanded. She still couldn't quite seem to get her feet flat on the ground. He didn't respond. He must have been fed up with her stumbling and just lifted her over his shoulder as he hurried from the hall where it happened. She repeated herself, with no response. "Let me see him! Let me go! Let me see him!" she shrieked. She thrashed around, trying to twist herself away from his grasp. She was being moved further and further away from where Ash was, but she had to get to him. She needed him.

Her blindfold was lifted just for a moment, and she was met with her captor's single eye. "I see my brother's head dashed across the battlefield every day and night in my memories. You won't have to." He said soothingly in his baritone.

She broke. Her heart broke and her hope broke. She shook her head and tried to reach out to the one-eyed man, seeking any comfort, though her hands were still tied. He wrapped her in an embrace and pressed her face against his chest.

"They killed him? They really killed him?" she sobbed to him.

"I'm sorry, yes. Let's get you out of here, girl. I'll keep you safe."

He began to lead her away. Her mind felt like it was full of muddy water, confused and painful. She couldn't accept his words. She wrenched herself away from him suddenly, though she was unable to see and immediately found her feet tangled. She fell to the ground, her face smacking against the floor as she was unable to catch herself with her bound hands. She ignored the throbbing pain in her cheekbone and rubbed her face against the stone tiles until the blindfold rolled up above her eyes, but all she could see was a uniformed body on the floor, blocking everything else in the hall. By then, the one-eyed man was already picking her up.

As she rose, she saw. She saw him. She started screaming. It was his face, but it wasn't his face. The one-eyed man quickly pulled the cloth back over her eyes.

"I was telling you the truth. Now you'll be seeing that the rest of your life." He said to her, with less sympathy than before.

She was lost. Everything was lost. Everything she had gained, everything she had built was crashing down. All of the steps forward, undone. She had no direction, all she could do was coddle her broken heart.

28: HOPE

THE INSURGO BASE

Ronnock looked down into the yard as the sun rose. It was a red sun this morning, fitting for the violent night before. He couldn't hear Krisae from where he stood, but he could tell by her body language that she was giving instruction to the surviving Insurgo. No one had heard a word or seen a sign of Iratez, and everyone assumed the worst.

He turned from the yard to the halls of the West wing. The Valehoutton base was lost. There was no rebuilding; not the structural damage nor the human loss. Less than a hundred remained when they had once been two thousand strong. He tried to be grateful that he and Krisae were among the survivors, but the guilt of coming upon the base at the end of the battle was unbearable. He couldn't help but to feel suspicious that the commander had sent them away hours before the attack.

Krisae, the interim commander, had graciously granted him the task of searching for people of interest among the dead. She did so because she knew he was restless and desperate to find Venell, but also didn't want to give him special leave. She had to be disciplined, now more than ever.

He had seen no sign of either Keoneo, Nalahi, Mayan, or the captured Redal girl that likely sparked this retaliation from the Darkstar. The conversation he had with Mayan before he snuck out to the plains with Ash haunted him. He couldn't help but to feel that he was to blame for all this death. He could've dissuaded his nephew, and that girl would be with her own fucked-up family so that he could be with his.

He continued turning over each body he found, writing down the name of each face he recognized as he went. He had a sinking feeling in his stomach that with their few numbers, they would be unable to bury all of them. Hestys. Rigel, the kitchen boy. The next one he couldn't identify, his face and head smashed in. He tried to be meticulous going from one corpse to the next, but sometimes he would see someone he had known well and would be drawn to say his goodbyes. It wasn't getting harder nor easier with each. As he rose from the destroyed skull, writing down details of the man's clothing instead, he caught a familiar scent amongst all the blood. He couldn't quite pin it down, so he followed it, leaving the task at hand for later.

Then he saw him. Laying in a pool of his own blood, likely mingled with that of all the dead around him. His shoulder was broken, and his arm jutted out at a terrible angle, but worst of all the left side of his head had been struck clean off. The damage aligned almost perfectly with the shaved line of his hair. His left eye was gone, caved in to the rest of his skull, but the right was frozen open with rage and defiance.

He went out the way he lived, Ronnock thought. He tenderly placed his hand on Ash's face and closed his remaining eye with his thumb. His fingers rubbed over the stubble on the side of the boy's head, and for some reason Ronnock felt himself close to tears. After finding all his friends and comrades dead in the halls, this angry boy was the one that got him emotional. It was not for his own grief, but for Venell's, unless she was dead too. He wiped his eyes and moved on. He tried to concentrate on documenting more of the fallen, but now his mind clouded with sorrow.

His foot kicked something small and metal that clinked repeatedly as it skidded across the otherwise silent corridor. He stooped to pick it up and saw it was a necklace. Stunned, he rushed back to Ash's maimed body. He felt around the boy's neck, trying to ignore the cold, slick texture of his crushed shoulder. His fingers grasped the metal chain and pulled.

He held up Ash's pendant in one hand, the same one he had returned to Venell in Bardon, and the necklace in the other. They were the same size, but this one instead depicted the sun with an inlay of orange agate on the copper pendant. He could faintly smell her on it. He recalled it sitting just below her collarbone when she lay in bed with him two nights before.

He held it to his chest over his heart and allowed himself to cry again. He had to believe she was alive. He had to hope that she hadn't seen what became of Ash. When he awakened from his daze, he realized how close he was to the commander's office. The door was open, a bad sign, he thought, but the office was empty. Not much seemed to be out of place, other than the desk lamp missing.

As he approached the other side of the room, he was taken aback for a moment when he saw Iratez's body seemingly stuffed beneath his own desk. Blood stained the clothes across his gut and chest. Ronnock wasn't sure which thought he had was darker: that the wounded commander had cowardly hidden from battle and died, or he was murdered in the commotion and the killer tried to hide their deed. The commander's huge body would not have been easy to drag into such a small space.

Nonetheless, Ronnock held his fist over his heart. "May your soul be at peace, sir." He said to the man who had taken him in at the lowest point of his life. As he rose, he decided he would go tell Krisae of the commander's fate rather than continue his search.

It was then that he noticed the opened trapdoor against the back wall. A cream and blue rug had been tossed aside and the wood door lay agape, revealing an underground staircase. He looked up to Iratez again, as if the late leader could tell him something. He died trying to defend a secret, it seemed, a secret that had been found.

Ronnock approached the staircase. As he peered down into the darkness, he understood why the desk lamp was missing. After retrieving another, he returned to the passage. Small specks of blood flecked the stone steps that descended to the dirt path below. Someone that passed through had been wounded, though not grievously. He tried to identify the smell of the blood, but it was dry and the scent was gone.

The tunnel looked very much the same as he continued: a straight path, no alternate routes and a low earth ceiling that began showing signs of vegetation above. One look at his compass let him know the course was taking him south. A rotten smell suddenly began to fill the stagnant air. Ronnock gagged as it took him unsuspecting. It wasn't the smell of death, of that he was glad, but it was unbearably rank. Then he saw a body. He didn't know who or what he had expected to find, but it wasn't this.

He took his nephew in his arms. It was infinitely unfair that such a clever and caring young man had his chance to learn and live snatched away. The boy's throat had been penetrated with a jagged blade. A bloodied coat was wadded up near Mayan's body, as though someone had been using it as a compress. At least he hadn't died alone. Rheena was going to be devastated; her husband and her eldest son were both gone.

At a dead end, Ronnock looked to ceiling to see an open hole. The floor was riddled with booted footprints, indicating to him that the Darkstar's men had also found the passage. Whether it was before or after Mayan had, he couldn't say. Then he saw that one set was barefoot: Nalahi. If she had come through the passage, hopefully one of the other pairs of footprints belonged to Venell. He tried to soothe himself with the knowledge that she could be safe, but he couldn't quite settle his doubts. The bare prints didn't double back, so she either escaped or was carried. Mayan's slight frame was easy for Ronnock to carry back.

He placed his nephew upright against the wall and closed the trapdoor. With morbid curiosity at his hand, Ronnock pulled out the top drawer of the commander's desk. It was empty besides a loaded pistol. Ronnock placed it in his pocket and opened the next drawer. He found letters to Rheena and Inca, along with a portrait Rheena from when she was a teenager. Another drawer was full of cigar butts, as if the commander was trying to hide his habit. He began to close it, but he thought the weight of it seemed odd.

 He reopened it, and knew his face twisted in disgust as he forced his fingers down into the wet ends of the cigars. He felt a crack within the wood and gently lifted the false panel. He withdrew a handful of papers. He felt a lump rise in his throat without even opening the first one. The commander obviously had something he was hiding, and Ronnock had a terrible feeling about it.

 He sat back against the wall across from where the bodies were laying. He hesitated unfolding the packet. Maybe he didn't want to know what was within the pages. He inhaled deeply and opened the first to find a letter. Whatever was within it was more important than him and someone had to know. He couldn't believe what he was seeing. His eyes flew over every word as he fervently unfolded each subsequent letter.

 The papers were correspondences between Iratez and either the Darkstar or her right-hand man, Basaulte. The commander had been seeking a lasting peace with the Redal heiress, promising the Insurgo's loyalty to her if she should ascend the throne. The diction made Ronnock believe that Iratez both feared and admired the Darkstar. He was clear in his rejection of Kras as a ruler, but not to the Redals as a dynasty. He felt tears for what seemed like the hundredth time today. While he could understand what the commander was searching for, he knew that most of the Insurgo would reject any Redal alliance.

And it was the Darkstar that infiltrated and destroyed the base. He had seen Basaulte on a far turret the previous night with his own eyes, the man's hulking frame and flowing raven hair was impossible to mistake. Why would she have betrayed their agreement? Was is her plan from the beginning to destroy them? Their support would have benefitted her claim, it didn't make any sense.

He refolded all the letters and placed them back into their hidden compartment. He dug the commander's husky body out from its place under the desk to the wall where he had placed Mayan. He covered both their wounded bodies with the blue and cream rug. As his gaze rested on Mayan for a moment, he thought of the clash his nephew had just had with the Darkstar the previous month, and how furious Iratez had been when he had heard of it. Ronnock hoped the skirmish had nothing to do with the attack. He lit a cigarette with his shaking hand, then went to find Krisae.

She seemed utterly exhausted, a strange expression to see on her, but an understandable one. After their entirely unsuccessful investigation in Bardon, they returned to find themselves in battle. Now Krisae was the one left to make all the big decisions about where the Insurgo went from this hellish pit. The weight of personal tragedy was an additional burden, though Krisae was one that could bear it.

He saw her slip from her commanding character for just a moment when he reported to her that both Iratez and Mayan had been killed. He said nothing of the letters. She quickly wiped away the tears forming and steadied herself. "I had a feeling about the commander." She said stoically. Ronnock knew that she had still been holding on to secret hope that her newest father-figure had survived.

"Despite the risk I face myself by returning to Snanka, I think it is best for the Insurgo that we join what remains of our force with larger numbers." She said matter-of-factly. "I know you face the same risk, but I hope you'll accompany us nonetheless."

The king of Snanka had massive bounties placed on both him and Krisae. They wouldn't be safe anywhere in the country. Even your staunchest ally would turn you over to the enemy for that many riches, and more than just death awaited them should they fall into King Nordin's clutches. However, that wasn't the reason Ronnock was struggling to commit to escort his sister to their homeland.

"She's out there somewhere near the Capital."

"Mayan's dead, and the Redal girl and Nalahi are missing. They may have taken her captive."

"Even more reason to get to her."

Krisae gave him a pleading look. They both knew the dungeons at Star Palace were impenetrable and attempting a rescue would essentially be a suicide mission. The fact meant little to him, however, especially when he thought of the soft sound of her voice. Ronnock would die for her a hundred times. His life meant nothing if he could give her safety and happiness.

Ronnock embraced his sister tightly. She veiled a sob against his chest, making sure that she looked strong in front of the tattered men she had to lead across the country. "God, please don't get killed." She whispered to him. "I love you, Ron. Please don't do anything too reckless."

He held her under her chin and smiled, "You're the reckless one, don't worry about me." Her eyes were still glossy with tears that she was holding back. He kissed her on the forehead. "Love you too, little sis."

Ronnock mounted Khazar within the hour and rode south with the heavy burden of hope in his heart.

29: THE TRUTH

AUGUST 1849: WEST OF THE CAPITAL

After trekking across all of northern Valehoutton, Jayen found herself nearing the capital. She followed the stars of the Matricider along the spine of the Crags until she was in the southernmost region of the country. As night fell, she took shelter in a grassy area beneath the cover of a jutting rock face. She sat cross-legged under the awning, still in the sights of the Matricider.

She had pondered little besides the reason that the Deep of the earth had chosen to spare her life. She kept trying to shake the feeling that she was unworthy of such a gift, but who was she to question the verdict of the higher powers? She closed her eyes and slowed her breathing.

She was in the throne room of Star Palace, but it was unlike what she had seen in her previous vision. Moth-eaten curtains hung over the windows. A stuffy scent of sweat and mildew overwhelmed her senses. The throne itself was leaning to one side as its base rotted. The grand doors at the opposite end were closed and slathered in a thick coat of red lacquer.

Sudden screams drew her out of the room. She saw a dark-haired woman being attacked by a skinny, scarred man with a shaved head. The woman's face and chest were pressed against the glass of an uncovered window. Jayen could hear the sizzle of the woman's skin burning in the light. A statuesque man with flowing black hair tore the assailant away from the woman. He crushed the smaller man's throat with his bare hands, then took the woman into his arms.

The smell of sulfur overpowered the rest of her senses as she found herself in a strange, dry wood. A towering figure shrouded in dark blue robes offered his hand out to a small girl with blood staining her chest and hands. She was unwounded, it was not her own blood. The child's golden eyes narrowed into cat-like slits as heat swelled under her skin.

She opened her eyes and felt the lush grass beneath her. Someone was coming. She hid herself behind a twisted tree, opting to observe who was passing through instead of attacking. She cautiously glanced around the side of the trunk. There were three people: a man and two women. One of the women seemed to be grievously injured. Jayen chose to make her presence known and revealed herself to the group.

The golden-haired woman was immediately on the defense, while the man was laden with the weight of the wounded one. Her fierce eyes burned like molten metal. They sparked Jayen's memory. Four deep claw marks on her face let Jayen know that she had recently done battle with a greth. She had been right to show herself. She raised her hands to show that her weapon was sheathed. "I heard you coming. I'm of the Godsmoors. I mean you no harm."

"You'll be dead if you do." The woman growled in response.

"Nalahi, we can't keep moving." The man said. The red-haired woman wavered as she began to lose consciousness. A flowering of blood appeared on her light pink dress near her thigh, though she held her lower stomach with both hands. As her arms fell limply to her sides, Jayen saw that the woman's abdomen had been sliced open. The wound was dreadfully reminiscent of the one that Jayen had barely survived.

The man laid her out upon the grass. Jayen delicately lifted the dress where it had been torn. As she lowered it, she looked to the two conscious travelers. "She won't make it through the night." She said softly.

The man drug his hand down his face, visibly upset. "I couldn't fight them all off, we were outnumbered with the low ground..."

"Then we'll have to leave her." Nalahi replied firmly. Jayen could tell she was trying to appear more unsympathetic than she was.

"It would be cruel to leave her to die alone." The man responded.

The red-head suddenly regained consciousness with a strenuous gasp. Her pale green eyes looked worriedly from one of them to the other. "I lied to the Insurgo when they questioned me, someone has to know." She frantically blurted out. "My father is dead. A sickness carried him away months ago, but we kept it a secret so his supporters would not lose faith or flock to Kras."

"That would make Delinda the heir since no males remain." The man said to Nalahi, "The woman that just destroyed the base."

The red-head grabbed onto Jayen's arm desperately. Her breath was labored, but she was trying to tell them something important. Jayen looked down at her, waiting for her words with a soothing gaze. She held the girl's hand softly.

"The Caeruleans: there are two. There are twin boys with my aunt, Iris Baras, in Southern Mesa. They're direct descendants of Bethell and Raytara. My father hid them there, he had been planning to support the eldest's claim ever since Kras ordered Cynn's destruction. They have the eyes... the Caerulean eyes." She paused and closed her eyes. She was losing consciousness.

Jayen's destiny was becoming ever clearer. She had seen those boys in her dream when the Deep of the earth had spared her. The girl didn't reopen her eyes. Her chest rose and fell a final time and she laid still. She had passed the burden of her knowledge on to someone else, and now she could rest. Jayen touched her face, which was quickly becoming chilled in the falling night air, lamenting silently on yet another young life gone too soon.

"The stars have been leading me to the Caeruleans, and now I cross paths with this poor child." Jayen said as she rose. She met Nalahi's suspicious gaze, careful to look the woman in the eyes instead of the jagged wounds on her cheek. "I'll be going to Snanka to seek out those boys."

Nalahi didn't speak at first. She just stared at the girl's lifeless body with hate in her eyes. Her fists were clenched, and teeth gritted. Jayen could see that even through her fiery anger, she was thinking clearly. "We're going to Snanka as well, to the Insurgo headquarters, but first..." She looked back to the sandy-haired man. "We're only a few miles from Star Palace. We could end this. We could open the door for the Caeruleans." Jayen was not following what she meant. "Giness has been within the walls, he knows how to get into the inner keep."

"You speak of revenge." Jayen said.

"Don't act like you know any of my intentions," Nalahi snapped at her. "I understand this is much bigger than my desires." She looked from Giness to Jayen. "If either of you are coming, don't slow me down."

"You were Aldrion's for some time, but not anymore." Jayen found herself saying. She couldn't mistake the towering figure she had seen with what she had been told from legends from her youth.

Nalahi stopped in her tracks. She didn't turn to face Jayen when she replied. "Not anymore." She repeated. "I don't need him to fulfill this."

"The Darkstar has returned to the Capital." Jayen warned.

"Then she can fucking die too."

Giness shrugged and followed Nalahi. Jayen sensed he liked her volcanic demeanor, it fulfilled what his quiet nature could not. While she was unsure of the Keeper's abandoned protégée, Jayen thought there would be no other reason for the Deep to show her Nalahi's past just before their meeting. Unless, perhaps, it was a warning. She followed the pair regardless.

They reached the palace just before daybreak. The sky was still blackened, though a streak of indigo was beginning to appear across the horizon. Giness led them to the western wall, claiming there were footholds to scale the wall enough to reach one of the narrow footbridges that led to the inner keep where Kras' chambers were.

"And the sun is rising," he said gesturing to the horizon. "She's called the Darkstar for a reason. We'll only be dealing with the weaker of the two Redals."

Jayen's body still felt strong and invigorated, even after her long journey from the North. She went first up the palace wall, working slowly, but without faltering, to find an alcove between one of light, sand-colored blocks to the next. She was also cautious to avoid the narrow, stained-glass windows that dotted the second through fifth stories. They called Star Palace impregnable, it had always been so. Jayen recalled how easy it was to create false truths with words, for she could see now that even someone less skilled than she could make their way to the footbridge. The skinny Giness Anshee only a few feet beneath her confirmed this.

The light of the rising sun was making the wall easier to climb, though Jayen also knew that they would easily be spotted from the ground now. Their time was running short and they would be easy prey clinging to the rampart. She risked a glance down. They were nearly fifty feet from the ground, certainly enough to waste the Deep's gift if she misjudged a step.

She was even with the footbridge now, a skinny passage leading from a single, fortified door, across the courtyard below, to the inner keep. It was only wide enough for one person to cross at once, making invasion from an army impossible. But it was not impossible for Jayen.

She had to climb sideways to get herself close enough to the bridge to pull herself up. The arched stone was just out of reach now. For the first time during her ascension, she felt fear bubble in her throat when one of her feet slipped within the nook she had shoved it into. Rubble from the hole shook loose and fell to the ground below. All three of them froze in place, hoping there was no one below.

The tinkling sound of the pebbles hitting metal alarmed her even more. She peeked down into the courtyard through the gap between her arm and the wall. A pair of armored guards, both drenched in rich scarlet capes, exchanged glances.

"This fuckin' place is falling apart." One said to the other. His counterpart nodded, and they both turned back to face the yard.

Jayen exhaled, almost not believing her own fortune. She grasped onto the smooth stone of the bridge and hoisted herself up. A small platform outside the door leading into the main palace had enough space to allow the three of them to stand and regroup. She helped Giness onto the bridge, though Nalahi declined her aid. The woman with eyes like molten gold glanced down at the pair of guards, then to Jayen crossly.

"You almost gave us away!" she hissed angrily under her breath.

"Now you are." Jayen whispered back to her. Not much broke her patient demeanor, but this woman's constant irritability was testing her.

They all fell silent again as the sound of a door opening and metal clanging broke the silence of the early morning. The castle was beginning to wake up. The two guards below them both went inside the main palace, leaving the trio with no more obstacles.

"You didn't have to come, why are you even here? Why were you so close to the Capital anyway?" Nalahi snapped, risking her voice to be a little louder now that they were alone.

"This is not the time, you're sabotaging your own undertaking." Jayen replied as coolly as she could, though she could hear the sharpness in her own tone.

"Not the time? What are you hiding? Only a liar would avoid an answer." Nalahi spat accusingly.

"Ladies, please, there's no need-" Giness began to interrupt.

"Shut up!" Both she and Nalahi practically shouted, each of them growing more venomous than the other.

He stood between the two of them as they continued their vehement, accusatory argument. Jayen couldn't even recall the last time she had been so heated, she had forgotten what passion was like.

The last thing she remembered saying was along the lines of threatening to throw Nalahi from the bridge, but she didn't get to finish. The metal-plated door that led into the main palace suddenly creaked open, and the rhythmic sound of soldiers' steps made Jayen's heart sink into her stomach.

30: AN UNKNOWN SOUND

AUGUST 1849: STAR PALACE

Kras held his loose fist to his mouth as he rounded the long table towards Delinda. His long, jagged fingernails threated to cut into his palm if he tightened his grip. His ragged, wet coughing echoed loudly through the hall. Delinda looked from one advisor to the next, as they all pretended not to notice the mortality of their king ringing through their ears.

"So, dear, sister," the king hacked, coming within inches of Delinda, speaking to her as though she were deaf rather than mute. "It appears that once again, I succeed where you have failed."

Delinda had no idea what he was referring to, but she should have known the reason she was summoned to the small council was because her brother was no longer feeling threatened by her.

She may not have found their cousin, but that was a small matter in comparison to defeating their staunchest opponents. The remains of the Insurgo were scattered to the wind: either abandoning their cause in full, like the undisciplined boys they were, or crawling back to headquarters in Snanka. Of course, he made no mention of this as it was her victory.

Nor had her brother ever made any comment on her attempted assassination within the palace walls, or her health as she still arrived with her forehead and cheek covered in cold, damp clothes to soothe her itching, healing skin. Her hands she left exposed, though the flesh still often felt taut and dry. Under her collared tunic she had another compress, soaked in soothing ointment, wrapped against the right side of her chest that was healing the slowest.

Kras continued after she inevitably did not reply. "Your lack of effort, Delinda, makes me feel that you are not only incompetent, but that you care nothing for my throne's security." He ironically coughed up thick, green mucus into his handkerchief before he could finish his gloating. "And that is a dangerous, treasonous thought..." he managed to finish before his lungs gave out. With a labored inhale, he waved his hand to the guard at the lesser Eastern door, the only way in or out of the hall apart from the grand, carved doors that led to the main foyer.

Delinda could smell the rot death as soon as the tall scout, Dierk, she thought his name was, stepped into the room. A body was wrapped in a rough, stained cloth and slung over his shoulder. Dirty, white bare feet hung out the bottom of the shroud near Dierk's knees, swinging back and forth with each step. He approached the council table as all eyes looked upon him. Most were wide with fear: fear of seeing a dead body, fear of who was under the shroud, and fear they could be next with the wrong words.

Delinda could've laughed at the pathetic lickspittles. She could see the show her brother was putting on. They would reveal the face, Kras would brag about how it proved his victory and perhaps close up by threatening anyone that thought to cross him.

Dierk slammed the body onto the table, resulting in fainthearted gasps from the councilmen that recoiled from the sound and the smell of wet, dead flesh. Small droplets of water flew off the shroud and scattered onto the table. Clear water, she noticed, and only on the outside of the shroud. The body had been left outside through the night and discovered in the morning by the scouts. They didn't kill whoever was beneath the cloth. Kras hobbled his way around to the head of the body and flung the off the cloth.

The ghostly face was barely recognizable with paper white skin that looked like it would crumble at a touch. Her eyes were beginning to sink into her skull, and the tips of her nose, lips, and extremities were blue. The cold had helped to prevent decay in the damp weather, which Delinda was grateful for. From her navel down the body was slick with crimson.

"See? SEE!?" Kras shrieked and began to laugh maniacally. "I have done what you could not! I have secured my throne; I have secured Redal power for the rightful son! Diar's line has ended and supporters of this pretender will scatter." Kras turned to his councilmen. "Do you see that no one escapes me? Not just traitors, but the children of all traitors will be thrown onto this table JUST LIKE THIS!" He shouted as he shook Apsonne's body by the shoulders, making a squeamishly slippery sound as her exposed insides were squished together with each tremor.

Kras words faded as Delinda focused on the body. She couldn't have been found that far from the palace, Dierk and his crew had been assigned to radius watch, she recalled. She could see her wound had been dressed, not to mention the body had been wrapped in the shroud last night before her corpse had been discovered. She must have had help to get so near to the palace, and that help could be out there, and close.

Court was adjourned, and Delinda took her customary position a few paces behind her brother as part of his escort back to the inner keep. It was a windowless tower that's only entrance was across the narrow wood bridge that could be drawn in the event of a siege. Thinking it was the safest place in the palace, the king spent most of his time there, but she knew his isolation was entirely unsafe. He carried on a one-sided conversation with her that she closed her ears to. He stopped for a moment to give her one final sneer before a young guard, with a helm much too big for him, hurriedly opened the red-lacquered door to let Kras out into the dawn. Even without the day touching her, Delinda had to shield her unadjusted eyes. The escort folded behind Kras leaving her behind in the shadows, when they suddenly came to a stop.

Delinda thought she heard women's voices, a sound foreign to the inner keep. Her feet stepped up to the threshold of the light, noting the sudden silence sweeping over the many muttered conversations. On the bridge, only a matter of feet away, were two women: One of the Godsmoors, and the other she recognized as the Viper Girl of the Saltwoods. They seemed to be caught mid-argument with each other, while a sandy-haired, slim, aging man in ill-fitted clothes was trying to appease them both.

Kras' highly trained bodyguards must have found themselves caught off-guard, she thought, smirking at her own joke. Her men wouldn't have hesitated to kill a stranger in the holdfast for even a moment, man or woman. Kras' seemed to be trying to make sense of the unexpected encounter.

"What are you standing there for?! KILL THEM! Kill all of them!" Kras squealed. "They're here for me! I told all of you they were coming for me! Kill them!" He fell behind his men in expected cowardice.

The three strangers were suddenly ignited into action. The skinny man drew his shabby sword too slowly. His eyes widened with the realization of his own mortality as Dierk's arm reeled back and withdrew his spear from where it punctured his gut. He fell backwards over the side of the bridge and into the yard below, drawing screams from the palace folk.

The Godsmoorian woman skillfully reflected the attacks coming toward her with a parrying knife and the broad end of her longbow, though she was unable retaliate. Delinda had lost sight of the Saltwoods girl; the golden-haired, golden-eyed little beast that constantly plagued their Saltwoods outpost. She drew her sword and took a step back further into the shadow of the keep, watching. She saw the plan: the Godsmoorian woman had drawn Kras' defenders away from him. He was only looking at what was right in front of him. He did not consider…

The Saltwoods girl sprung up behind him from the right side of the bridge. He still hadn't realized what was happening. Her hair, blonde-streaked and matted, was tied in a knot at the base of her neck, revealing a jagged scar down her spine. She was darkly tanned, as if she had been in the sun too long rather than it being her natural tone, though light spots of skin mottled her flesh at random. She raised her armed hand, not slowly, but with a sense of weight and purpose of her every move. Perhaps she felt that with that hand, she held all of Valehoutton.

Though it had not been her intention, Delinda stepped forward to reach that raised hand. As the sunlight touched her skin, it began to boil and smoke her newly healed flesh. It seemed like those few seconds lasted an eternity. With the short distance and the Viper Girl's back turned, she could have saved her only living family. Then she looked again at the girl's broad shoulders, bearing years of pain and labor, to the cowering man in front of her, and finally to her own peeling flesh. She clasped her burned hand and shrunk back into the darkness.

The girl gave up her stealth with a loud cry, a cathartic roar, which turned Kras toward her. The king looked like a rat realizing its foot was stuck in a trap. His pale, gaunt face drew even longer as he looked up into the eyes of the woman that would finally make all his fears real. She stabbed deep into his lower belly, digging the weapon in past its hilt and entering her entire fist into Kras' abdominal cavity. Like a true killer, she sliced upwards until the blade caught on his breastbone, spilling his royal innards onto his newly shined, fine boots. He sank to his knees, fell face-first into his own spread entrails, and died.

The Viper suddenly turned toward Delinda, sensing eyes upon her. Perhaps it was too dark through the threshold for the girl to see her, or perhaps she did not know who Delinda was. Perhaps she didn't care. Delinda could have sworn her own eyes met with those fierce pools of molten gold, but it was impossible to know. Regardless of what she had seen, the beast turned away and called to the Godsmoorian woman. The cocoa-haired native easily slipped away from battle over the side of the bridge.

The Saltwoods girl paused for a moment, looking down to the droves of palace-dwellers below that had stopped their daily bustle to stare up to the sounds of violence. "Make no mistake! Kras has committed mass genocide in the name of fear! Fear of the Red, fear of the Caeruleans, fear for only himself! Don't let them lie to you about Cynn! He massacred an entire colony because of fear!" She shook her head in disbelief, even after so many years had passed. "You've all forgotten Cynn. You all wrote it off as some unpreventable tragedy. I remember it every day. I remember that disgusting little worm of a man ordering my entire family to death!" She turned to spit on the corpse of Kras Redal. "You didn't kill me." She climbed over the side of the bridge and disappeared as the Godsmoorian woman had.

Delinda flashed back to the children she pulled from the window of the Daaine family cell; The twin boys, sniveling and clueless, and the fiery-eyed girl with firm, knotted brows and seething with wild anger. She began to hear laugher slowly growing in the hall. It was a laughter of disbelief, but with an underlying cruelty. A woman's voice, but the grown Daaine girl was much too far away to be heard by now.

That was when Delinda clasped her hands over her mouth. She felt she was going to lose consciousness, because the laughter, that sound, was coming from her.

31: THE DEEP

AUGUST 1849: THE ORCHANE FOREST
Minortai was out of his body again. He was in the white void. Its utter emptiness was chilling. It was not just absent of objects and color: there was no sound, no smell, no feeling of air moving past his face as he walked. He felt no physical pain and thought only curious thoughts.

The Deep itself had brought him here. It wanted him to see this plane and to collectively bring his knowledge back to it. He was the Deep and the Deep was him. It was the energy of all organic and inorganic matter. It was the flow created from physical and kinetic events, and it connected all planes of existence. The empty white beneath him faded away and became the night sky. He continued to walk through the cosmos, seeing constellations he recognized and many that were strangers. Eternity stretched on before him, behind him, above him, and below him.

His past self, the smallest child his age in Tiver, sat wide-eyed listening to his uncle's stories of the beginning of time. Nehlas scoffed at the legends from the other side of the room, his face only dimly lit by the fire roaring in the hearth. Across the stars, Minortai saw his future self sitting with his chestnut-haired daughter on his knee as he told her the same truths. Her little hand played with his greying beard as he spoke. No stars marked her face. Minortai felt confusion upon seeing his own triangular marking had disappeared from across his aged skin. Was it himself? He knew it was.

They spoke of the Keeper of Life, Valkenon. He could create life, but he was also the giver of punishment when the Deep flow was misused. It was he who created all mortal life, but the Godsmoorian people were his true children, created in his image. They are reflections of himself in both appearance and in their connection to the Deep that other mortals lack. The flow was closest to the surface in Ellinhall and the Godsmoors of Valehoutton, leading Valkenon's children to flock to these holy meccas.

Both Minortai's memory and future began to fade back into the stars. He saw another future where he was the last Godsmoorian, dying alone and far from home. The scenery surrounding him was shrouded in flame and shadow. The Deep sighed with mourning as the land burned. The vision was swallowed back into the universe.

Both futures and more were real, and all existed simultaneously. Minortai felt no alarm as he kept his stepping silently forward. Life and death were opposite, but not at war. Each needed the other. The Deep requires both to be in balance.

The cosmos led him to another scene in another time. He recognized the aged, faded decor within Dust's Plateau. Hellan crossed the dark stone masonry of the corridor with hurry beneath her heels. Her steps echoed loudly in the emptiness. As Minortai followed her, he found the boiling bricks were under his feet as well, and he could smell the musty, old furniture in the parlor. Dust and cobwebs covered every surface. Hellan opened a door of splintering, black wood and closed it behind her as she descended the stairs within it. Minortai stepped through the door as if it was only a shadow rather than solid ebony. It seemed that this time she was unaware he was there.

The underground chamber was cooler, locked away from the desert heat. The light warmth of candle flame and the scent of melting wax filled the room. The candles were arranged in circles around symbols painted on the floor. The resemblance of the red paint to blood made him feel unnerved. Hellan opened a dusty tome to a bookmarked page and inhaled nervously. As Minortai stepped around her, he saw that she was much younger than he had seen her in their other meetings here.

"Keeper of Death. Taker of pain. Alash tad al-ash tal ashtu. Daimos Muerte, I call upon thee for a trade. Soul for soul."

The candle flames all simultaneously went out and he and Hellan were alone in the darkness with a mysteriously terrifying laugh. "Child, what makes you think you can control me or the Deep?"

"You mistake my intention, I wish to keep balance and give you something in return." Hellan replied in a higher-pitched voice than Minortai had heard come out of her older self.

An all-white, ghostly figure appeared in the center of Hellan's circle. His glow dimly lit the room. He wasn't particularly tall, but he was slender and ethereal. His white-blonde hair flowed to his knees and blended into loose robes. "What makes you think you can offer me anything that even piques my interest?"

"I know I am your progeny. You fathered a child with that poor Reven girl a hundred years ago: my ancestor."

Daimos tsked approvingly as he began to circle around them. Minortai began to have the sinking feeling that he could be seen by this being. "My little Hellan, you have done your research." He moved her heavy raven hair out of her face. Her dark grey eyes were unmoving, while Minortai felt a shiver creep up his spine. "How does it feel being a descendant of the Keeper of Death, then?"

Hellan ignored his question, "I know you've kept my mother's soul. Return it to this plane, return her to a physical body here."

"And what will you give me?"

"My eternal soul. I will do your bidding, I will return to you after death. A soul for a soul." Hellan said firmly.

Daimos cackled, and the candles began to relight one by one. Minortai could feel the warmth of the flame all around him, rising like the fear in his gut. He felt as though something very wrong was taking place. "I will take and give in the same act, and our trade will be sealed. Do you agree, Hellan Ukon?"

"I agree."

Daimos began to approach Hellan with lascivious intent. Minortai tried to grab her by the arm to pull her away, but his hand passed through her just as his body had passed through the door. Daimos began to disrobe her, and Minortai helplessly backed away. What he was seeing had already happened, there was nothing he could do to change it.

Then Hellan's grey eyes rested directly upon him. She frowned with confusion but was soon distracted as Daimos forced himself inside of her.

Minortai's next step back sent him falling backwards. Instead of hitting the floor, he kept falling. The stars were around him again, though he could not walk as he was before. He couldn't stop his eternal descent into the cosmos. He grasped outward as though there was something he could catch himself with, but there was only emptiness.

A decrepit old woman lay in a bed much too big for her frail body. A heavy crown adorned her head, though she was nearly bald. A young man sat at her bedside grasping her hand, looking lost and desperate.

The woman snatched her hand away. "To think my dynasty will be left to a sniveling fool like you."

"Queen Freyjonne, you've taught me well. I'll be a good king."

She scoffed, "You were one of many. You mean nothing, you're just the only one to outlive me." She raised a bony finger to him. "So I suppose, long live the Caeruleans."

Minortai was still falling. He felt as though he couldn't breathe. The visions were becoming too much. His brain felt overwhelmed, too saturated with information for him to process it all. He tried to close his eyes to get it to stop, but it made no difference, the scenes kept playing.

A young woman with bouncy, short hair and an angelic face led a company across the Eastern Crags, not far from the pass that he and Kaj had just taken. Her silvery eyes were wavering, yet strong. Her pouty lips were set in a determined grimace. She turned behind her to shout something to the group of nearly a hundred young men that she was leading through the mountains, but Minortai could not hear her.

In darkness, he heard the rattle of chains accompanied by the smell of burning herbs. The sound of a woman quietly weeping echoed through the room. A single white flower was dying without the light of the sun.

"There is nowhere safe anymore! You should know that better than anyone!" A different woman spat. A golden-haired woman with eyes like molten gold walked alongside an older, dark-skinned Godsmoorian woman with dreadlocks braided down her back. They made quite the odd couple.

The Godsmoorian woman was cool and collected, especially in comparison to the younger woman's temper. It seemed this opposition only fueled her fire. "Our choices are hiding in the wilderness or crossing the border to Snanka. Ellinhall is forsaken and the Tuaegians will kill us on sight."

"Fuck the wilderness." the golden-eyed woman seethed.

Far behind her, a towering hooded figure stood watching. He was over seven feet tall, and his face was concealed by a white, porcelain mask. The mask turned to look at Minortai and his fall began to slow until it eventually stopped. He was standing in midair, and his vision began to bring him back to the void where he first awoke.

He was alone in the empty white with the giant. He spoke with a booming voice that made Minortai feel smaller than he ever had before. "I don't see many mortals here, Minortai Silverstar." he said.

Minortai was at a loss for words. He somehow knew that this was who Kaj had been seeing in her dreams.

"Thank you for leading me to Kajonne. Open your eyes, Minortai. Open your eyes..."

Minortai jolted awake under his bloodstained furs. He was still in a panic, his chest heaving and his palms sweating. He searched around for Kaj in the dim light from the rising sun peeking through the ancient trees of the Orchane Forest. White morning glories greeted the day with much more fervor than Minortai did.

The previous night Kaj had told him how much this forest reminded her of Ellinhall. Its quiet age and frequent rain made it both comforting and eerie. It felt as though the forest had a consciousness and wisdom of its own, silently observing passersby in its midst. She said it smelled like life. To Minortai it just smelled of damp earth.

Now Kaj was sitting up, though still wrapped in her sleeping furs. Moss stuck in her auburn hair where her head had been laying against the earth. She looked to the edge of the woods, her mouth agape with wonder.

Minortai could also feel the omnipotent presence. The morning air was thick and stagnant, his skin prickled unwittingly. He ungracefully rose to his feet, stumbling as he was cruelly reminded of his injury after all the time he had spent wandering painlessly in the astral plane.

"What do you want?" he said to the hooded man.

"I am Aldrion Salougian, Keeper of Time. I have come for you, Kajonne Maheil Wenn Dell."

Kaj's bottom lip was trembling, "I know, I've been waiting." She whispered. Minortai was near and he could barely hear her, but Aldrion seemed to hear her just fine from his distance.

He approached them, his long, dark blue shroud dragging on the damp earth and concealing his feet, making it appear as though he was gliding across the ground toward them. His towering figure loomed over the two of them, even more intimidating up close. Kaj rose to her feet, her head barely reaching his shoulder.

"You haven't lost everything. You have yourself, and you can dedicate yourself to the realm.

You will gain some of my power to aid your intentions, but only for the time that you remain in my service." Aldrion boomed.

Kaj had tears in her eyes, but they seemed to be sprung from awe, not sadness. She reached out to take Aldrion's hand, sealing their bond. Wordlessly, he began to lead her away, deeper into the Orchane Forest.

"Wait, Kaj, don't go," he called to her. Neither she nor Aldrion turned back to give him a second thought. He hobbled after them, though he could not keep up with the giant's strides. "Kaj! Please don't leave me! Please don't take her!" he shouted more desperately.

He burst through a twisted thicket of trees that had been blocking them from his sight. No one was there. His feet splashed into a clear, still body of water. Small lily pads capsized as he caused crashing waves upon the placid surface. The thick feeling in the air had lifted and the hum of the forest life returned. His leg was throbbing from the movement he had just forced upon it, yet it was not nearly as painful as the fact that he was completely alone.

Siyah. Nehlas. Kaj. He had crossed the entire country only to end up on his own. He felt listless as he wandered back through the forest, dragging his leg as he went. It all seemed hopeless until he suddenly found himself surrounded by sunlight. He shielded his eyes, and as they adjusted, he was able to take in the sight before him.

The wind was still and the white sun blazed onto the black sand, glinting like grains of glass. The rising and falling waves of the desert were void of any green life. The sky looked red and hazy in the distance, and far into the horizon, a single black tower rose from the sand. As he stood before the ominous sight, a burst of wind kicked the black particles into the air, whipping around him with stinging grains and blurring his vision momentarily. Above the tower, the stars of the Matricider appeared skewed and out of order, shining dimly as they faded into the morning sky.

This was no vision, this was real. He stood before Dust's Plateau, and Hellan awaited him.

32: LOYALTY

THE CELESTIAL CAPITAL

The South was sultry and uncomfortable compared to the Plains, where the cold, night winds would drop the temperature and bring refreshing aromas of dry grass and distant pine. Ronnock's clothes stuck to his sweaty body, chafing and vexing. Either lush grass or dark peat carpeted the ground, with some groves of short, emerald-leaved trees that barely topped his head when he was dismounted. He could tell by their shape that they had once been manicured and cared for, but now grew wild in their abandonment. He stopped Khazar near one of the groves and dismounted to take a rest. The weight on his mind was heavy. He took a swig from his water skin and was unable to ease his worries.

It was cosmically unfair to him that she was stolen out of his life just as they had finally begun to unfurl their love. Ronnock tried to push aside his apathetic thoughts: thoughts that he would never be happy, as every light in his life kept getting snatched away just as it began to shine, but they kept circling back around in a cruel, endless cycle.

He smelled blood before he heard the screams. Grown men only screamed like that when they were staring death in the face. He abandoned Khazar in the grove and cautiously began to follow the scents and sounds of violence. He hurried between groves, making sure to stay hidden as he approached. The gutteral, animalistic growls were all too familiar to him. The sound flashed him back to being outside the walls of Dust's Plateau. He was suddenly ten years younger in the black sands, struggling to keep Khos' salivating mouth away from his throat. Those monstrous, blood-thirsty eyes that struck terror deep in his soul now lived within him.

A man and two women ran fleeing from the rotting figures of the infected. The mass of six Red hurriedly hobbled after the trio as quickly as their decaying limbs could manage. Ronnock always found it odd that these Red seemed to find each other, he rarely saw them alone. He couldn't make out where the trio was from, or what their business near the Capital could be. The smart choice would to be to return to Khazar and continue his quest for his lover. Then he saw the bundle that one of the women was clutching was not just blankets, but an infant. His choice was made for him.

He drew his sword and exposed himself from his tree cover. He shouted loudly to the Red, trying to draw their attention. Two of the six abandoned the faster prey and turned instead to him standing still. He stood his ground and easily cut down them down in the midst of their rush. He flicked the blood off his sword, splattering it across the grass like crimson paint. He ran across the thickly vegetated field to close the space between himself and the remaining four Red. One of them, hunched over and maimed, slowly turned toward him just in time for him to drive the point of his sword through its mouth and out the back of its already mushy head.

Three to go, and he spun to face his remaining foes as he withdrew his blade from the creature's rotting skull. He was so overwhelmed with adrenaline that his ears had blocked the constant wails of the fleeing human trio. Two of the Red had one of the women on the ground and were sharing the feast of her entrails. The man was still clutching her hand, as if he could still pull her to safety. The remaining woman, still clutching the infant, stood screaming for the man to rejoin her twenty feet ahead. It was the first time Ronnock heard the infant cry in all the chaos. The third Red...

Ronnock heard rough panting behind him. He turned and grabbed the monster's throat with his free left hand, crushing the soft flesh under his fingers and feeling its windpipe collapse. It made no difference, however, and kept reaching for him with its wagging, black tongue. He kept a firm grip on its throat, then kicked the rest of its body away, leaving only a thrashing head in his hands. He felt his gums tingling around his eyeteeth as he tossed the head to the side, rolling it across the grass like a morbid lawn game.

The beast was getting louder as he abhorrently relished the slick feeling of blood on his hands. The scent of the dying woman's spilled blood proved to be too much for him to restrain his own monster. His fangs were bared as he tore into the remaining two Red, though he was himself enough that he avoided ingesting any of their rancid blood. Their minds were so far gone that they showed no pain or fear even as he ripped them apart. Their bodies lay strewn across the clearing, mixed with the insides of the woman they had killed. Ronnock picked up his sword from where he had forgotten it and impaled the woman's head. He didn't want to risk her coming back Red.

He turned to the couple and asked if they were all right. The woman screamed and clutched her child tighter against her chest. The man put his arm around her in a protective gesture, though his wide, shaking eyes told Ronnock differently. He reached a bloody hand out to them, but they jumped back fearfully, the man quickly brandishes a knife with a trembling fist.

"Leave us be! I'm warning you!" he said in a frightened voice that quavered as much as his hand.

Ronnock withdrew his hand, suddenly conscious of his appearance. The shame made him hastily withdraw his fangs, and he felt the Red leave his senses. Without a word of thanks, the couple fled the gory scene with their lives and their child. Ronnock was left standing alone amongst the carnage, as usual.

His heart heavier than before, something he had thought impossible, he returned to the grove where Khazar patiently awaited his return. The stallion snorted and recoiled from him. Ronnock wasn't sure if it was the scent of blood, or if the horse sensed the evil beast that festered within him.

He was less than a mile from the Capital, he supposed he could continue alone. Ronnock reached out to the statuesque, black stallion again. The horse exhaled heavily through its velvety nostrils, but allowed itself to be touched. He wrapped Khazar's reins and bridle neatly around his hand before placing them in one of the pockets on his saddlebag. He rubbed the stallion's face where the leather has been sitting against his coat for the last two days. The chance of him entering the palace undetected would be greater if he approached on foot. However, he would have to wait until nightfall to approach, though he wasn't entirely sure the cover of night would be enough for him to get past the sentries. Once he was inside Star Palace, he'd need pure luck in addition to skill. He could very easily end up in the wrong place at the wrong time and die for it.

Khazar became smaller each time he looked back over his shoulder. He stood waiting curiously for some time, but when he was almost out of sight,

Ronnock saw the midnight horse begin to make his way home. Ronnock wondered if he would return to the Whispering Plains, or to wherever his home was before.

The biggest, frontmost building that made up Star Palace was not defended by an outer wall. The light beige stone was a fortress itself, thick and impenetrable. Blue and white stained-glass windows lined the upper stories, one of the old Caerulean palace details that the Redals couldn't cover with red paint. The palace stood in front of a steep, deep gorge, and the inner keep behind it was seemingly an island of rock within the dry moat. Only narrow, stone footbridges leading to guarded areas of the palace allowed access to the inner keep. Armies could easily be cut down one man at a time trying to storm the palace. Luckily, Ronnock was only one man. He paced the edge of the gorge, contemplating his next move.

His attention was caught by the tinkling of small bells and the familiar scent of spiced cinnamon. He still recognized Nai's smell, and he almost groaned at the notion of rescuing her once again. He thought he had finally rid himself of her. He leapt to hide himself around the adjacent wall of the palace, though risked a glance around the corner to watch her approach. She was walking alongside two well-adorned Redal officers dressed in red. Nai was wrapped in what appeared to be brand new pink silks, and her hair was braided back and interwoven with golden adornments. She didn't seem to be a prisoner.

"I assure you, the western chambers are some of the most luxurious in the palace. You'll be most comfortable there. It's a fine reward for the lady that helped deliver the Insurgo to Queen Delinda." The younger, dark haired officer said as he walked with his hands behind his back. He was confident in his own safety.

"But they are safe?" Nai's accented voice replied. "Even the king's chambers were not safe from those savages."

"Things will be different now that Queen Delinda reigns, at the Capital, and across all of Valehoutton. She is a capable leader and does not allow rebels to run rampant across the country. The two remaining assassins are being tracked and will be killed on sight. The remnants of the Insurgo will go crawling back to suckle at Rheena Ukon's teat in Snanka, but the Queen has already gathered men to put an end to the traitors once and for all. No one will dare to rise against the crown after we crush them in Snanka like we did Bardon." The older officer continued. His speech became more impassioned as he went on.

It was almost too much for Ronnock to take in. Kras was dead and Delinda was queen, Nai had something to do with the Insurgo's downfall, and now the Redals marched for the headquarters in Snanka. He scanned the area for witnesses, then acted quickly. He leapt around the corner and slashed the throat of one guard, then the next. Nai barely had time to scream before his hand was over her mouth.

"You're not going to make a sound unless it's answering my questions." He growled at her. The burning he felt was not the Red, but his own anger.

She looked up at him with fearful yellow eyes. She had seen him kill enemies before, and now she was an enemy. He had barely lifted his hand when she began to shriek. He braced it back down over her face and grasped her throat tightly with the other. "So you'd rather I just kill you now?" he growled her.

She began to cry as she tried to speak from under his palm. He risked lifting his hand again, though he kept his grip on her neck. "Please don't hurt me, I didn't have a choice." She mewled out.

"What exactly did you do? How much did you tell them?" he demanded. She replied so quietly he couldn't hear her. "What?" he questioned roughly.

"I let them in." she repeated just loud enough for him to hear.

His vision went white for a moment and suddenly both of his hands were around her throat. "Do you know how many people are dead because of you?!" She didn't answer. Her eyes just widened as she felt the pressure of his fingers on her windpipe. "Why? Why would you condemn us to death after we took you in?"

Now her eyes narrowed and shifted to a light, angry green. "You brought me there and trapped me. You brought me there with a promise of love and abandoned me for that plain, boring girl! How could you choose her over me?!" She looked over his shocked expression and he saw a smirk cross her face. "Any blood spilled is on your hands, Ronnock Ukon."

She died with that vindictive, satisfied sneer on her face as Ronnock snapped her neck and let her body fall into the dirt. He hadn't realized how hard he was breathing or that his hands were shaking. That bitch. That hateful, evil bitch. He should've left her chained to be sold in the streets of Bardon.

As he began to take steps away from where he left Nai's body, he felt each becoming more difficult. Venell could be just on the other side of the stone wall, imprisoned and frightened, but she could be anywhere else. She could have escaped with Nalahi, her captor's may not have yet arrived at the Capital, or they could have killed her on the road. Breaking into the palace chanced capture and death, and he could die with the knowledge he had just gained, leaving Krisae and the remaining Insurgo to march straight to their deaths. Even Rheena in all her wisdom would be caught off guard by a full-fledged attack, especially with a force led by the Darkstar herself.

But these were just thoughts to comfort himself from the consuming dread that he was indeed leaving the woman he loved to suffer and die in the Redals' captivity. He had to hang onto the hope that she was free somewhere with Nalahi, or the guilt may kill him long before any sword did. Ronnock had made his choice. He had to do the right thing. His walk from the side of the palace walls turned to a run, as if he could outrun his fears. It would be a long journey to the black sands of his childhood without Khazar.

33: PHOENIX

SOUTHERN MESA, SNANKA

Samirael Vaes jolted awake. Her neck was stiff from the awkward position she had fallen into. Her letter she had been writing was stuck to her forearm where the dried ink had bonded the paper to her skin. She shook off the parchment to find all the words were smeared and unreadable. She groaned and rubbed her eyes. It was the middle of the night. She had fallen asleep with her light on, wasting expensive oil. She crumpled up the ruined paper and added it to the growing pile of identical balls of imperfect letters on the floor of her room. She shut off her light and lay back on her bed. Of course, now she was wide awake.

Her window was open, allowing the warm breeze to fill her room with the scents of citrus and earth. She could see a light in the neighboring house. Someone else was awake in the dark hours before sunrise. She rested her arms on the windowsill and wondered if she would catch a glimpse of him tonight. A family with two sons around her age had moved in near the end of last summer. Both had dark hair that grew in tightly wound curls and skin the color of oiled bronze, though one was taller and leaner than the other. She had not seen the taller one up close, but she accidentally met the other.

It had been almost year since she had tried to run away to find her father. Her mother's new husband made her life unbearable, and she dreamed of what her life could be with her other parent. She loved her half-siblings, the twins Gemini and Dallie, but their father, Malachi, was a cruel drunk that harbored contempt for his bastard stepdaughter. Her mother had stopped standing up for her and let him make his painful japes as he pleased.

The citrus trees had been in bloom then too, when she had climbed out of her second-floor window and stole across the orchard. She had been looking over her shoulder to make sure she wasn't being followed when she ran into him. Her face hit his shoulder and she fell back onto the ground. She hadn't known he was her new neighbor then, she mistakenly thought he must have been some sort of night guard. His brow was heavy and his curls stood out so far from his head that the shadow they cast over his face covered most of his features. As he lifted his face to look at her, she saw his soft, blue eyes looking at her. He apologized to her as she turned and ran back home. A few days passed while she moped about, until she saw him through the open window next door. That was when her habit of staring into his window from hers began.

  The curtain in his room was suddenly pulled back and he appeared before her. He must have been trying to get the rare breeze to blow into his room just as she was. His dark curls were pulled into a bun on the top of his head. Somehow, Sami found some courage within herself. She pushed aside all her crumpled letters and found a fresh parchment. She simply scribbled down "Hello, I'm Samirael." She folded the letter and tied it around a wooden spoon that she had still not taken back to the kitchen. She leaned out of her window as far as she could and threw it into his open window.

  The noise startled him, but he closed his book and looked around for what had dropped on his floor. She saw him pick up her note and read it.

He approached his window, and for once, he was looking back at her. She smiled and waved. He looked worried. He closed the curtain and the candlelight went out. Her heart dropped into her stomach. Did he find her strange? Perhaps someone had already told him she was a bastard child? Her throat was still tight with disappointment when she turned off her lamp and tried to go back to sleep.

A heavy thud woke her up the next morning. She sleepily sat up, thinking someone had been knocking on her door. As she put her feet on the floor, she saw something wrapped in parchment. She opened it to find that it was a note wrapped around the same wooden spoon. "Come to the orchard tonight. Raliden."

She held the paper to her heart. "Raliden..."

Night could not have come fast enough for Sami. The fireflies were slowly disappearing as the dry heat of the late summer persisted. Sami remembered them being numerous in her youth, but as the drought went on, the night-time lights disappeared. It was nearly magical for her to see even a few twinkles as she tiptoed off her family's back porch. The scent of the citrus blossoms was so overwhelming she could nearly feel the sweet grit of sugar on her teeth. She alternated from a quick walk to jogging as she hurried through the orchard, rushed by the thought of being followed as well as the fear that he had not come to meet her.

There were so many reasons she could be left on her own tonight. He could've been stopped. He could've changed his mind. He could've tricked her. Why? For his own amusement, or for something more sinister. She looked up quickly at the sound of footsteps.

"Raliden?" she risked saying.

"Uh, Ral-ih-den, actually." He replied, awkwardly scratching the back of his head. "It looks different on paper." He offered when he noticed her embarrassment.

Silence.

"You're Samirael." He said. He couldn't think of anything else to say. She smiled anyway. Twinkling lights began to appear around them. Sami felt the air breathing magic into her as she looked into Raliden's eyes and realized that they were not quite the same color.

She loved to think back on that night. It was a perfect dream, and it was the start of their love. They spent many more nights in the orchard, laughing and kissing and talking, but none were quite as enchanted at that first one that set her heart free. Being with Raliden made everything around her more bearable. Dallie and Gemini would tease her for having her head in the clouds, but it didn't bother her in the least, for it was true. He made her feel like she was walking on air. Her mother was relieved that Sami was out of the house often and away from Malachi, though Sami wasn't sure if her mother fully knew what she was up to.

After her sixteenth birthday passed in spring, they started to show their love by more than just kissing. Sami feared bringing a bastard child into the world, she would never want anyone to be mocked the way she was growing up, but Raliden made her feel so safe. He would care for her always, she knew.

She lay back on her bed after sneaking him in through her window late on an autumn night. His hands slowly moved up her sides as they lifted her shirt. She loved the way his dark skin looked against her pale flesh. They had kissed until all their clothes were off, and now Raliden hovered over her in their moment of truth. It couldn't possibly be wrong if it was with Raliden. She felt her fears and doubts lift off her. He smiled wide and kissed her again. She loved looking back and forth between his mismatched eyes: one pale blue and the other a swimming green. "Are you sure? Are you ready?"

She nodded, "Yes, I want to be with you like this. Forever."

He nuzzled his head into the crook of her neck and thrust inside of her. It definitely hurt, just like all her friends said it did, but then she began to feel hot. She closed her eyes and let the feeling rise in her. Raliden's breath was heavy as he whispered to her that he loved her. Her whole body was sweating, and the heat was becoming unbearable. She opened her eyes, and Raliden must have seen the worried look on her face.

"I can stop." He told her quickly, yet gently.

"It's so hot," she panted out.

"I can open a—" Raliden never finished his sentence.

Ecstasy took over Sami. She felt as though she was floating in a soundless, weightless space. The world around her seemed to be crawling though time. Bursts of red, orange, and yellow danced across her eyes. The burning heat she had been feeling was released. Flames painlessly licked across her skin, leaving her unmarred and euphoric. They flickered from her body and radiated around the room. They snaked around Raliden, licking his skin as they had hers.

But his beautiful, smooth skin began to blister and peel. His hair was consumed instantly, and his lovely blue and green eyes turned to liquid and bubbled down his fleshless cheeks. Time suddenly caught up to its usual pace, and all she could hear were Raliden's shrieks of agony. The fire spread across the bed and to the carpets. She screamed and tried to beat the flames away from Raliden. His anguished cries diminished as his tongue and throat burned away. Sami cried for help, screaming for anyone to come to his aid. As she stepped off the bed, the fire followed her onto the floor, leaving embers where her feet touched the carpet. She swatted at the blaze, but her every movement just spread it more.

Dallie suddenly appeared in her doorway. Sami couldn't hear what she was saying over her own cries. She covered her naked body as best she could with her hands, the flames still swirling around her and now reaching their fingers toward the ceiling. Dallie began beating the flames across the carpet with a towel, but for each spot one she put out, Sami started another.

Gemini and her mother burst into her bedroom. Gemini was the first to see Raliden's body, now charred beyond recognition, smoldering into ash on what was left of Sami's bed. Her mother was crying. She reached out to Sami, but Sami shrieked and jumped back, "I'll kill you too! *I'll kill you too*, don't touch me or you'll burn too!" She wept as she fell back onto the ground.

She could finally hear their voices and the crackle of the fires Dallie and Gemini had yet to extinguish. Her mother touched her cheek, and her hand felt terribly cold. She became increasingly aware of her own nakedness and quickly pressed her legs together and covered her breasts with her hands. Her skin was still burning hot, but it was completely unharmed. Sami looked up into her mother's wavering green eyes. She had never seen such fear on her mother's face, not even when Malachi had pushed her down the stairs on her tenth birthday.

"Oh, Sami," she said through her tears, "What have you done?"

ACKNOWLEDGEMENTS

Thank you to my parents for your unconditional love, even though you generally have no idea what I'm doing.

Thank you to my dogs for the same reason.

Thank you to the Eickmann side for the introduction to Nerd World. It makes me weird little heart happy to share it all with you. Thank you for the music and love, I'll sing with y'all forever. I was going to name all of you individually, but that would take, like, six pages.

Thank you to the Hostettler side for showing me what friendship is. The blood of the covenant is thicker than the water of the womb.

Thank you Natsuki Takaya and Hiromu Arakawa. Your work changed my life.

Thank you Jessica for being my first editor in 8th grade. I miss you.

Thank you Chico for being the best city in the USA. My friends there touched me forever: The Olive street crew and GO people.

Thank you to the love of my life for making me feel deserving, rain or shine.

Thank you to me for pulling this shit all together from an origin point of 1999. The original was a handwritten 20 pages long and consisted of all Japanese names. I imagined plot pieces everywhere from doing warm-ups in middle school PE, to on rides at Disneyland. I laid awake countless nights thinking: "I have to get all this out somehow." It was an on-going life project I thought I'd never finish, much less ever share with another living soul out of sheer embarrassment. But you did it! Now, do it again.

Dana says: Wine glasses are for peasants

Made in the USA
Las Vegas, NV
11 October 2022